The Insomniac Booth

And Other Stories

Clive L Gilson

For Sophie & Jemma

CONTENTS

Rag Trade Gepetto

The Politician's New Speech

The Insomniac Booth

Beginning with Smith

Heirs and Graces

Fergus on A Bridge

The Starving Wolf

Fancy and the Flutter

Towering Dreams

Do Unto Others

The Mobile Phone

For The Love Of Comets

The Tender Kiss

Only The Names Change

Jamul's Happy Day

Jack and Jill Went Up the Hill

Where the Grass Is Greenest

Hesperus Wrecked

Picking the Wings off Crane Flies

Lord of the North Wind

The Assistant Shop Manager

Pigs and Dogs

Bastille Day

The Last Watchman

This Song is for You

About the Author

Rag Trade Gepetto

SLEEP WAS A STRANGER to David. Our gentle friend, that warmth of embrace and soft comfort at the end of a long day, had always seemed to be at one remove from his soul. He tried in vain to count sheep, failing miserably each night to imagine any flock big enough, and through that imagination to will his limbs to slumber. David lay at night amid the intermittent tics and spasms of sagging brickwork and leeching pipes. Minutes might turn into decades of waiting, during which time he focussed on liver spots on the painted ceiling above his dishevelled bed. He always returned to the same theme, and in so doing he inevitably banished all hope of that slow decline into the unconscious world of the dream king. And so, wiping the grit from the corners of his eyes, he would rise, usually around two in the morning, make a pot of tea, and sit in front of the television flicking between the educational and the banal.

On occasions David tried alternative tacks, pouring himself liberal measures of cheap brandy in an effort to knock himself out, and but for the persistent worry that his liver would explode, he might have considered alcoholism as a cure for insomnia.

Fridays were his favourite tipple days, as he generally did not work on a Saturday and then had time to recover before Monday. Even here, though, when sweet oblivion coursed through his veins and he collapsed on the sofa, he couldn't ever say that he slept. Rather he entered a twisted world where the great theme of his life was made real, and the tempting began all over again. In some ways, these weekly diversions seemed more real to David, full of the visceral sharpness of existence, than did the mundane world of rag trade cutting on Eastcastle Street in London's West End.

David's inability to enter the altered state of mind that brings mental recharge and balance was caused directly by his chosen trade. David worked the cutting benches for those 'B' list designers who stitch their way through one financial crisis after another at the back of Oxford Street. He spent his days surrounded by fittings, by models, and by the spike-tongued hopefuls trampling their way towards the catwalk, and all of them, the girls, the boys, the madames, the couturiers, only ever saw him as a pair of sharp blades.

David, however, saw beyond the chalk line and the pattern book. David saw girls and women. He watched them move and twist within their fabric shrouds and surrounded by skin and bone and muscle and the imposing beauty of the fashionista, he wept internally. Summer was the worst time of all with acres of breast exposed to draw his gaze down into the realm of the lascivious. David was one of life's luckless men. He smiled and made a threat of it. He laughed and drew fingernails across a blackboard. He held a woman's hand for just a moment too long. He tried too hard.

He was barely thirty years old, skilled and adept at his trade, but he was already balding, noticeably overweight, had crooked teeth and one eye that stared manically out of its socket. He knew instinctively that he was never noticed for who he might be, but only ever for what he could do. Those paragons of perfection who employed him would not see the man because his flesh offended them.

At night, David thought about one thing; his ideal woman. In spending his sleepless nights imagining perfection, and then in the morning looking at his own reflection in the bathroom mirror, he committed himself to a cycle of despair that he was convinced would only ever end when he put out the lights…permanently. It wasn't as though David wanted too much of the world. He recognised in the sea of fake perfection that ebbed and flowed around his salt bleached rock, that beyond the make-over shores, where bleary eyed beauties awoke in their raw state, there might be a little nook or tight cranny where he could find happiness. All he wanted was a cuddle, was warmth other than his own in bed on a cold night, and in the throes of such thinking, when the alcohol finally bit, his dreams took him into strange encounters with girls made of glass and wax, girls who beckoned to him and then shattered at his touch. He dreamed of feminine peacocks, creatures of fan and feather and piercing shrillness. He dreamed of the hunting tigress with cubs mewling in the undergrowth and he knew the bite of her rancid fangs. David also dreamed of a man, who sat at the edge of the disillusionarium that his drunken world inevitably became, a man who never spoke, who never moved, but watched and waited, and waited and watched, a man dressed in the threads of deep, black time, threads woven into a riverboat gambler's brocaded frock and embroidered waistcoat.

It was on one such Friday amid the high heat and low-cut bosom of June that David forsook the usual Fundador and splashed out on two bottles of Grouse. He never drank Scotch. It made him unduly maudlin, but, he decided while wandering disconsolately down the drinks aisle at his local Tesco Metro, that it had been a fucking maudlin day, and the cause of his melancholy was the new girl on reception.

During a quick introduction by the owner of the salon, David had let his gaze linger too long on the new girl's breasts and rather than the usual snort of disgust he'd received a round, heavy slap in the face. The sound of her palm on his cheek filled the air with thunder, rattling across the downstairs showroom, and he had fled in horror to the workshop on the first floor. No matter how large the stone he overturned, he found no place to hide, and blushing crimson the day long he'd chalked and cut and made one ham-fisted, embarrassed mistake after another, until She Who Must Be Obeyed had waved her finely manicured hand at him and told him to go home. The fact that she added words like creepy and weird and skin-crawling to the usual terms of abuse that he periodically suffered was, he felt, a little gratuitous. He had never actually touched a girl's breast, nor would he dare to do so, but sometimes he just couldn't help where he looked, afflicted as he was with the blow of the birthing ugly-stick.

"It isn't weird or creepy", he told himself repeatedly as he stared at the rack full of spirits in Tesco. "I just lose track of where I am looking sometimes. For God's sake!"

David caught sight of another shopper looking at him as if he were the nutter on the bus, so he picked up the two bottles of scotch, bowed his head, and walked quickly to the check-out counter.

*

Slumped on the sofa, with the world drifting into an amber haze fuelled by an empty bottle of the blend, David closed his eyes and fell asleep immediately. All he wanted on this night of all nights was the blackness of absolute torpor, but even in his befuddled state he still staggered into the kingdom of impossible dreams. David stood on a beach watching the waves crash in, swaying in drunken rhythm with the surf.

In the distance he saw his alter ego, Mister Darcy on a white charger, galloping along the shoreline with whipping hair and muscular abandon. Unlike his previous dream incarnations, however, there was no immediate object of the chase, no impossibly fragile maiden to save. Instead, his imagined avatar turned the horse to face a rocky spur at one end of the beach, and there he saw the man in black. Again, breaking with all tradition, the usually passive and silent man stood, climbed down from the rocks and started to walk towards the Darcy figure, who dismounted with a jump and a flourish. The two figures met in the curl of receding water at the shoreline. They stared at each other for a moment before Darcy spoke.

"Are you the Devil?" he asked. "Have you come to make a pact? Is this my Faustian temptation?"

The man in black looked down at the wet sand and shook his head. "Nothing to do with me, mate, all that Devil nonsense".

He looked up and pointed back along the beach to where the true-to-life form of the dreaming David stood watching them. "There's no magic can make him any less ugly than he is."

"We know," replied Darcy, "but we'll do anything for just one chance. Souls aren't much use when you're as disappointed and as lonely as we are."

"That's true enough," said the man in black as he kicked at a pebble embedded in the soft, wet sand. "But it won't change anything. When he wakes up he'll be just as unattractive as he was yesterday. More so, given how much he's put away tonight. Anyway, I'm not in the soul business. I'm just a gambling man."

Darcy moved in a little closer and looked hard and long at his companion on the beach. "So, what are you doing here? Why are you always in our dreams?"

The gambling man shrugged his shoulders. "Waiting for the moment when you get off the horse and ask that very question. I feel sorry for you, for him."

"But according to you there's nothing that will change our life?" asked Darcy, looking confused.

In the dream David and Darcy started to merge together, so that, as the man in black watched and smiled sweetly under the towering blue sky, the impeccable and imposing rider of the white steed twisted and decayed back to his sad and depressive core component part.

The man in black waited for the metamorphosis to complete before speaking again. "I didn't say that. I said you'd still be ugly in the morning. I never said anything about not being able to change your life."

With that the man in black took David's hands in his and turned them over as if inspecting for warts and calluses. "Hands of a craftsman, mate. I don't think you have any idea just how skilled you are. Think about it. Tomorrow, when you wake up I'll give you this – no hangover, nothing but the fresh breeze of a summer morning, and you'll feel great. Think about what you can really do with these hands." He paused. "And with what's in your heart."

The man in black smiled and let David's hands fall to his sides. "As I said, I'm not looking for a soul. Not looking for anything of yours. You live your life, mate. If there's anything to collect it'll be done long after you've stopped shuffling through this mortal soil."

With that he turned on his heel and walked back towards the rocks. David felt tears stinging his eyes as they welled up and then fell upon his ruddy cheeks, and as his vision blurred so did the image of the walking man. David wiped away the tears with the back of his hands, but when he finally saw clearly again, there was no gambler, no Darcy and no white charger on the beach. There were no fantastic images of women, no wheeling gulls, nor was there the reassuring sound of surf. Slowly a dusky darkness fell, and for the first time in years David slept truly, like an innocent child.

*

Despite the evidence around him, the empty bottle of scotch, an overturned tumbler, the crick in his neck and the taste of deep sleep in his mouth, David had never felt quite so bright and alive of a morning. It was still early, the clock hands reading just seven o'clock, and already the summer sun streamed in through windows against which no curtains were drawn. He stretched out on the sofa, yawned, considered his options and realised that he was hungry, as if he had been walking in coastal air all night.

He remembered nothing of the dream, but he felt a tingle in his fingers, as though they were trying to speak to him. David made himself a cup of tea, sipping the hot drink slowly, and all the while he basked in the warming sunlight that flooded his meagre little flat. He had an idea, but first he must shower and then, rather than hunt for a dry crust in the bread bin, he would walk down to the coffee bar on the corner of the street and eat Danish pastries. For some reason it seemed to him that this was a good day be alive. To Hell with the bloody women and their bloody dresses, he thought.

The rest of the weekend saw David working to liberate himself from the squalid mediocrity that had coloured so much of his life to date. He cleared the flat of rubbish. He swept and dusted and hoovered. The bathroom gleamed as never before and the whole place bloomed like a summer flower bed bursting through mulch. He washed clothes, bagged up old items for the charity shop, and without quite knowing why he put aside the best cuts of collected redundant cloth for some future use.

During Sunday afternoon he started to move the furniture around so that he could create a working space, and there he placed the tools of his trade, his scissors, his needles, his threads, his bodkins, together with his one pride and joy, an antique hand-cranked Singer sewing machine. Finally, come Sunday evening, when all was set and clean and fair, he took himself off to the bathroom and scrubbed himself with a vim and vigour that suggested in no uncertain terms that David wanted to scour away the stain of disappointment that had soiled his life so far.

Although the previous working week had ended in personal embarrassment for David, the one saving grace in all this was his skill and his craft. He might have been ridiculed the previous Friday, but he had not been sacked. As he walked up the stairs at Oxford Circus station and headed along towards Eastcastle Street, he felt serene and relaxed.

He bought flowers from a stand by the old Post Office. The morning girls, all bright and rouged and clad in their summer skimpies, simply didn't interest him. He entered the building where he worked, handed the flowers to the receptionist and apologised for his previous indiscretion. He skipped up the stairs in the full knowledge that mouths hung open behind his back, and when the Madame appeared to ask what was going on he simply smiled at her and told her that he had thought long and hard about life and that he was now a changed man. David couldn't quite tell what they believed and what they disbelieved, but then he didn't care. A plan was forming, a scheme of divine proportion, that would take away the edge of his physical and emotional hunger forever.

The plan was nothing more than a vague shape in the early moments of Monday morning, but by degrees, as he worked through the day, smiling and whistling to himself, the bones of the thing began to form. He surveyed the fabrics in the workshop and saw in lycra and toile and cotton the shapes of limbs. In taffetas and satins and wools he saw skin tones and contours. The mannequins upon which hung Madame's latest creations gave form to the coagulation of shape and sinew, and in his hands he held the means, held the tools that might bring life to the ideas floating dimly in his head. By the end of that first working day after the disaster and the dream, he was resolved to act. He would borrow a mannequin and, at the end of each day working the cloth, he would take home off-cuts. David would fill his evenings with the sound of the Singer.

Over the next few weeks there appeared in David's flat a succession of patchwork skins, each one crafted on the old singer and fitted over the mannequin like a Lycra glove. Colours and shades entwined, with gold and silver threads catching the light, but none of the textures and the patterns, made up from off-cuts as they were, could ever quite conform to David's aesthetic. Her skin had to be perfect before he would consider the next steps.

Days merged into nights and back into the rising light of late summer and then early autumn. David worked all day at his trade, a changed man, happy and discrete and gentle. At night, with his latest captures from the cutting room floor, he became a fevered creature, bending over his old sewing machine for hours in an effort to sew the smallest and the finest seams. David never drank now, but the hours and the days spent spinning the sewing machine wheel in both directions inevitably took its toll on the man.

Towards the end of September, just as the Devil spat on the bramble bushes in the courtyard behind David's flat and the Hawthorn in the local park hung heavy with blackening sloes, David began to realise that something had to give. His search for perfection was driving him towards the madness of insomnia again, and he had either to finish his dream project or abandon happiness for all time. On the last Friday of the month, as he yawned over his scissors and counted the minutes down until lunch time's sweetly fresh air, the Madame entered the cutting room. Across her arm she held a bolt of the finest golden Escorial, which she laid gently on David's table.

"For that singer, you know, hot little arse but slight nasal whine on the high notes…touring at Christmas and wants this ready for dress rehearsals next month." she said, smoothing out a crease in the material. "I'll send the drawings up later. Usual stuff, patterns and cuts, and I know you'll do your best. Beautiful isn't it?"

David simply stared at the sheer brilliance and the tight but elastic weave of the Escorial. It was, indeed, beautiful. He nodded his agreement as Madame turned and headed back down to the lower floor. The Escorial was perfect.

True to her word Madame sent up the relevant drawings, a design for a light and skimpy halter neck dress, cut low at the front and back. It was all so depressing, he thought. Here he was, staring at the most stunning bolt of cloth just when he needed it, but judging by the drawings he would have to be profligate with the material. While the line was simple, there were so many flourishes and twists and hints to be cut for the associated dancers that there would nothing serviceable left of the Escorial, nothing worth taking home for his darling girl. It would be a tragedy, but, as he turned the design round in his hand, desperately trying to find economies within the pattern, David decided that it was time to sink or swim. He had to finish his dream girl, and only the golden Escorial could possibly do. The entire bolt of cloth would be required, but from it he could cut a perfect skin, and then he could really begin to make his dreams come true.

David spent his entire lunch break walking the diesel fumed streets that ran around the John Lewis store at Oxford Circus in a vain attempt to clear his mind. This would be the last straw as far as Madame was concerned. David tried to talk himself back towards a land of common sense, but he was, he knew, already too far gone with his new enterprise. Eventually a grimly determined David returned to his cutting room, gathered up the golden skin, stuffed it under his arm, and, taking one last look around his place of work for so many years, he boldly marched out of the building and took the first train home.

Never in any folk or fairy tale did a man work as hard and with such concentration as David did that Friday night. No elves, no pixies, no faeries, not a single creature, not even Tom Tit Tom, could have sewn and measured and cut with such care and deliberation. David could feel a fever brewing up in his blood, but it was, he knew, a fever of the heart. This skin would become flesh and blood in his hands. He was a chalice filled to the brim with love, and he alone possessed the skill to make that love real. By Saturday morning the skin atop the mannequin was complete and without blemish. He ran his hands over the perfect material, sensing the warp of the fibres as though they were pores, and David shivered with delight. The skin fitted every contour perfectly, revealing a proportioned ideal of womankind, full of breast and slim of waist. He could not rest yet, however. As perfect as the skin might be it was still many hours and days away from being his darling girl.

Where before David might have sought out alcoholic remedies for his nocturnal restlessness now he revelled in the fever of work. The only time that he left the flat was to buy threads and cottons. He spent nearly twenty-four hours embroidering just one eyebrow. She would take time and effort and skill to complete, all of which David devoted to her making without care or thought for his own state. He embroidered full lips of ruby red, eyes of a deep, longing brown, toes that were flawless, fingers that were slender and golden, and ears that were faultless and delicate. He spent days bent over an embroidery hoop, barely remembering to drink the meanest cup of water or to eat even the most frugal morsel. Every ounce of David's energy, every luminescent molecule of his soul, fed this unbridled passion. He was determined, come Hell or high-water, that he would create the perfect woman, the ultimate partner in life.

It took almost three weeks of the most painstaking work to complete the embroidery, to carefully add elements to the skin that would enhance her beauty, and finally to make the prefect little black dress for her to wear. By the end of his labours, David was blindly in love with his fabulously fake creation, seeing in her weave and in every stitch the embodiment of everything that he could never be close to in the flesh of real life.

He spoke with her about love and truth and timeless bliss, imagining her voice as a soft and sultry summer night's whisper. He sat at her feet, gazing up into her embroidered mannequin eyes, and wept quiet tears for such beauty. In his heart he also wept because he knew that there was no such thing as a fairy god mother, no matter how much he wished it, no matter how loudly he wailed and pleaded. He suddenly remembered the words of the gambling man in his dream, a dream that seemed to exist in another lifetime. There was no soul. There would be no miracle. He would never meet his own Jiminy Cricket, nor would his darling girl ever come to life. For weeks David had denied this one simple fact while lost in the fever of creation, but now that this simulacrum of love stood rigid above him, he had to admit the truth, and with that admission the last of his strength began to drip away.

But there was yet one decision that David had to make. He understood that if he were to die for love, he would leave the girl standing as cold as stone in his flat, and that would never do. He had to find a way for them to be together, if not in this mortal world, then together in spirit, as one being within the eternal flame. Slowly David rose to his feet and, with the world swimming in black spots, he reached out and leaned on his work chair. Gradually the close horizons of his little working world steadied and he managed to focus. Where would they go, he asked himself? Where could they go? David was so tired and so run down and so exhausted of life that he really couldn't think clearly. Every spin of the cog wheels in his brain drained him of precious energy, so he took a decision. They would trust to Lady Luck.

Although rigid, the mannequin body was light. Without putting on shoes or coat, David picked up his darling girl, manoeuvred her down the stairs to the street door, and stepped out into a foreign world. When last he'd been out it was autumn and blustery but still warm. The world around him now was white and thick and diamond clear. Snow had come to blanket the world outside, marking the end of living time for another year with the coming of the sterile freeze.

David felt the cold for just a moment as the snow underfoot melted into his socks and the cold air scratched at his throat. The only question in David's mind was where they should go. A church? A bar? None of the obvious places for seeking happy oblivion seemed appropriate. Instead, David and his perfect woman set off towards the south, heading slowly down from the smothered heights of the city towards the equally hidden river valley below. It was early in the morning, judging by the sense of quiet slumber that emanated from under the snow-covered duvet that lay snug upon the streets, something for which David was rather grateful. Even in his befuddled state he still remembered the tattered edges of reason that came with ridicule.

After a mile or so, David began to lose all feeling in his feet and hands. He nearly dropped his perfect girl while negotiating kerbs, and he cursed the fates that might yet ruin his work. To make the river meant another mile or so of heavy trudge through the soft snow, and David began to doubt whether he had the strength to make it. He forced himself to take another step, and another, until, rounding the corner of some municipally grey building, David saw the flicker of bright red and yellow flames in a brazier at the end of an otherwise isolated and dark alley.

"Oh, yes," he whispered to his love. "Forgive me my dear, but I need to spend a minute or two by the fire."

There was a pause, as though she was answering him, and then he replied, "I know, but the river will take us down to the eternal sea. Just a moment of warmth, my love, just one minute, and then we'll be on our way again."

David dragged both his own shattered body and his frigid lover towards the brazier. There was no one in sight, although signs of itinerant occupation remained; an abandoned overcoat, an overturned mug next to a half full bottle of cider, cans and cigarette butts, a ravaged pizza box, and what looked like a used condom. David shuddered and told his darling girl not to look. He spread the overcoat out onto the bare snow and lay down in front of the brazier, letting the feeble flames work their magic, but magic, as David had already surmised, does not exist for people like us. Slowly as the effects of hyperthermia set in and the cold and the fatigue settled into the unconscious descent to coma and death, David muttered one last word; "Soon."

Without strength and without a word from his one true love, he slipped away towards the great sea of eternity, sailing towards his death just as he had always navigated the oceans of his life; alone.

The world was silent for a mosment but then there came a footstep in the snow, followed by another and another. The footsteps were slow and measured. Slowly, taking shape in the feeble fire light from the brazier, the form of a man dressed in a black frock-coat and waistcoat appeared. He knelt down where David lay next to the perfect mannequin and placed a hand on David's forehead and then at his neck. He held his hand there for a moment and then with a shake of his head he turned his attention to the mannequin. In running his fingers along her seams, in tracing the contours of the plastic body under her dress, and in touching her fantastically embroidered lips and eyes, he marvelled at the workmanship. She was truly the most beautiful creature that he had ever seen.

He turned back towards David's body and said, "I knew you could do it. If anybody could do it, it was always you." He patted David's cold leg. "And I meant what I said. No souls. It's like Michelangelo, you know, that one great work, the one that uses up your life. Still, it's worth it, isn't it, mate. She's stunning."

The man in black turned back to the mannequin, took both of her rigid cloth covered hands in his, and to her he whispered that simple phrase that brings life to the world; "Love you, babe".

The air suddenly grew warm and tropical around the brazier, melting snow and ice in an instant. The golden cloth shimmered in the fire light. Every stitch and every thread strained and writhed as the inner plastic of the shop-window mannequin twisted and buckled and then snapped back into place. Textures mingled and changed, and the world suspended belief for just one second, during which the man in black stood up and helped a gorgeous young woman to her feet. She wore a simple black dress over olive-golden skin, her dark hair falling in long cascades about her shoulders.

He looked into her eyes and smiled. "Been a long time waiting for you, babe." He bent forward and kissed her on her ruby-red lips.

She smiled too and then looked down at the crumpled body of the cloth cutter. "What's that?" she asked.

"Long story, babe. I'll tell you sometime. Right now, I'd wager you're just a wee bit hungry. What do you say we head down to the river where I know a great all-night café?"

The girl prodded the body with the toe of her bare right foot and shrugged her shoulders. "Yeah", she said, "I am a bit peckish, now you come to mention it."

The Politician's New Speech

(Loosely based on Andersen's The Emperor's New Clothes)

POLITICIANS COME AND GO, passing through the revolving doors of power and celebrity, and sometimes even infamy, like eels sliding from a barrel. For the most part the good folk who take up the cudgels of representative democracy on our behalf are well meaning, hardworking souls armed with the sword of conviction and the shield of dedication. In recent years this combination of valour and commitment has been ably demonstrated by many of the parliamentarians who congregate at Westminster. During recent periods of parliamentary jousting one politician above all others has become synonymous with the ruthless pursuit of truth and the calling to account of those who would betray the allied boons of principle and practicality. He has made it very clear that he doesn't care for convenient little compromises and political deals, believing absolutely that a spade should be called a shovel. That he is no longer in direct control of the levers of power is a shame, but in his time of greatness he employed a whole army of secretaries and assistants, whose sole job it was to document every fact and every detail of every case and policy so that he could remain true to his principles. He was well known for his ability to quote chapter and verse, with a comprehensive range of interpretations, on any of the hot political potatoes of the day.

So renowned was he throughout the country, indeed throughout the world, that many famous and influential people came to visit him at his London home, from where the man worked so hard to forge his shrine to political verisimilitude. One day, attracted by the unrivalled opportunities being offered to skilled people by this new broom sweeping through government's old and crusty cobwebs of social patronage, two provincial public relations specialists arrived in the city determined to make their fortunes. They watched and listened in the marketplaces, taverns and forums, and then, one morning, they called an impromptu press conference where they made a grand announcement. They could, they said, write the most fabulously truthful documents in all the known world.

"That's right", they said to an amazed crowd of journalists and onlookers in the main parliamentary square, "we are the greatest doctors of spin ever seen or heard. Our speeches, pamphlets and white papers are guaranteed to cure all evils".

To cap it all, they claimed that their documents were so beautifully written and were so truthful that they had a very singular and wonderful effect. Their words, phrases and arguments were so truthful that they became quite invisible to any person who was unfit for their office or who was inadmissibly stupid. The great politician was stunned when he heard these claims. "What a wonderful thing", he thought to himself. "With documents like this I can find out which men and women in my government aren't suited for the posts they hold; I can tell the wise ones from the stupid. Yes, these men must become my secretaries at once".

Within a couple of days, the politician's grey suited emissaries employed both men at a very competitive salary and asked them to lend their considerable expertise to the production of a particularly difficult document that the governing party had to set before their parliamentary colleagues. The two men were installed in a bright new office full of the latest computers, printers and online, on-demand production facilities. They sat tap-tapping away for days on end, preparing this very difficult document from the politician's notes and the supporting data supplied by various agencies, committees and focus groups. They attended countless briefings with government advisors and other interested non-governmental agencies, demanding without ceremony or attention to etiquette or protocol, the finest paper, the most exquisite pens and a great largesse of expenses, all of which disappeared into their briefcases at the end of each long working day.

After a month, and with the deadline for the great politician's speech looming, he decided that he would like to see how the document was progressing, although, given the special properties of this document, he felt a little uneasy about reading it in person. He certainly didn't want to appear unfit or stupid. The great politician did not believe in conceptual attitudes like fear, but nonetheless he felt it best to send one of his advisors to find out how things stood. After all, the political and media establishment knew about the magic powers this wonderful document possessed and the great politician knew that these people, who generally failed to see the bigger picture, would be as keen as mustard to see how unfit or stupid various members of the government might be.

"I'll send my faithful old private secretary to see these doctors of spin", thought the great politician. "He's very capable and far from stupid, so he's the best one to see how the land lies".

Sir John Gladstone went to the rather tastefully decorated office where the two word-smiths were beavering away at their task, and as he perused page after page of the report he became more and more agitated. "Heavens above", he thought, his eyes wide with surprise and fear. "I can't see a single word on any of the report's pages". But he said nothing.

The two writers asked him if he thought the syntax was just perfect? They asked for his opinions on all manner of things, and particularly whether he thought the blending of fact, interpretation and style created the most stunning and persuasive of arguments? Then they showed him the latest section of the report, which was hot off the printer, and Sir John could do nothing but open his eyes wider and wider. He couldn't see anything but blank pages, for there was, as far as he could tell, nothing written on any piece of paper anywhere in the room.

"Great galloping synonyms", he thought. "Am I really this stupid? I've never thought so, and if I really am then no one can ever find out. And if I'm not stupid then I must be unfit for my post! No, it will never do to let anyone know I can't read the report".

One of the two men of letters asked the old man, "Well, what do you think? You're being very quiet"

"Oh, erm, it's wonderful, to the point, pithy but flowing, quite brilliant..." enthused Sir John.

"We're delighted to hear it", said the two men, beaming at him, and they proceeded to name the chapters, to summarize their arguments and to explain all of the most salient points they had made. The great politician's faithful private secretary paid close attention to everything the men said so that he could repeat it all verbatim when he reported back to his master, which he did directly.

After this visit, and pleased with their work, the two doctors of spin demanded an increase in their salaries somewhat above the prevailing rate of inflation. They also asked for a chauffeur driven limousine and a large apartment overlooking London's magnificently refurbished and regenerated dockland landscape, but not a word was typed even though they sat in their office day after day tap-tapping away diligently on their keyboards.

Not long after this, and with the day of the speech now very near at hand, the great politician sent another official to review the document and to report back on its progress, but exactly the same thing happened to him as had happened to Sir John. He read and he read, but as there was nothing to read but empty pages, he couldn't actually read a thing.

"Isn't it a beautifully constructed thing", said the two public relations wiz kids, and they explained every nuance, every intimation and every statement, overt or implied.

"Well, I'm not stupid", thought the official, "and neither am I unfit for my position...at least, I've always assumed that was the case. If I really am incompetent I must be careful not to reveal it".

And so, he praised the document that he couldn't read and assured all who would listen that it was perfect. "It really is your sort of thing", he said to the great politician later that same day. "It's direct, to the point and it's sure to knock your opponents into next week".

Every journalist and commentator in the world of newspapers, television and radio, together with every member of the chattering classes and everyone who was anyone in the established elite, were all talking about the soon to be published paper. Reassured by his aides and aware that the world's press was waiting with bated breath, the great politician himself now wanted to read the document, even though there were still some relevant facts to include and a few final conclusions to draw. Together with Sir John and his cabinet colleagues, the great politician swept through the corridors of power and into the office where the two doctors of spin were pretending to type away furiously at blank computer screens.

Sir John, aware that he had to make a strong showing in the midst of so many hawk-eyed, elected members, exclaimed, "Oh yes Sir, isn't it magnificent, so well argued, so concise, so irrefutably true. Please, Sir, take a look, read the executive summary". He took the great politician to one side and showed him page after page, reassuring everyone assembled in the room that it was only the stupid or the incompetent who wouldn't be able to read a word.

"Bollocks", thought the great politician, "I can't see anything at all on these pages. This is dreadful. Am I really stupid? Am I truly unfit for the great office I hold? This is the worst thing that could happen to me. There'll be a leadership challenge for sure".

Calling on every ounce of his experience and all of his blithe abilities, honed to perfection through dealing with cabinet crises and the terrier snappings of the gutter press, the great politician read through a few pages silently. Then he turned to his colleagues and said, "Some good points being made here. Just what I wanted. All as it should be. Couldn't have put it better myself".

Turning to his two new spinmeisters he said, "Yes, very good work, gentlemen".

The great politician nodded approvingly at the piles of papers that covered every desk and table in the room. He certainly wasn't going to say anything about not being able to read the bloody thing. It was then the turn of his cabinet colleagues to scrutinise the document, page by page, but they weren't able to make any more sense of it than their boss had been able to do. Yet, like the great man himself, they were all convinced that their own survival in office was at stake. One after another they made various comments of agreement such as, "Oh yes, I entirely agree...Extremely well put...A fine piece of work...A solid basis for policy..."

So pleased were the great politician and his cabinet, so convinced were they of the document's merits, that they promised the two charlatans a knighthood apiece if the document found favour in parliament and the policy became law. The gentlemen in question thanked the members of the cabinet for their generosity, pleased that their work was so well appreciated, and looked forward to enjoying the benefits that such preferment would bring. They were particularly interested in lucrative non-executive directorships and non-governmental agency sinecures.

The two masters of official prose worked like Trojans throughout the whole of the night before the paper was due to be published, collating pages by section and sections by chapter. They bound the finished documents in real red leatherette and hand embossed the government's coat of arms on each cover. As dawn broke they staggered wearily out into the early morning daylight for a well-deserved cigarette on the Embankment. They were just in time to meet the deadline for publication. The great politician's long awaited speech on the matter was just a few hours away.

During the course of the morning the finished document was delivered to every cabinet minister, to the media, to members of parliament and, of course, to the great politician himself. The two charlatans attended the cabinet and ran through the contents of the report with the assembled ministers of state, describing and explaining all of their arguments, summaries and conclusions in the clearest and simplest terms.

"It's such an easy read, though", they said. You'd think there was nothing here but blank pages were you a simple minded man or an incompetent fool, but that, of course, is the beauty of it".

For the rest of the morning the two men worked with the great politician, schooling him in the contents of the report. They made sure that he could cross-reference the relevant sections with his own briefing notes and that he could quote verbatim from all of the sections and paragraphs that would support the arguments he was to make in his speech. As the great politician tried out different tones of voice and different facial expressions, as he opened his stance and practised his smile, the two doctors of spin encouraged and enthused; "Oh, sublime, Sir...Well put, Sir...What a winning way with words".

Just then Black Rod, in his role as master of ceremonies, popped his head around the door and said, "Time, Sir. They're all assembled in the chamber".

"I'm ready", said the great politician. "Bring it on…"

He took one last glance at the executive summary and checked his notes. He checked that his tie was straight and that there were no bits of cabbage stuck to his perfectly white teeth. Then he proceeded to enter the great debating chamber in procession with the master of ceremonies. The place was crammed to the rafters. Every bench seat was taken and there were crowds of people standing in the aisles. In the galleries up above the assembled politicians there was a veritable host of media reporters, who were all fighting and scrapping for the best vantage points. On every lap and in every hand there was a bound copy of the government document, resplendent in its full red leatherette glory. Every copy was thumbed and smudged with sweat and grime where avid but confused readers had tried and failed to glean the document's meaning from its empty pages. There was a look of madness in every elected representative's eyes, and the reporters in the gallery, having assumed they were in some way mentally sub-normal, were ready to hang on every word that the great politician might say. There was a general air of desperation.

Following a brief introduction by the Speaker, the great politician rose from his seat on the front bench and the wild chatter that had filled the great hall subsided and was replaced by a hum of nervous excitement. All became still, except for the sound of a car engine being revved outside, followed by the squeal of tyres on damp tarmacadam. The great politician cleared his throat and raised himself to his full and magnificent height.

"Never before have we faced such a clear and present danger", he began, using his most authoritative and serious voice. "Never before has our resolve been tested to such limits…"

All around him members of the parliament shouted and cheered. "Hear, Hear…Absolutely…Come the time, come the man", they all exclaimed, waving their order papers in the air above their heads. Not one of them wanted to appear stupid or unfit for their position in front of so many of their peers and friends in the media. The great politician raised his hand for silence, but just as he was about to continue the otherwise usually anonymous member of parliament for Rutland Metropolitan stood up and spoke.

"But there's nothing written on any of the pages..." he said quietly.

The chamber was pregnant with silent expectation. The Speaker started to rise, intending to admonish the backbencher for his rude interruption, but thought better of it when he caught the great politician's steel grey gaze. For his part, the great politician broke off from his prepared text and brought his verbal guns to bear on the heckler, just as he had done with unfailing accuracy so many times before. He glowered at the meek little man who had dared to interrupt him, before breaking into a fatherly smile and saying, "There speaks the voice of innocence..."

Even as he spoke the great politician became aware of a whisper circulating around the chamber. Backbenchers on all sides of the house became more and more animated, while the press pack in the gallery repeated the words of the otherwise unknown political representative to their editors by means of their mobile phones. Suddenly, one of the great politician's own cabinet ministers leaped out of his seat and shouted, "There's nothing written here at all - that's what old Hester-Whatsisname is saying - there's nothing written here at all!"

His words turned into a chant. Every single person in the chamber jumped up to his or her feet. The air was thick with the maniacal laughter and the sound of pages being torn out of the beautifully bound document. The great politician was drowned out in a storm of derision, with shouts and cat-calls ringing out everywhere. Every newspaper and every television programme ran special editions and lurid news flashes. The great politician shuddered and sank back into his bench seat. He knew the game was up... except that he puffed and he blew and he managed, with the help of the Speaker, to finish his speech.

The rest, as they say, is history, although throughout his long years of retirement, when he published his memoirs and his diaries and tried to settle into a state of fatherly grace in the House of Lords, the once great politician told anyone who would listen that he had been right, that his opponents had been wrong and that a report with blank pages was exactly what he had intended all along.

The Insomniac Booth

JEFF HAD A DRIFT on, the sort of drift that blows dry leaves along the gutter, an autumnal mood swing. He caught the eye of the waitress and pointed at his empty glass. There was no need for words, for the awkward camaraderie of the lonely drinker and the working girl. It was a new bar, new to Jeff, but he had already established the most basic and essential form of communication. She knew what his usual tipple was.

The fourth shot. Another large one, no ice. He could hear the straining flat line of someone murdering Uptown Girl in the karaoke room next door, but it was all white noise. He shoved a plate of cold, congealing food into the middle of the table. He'd ordered a cheeseburger and fries, no salad, but his appetite was only a function of his conscience. Without hunger to drive his impulse to recognise the thing as food, he found the charred edges of the meat patty distinctly disturbing. He hoped the waitress would take it away when she brought his drink over.

He had got as far as unwrapping the knife and fork from their red paper napkin, but they lay clean and sterile on the polished wood surface of the booth table. Jeff picked up the knife and ran a fingernail along the serrated edge of the blade. He put it back down, making sure that the knife and fork were positioned exactly in the middle of the napkin. Obsessive, he thought. Compulsive? He had to stop the displacement activity.

"Is everything...oh."

The waitress stood over the table looking at the plate of untouched food. The inevitable question, to which all sane people nod apologetically, stuck in her throat.

Like that burger would if I'd tried to eat it, thought Jeff.

"No, no problem, not with the food, anyway", he said, smiling dispiritedly up at her. He couldn't leave it at that. "Not hungry". He shook his head.

She lifted a tumbler from her tray and slid his drink onto the table. She raised an eyebrow and as she stooped to pick up the plate Jeff moved his left arm onto the table so that he covered the naked cutlery. The woman made no attempt to collect it. They exchanged a quick glance before she reached out to clear the empty tumblers that had contained Jeff's first three drinks from the table, a simple, unspoken question and answer; "Should I?, "No, not yet".

Strictly speaking this place wasn't a bar. The karaoke room next door was for post prandial entertainment. It was amazing what people would do in the name of a good time, even at this late hour. The burger had been Jeff's way of getting another drink, of getting more drinks. He'd fulfilled his side of the bargain and now they had to fulfil theirs. That was the thing about licensing laws, even though you could, as a landlord, open for business whenever you wanted to now. In this part of town the bars killed the lights around one. Terminal soaks and insomniacs had a choice; club land or places like this; pierced eardrums or thinly veneered late night diners with a license. Not that Jeff had been on the sauce all night. He rarely drank before ten and never in daylight hours. He had things to do. The problems started when he ran out of things to do. Counting empty tumblers was as good a thing to do in the wee small hours as anything else and it beat the herding of sheep into a cocked hat for entertainment value.

Jeff liked being near people when he couldn't sleep. It wasn't for conversation, nor was it for the vicarious thrill of some illicit opportunity. Jeff liked sound and presence, but not proximity. He took a shot. Cheap Spanish brandy. It kept the wolves at bay. He felt the skin inside his mouth tingle as the thirty-five percent proof fire bit.

Once, in another bar, he'd tried to see if he could get full value for money by laying six empty tumblers on their sides. He'd waited for the sticky residue of drink that clung to the glass to succumb to gravity and room temperature, and pool at the lowest part of the curve. Would he get another shot? The trick that other late night drinkers missed out on was patience. Wire in the blood and all that. The bartender that night had started off by being amused, but Jeff's insistence on waiting the full fifteen minutes before stacking each glass in turn on top of his last drink, balancing rim upon rim to complete the job, soon ceased to entertain.

He hadn't quite decided whether to try it again tonight. Something about the way the waitress looked at him suggested otherwise. She was older than most of them, older than Jeff remembered them being. He twisted in his booth, resting his back against the back wall and looked out across the bar. The place was sparsely populated, mostly by kids, or people Jeff thought of as kids. They were probably in their early twenties, had jobs, needed dental plans and were already tripping merrily along the yellow brick road to a conservative middle age. That was when he noticed the difference.

There were three waitresses on the graveyard shift, dealing with the fallout from the clubs and Friday night excursions to satiate the munchies. His waitress was in her forties, very Frankie and Johnny. The kids got the pretty girls. He guessed it was something to do with the myth of freedom. Older men on their own in situations like this, in the witching hours, drinking alone, couldn't be trusted. Thank the power of the free press for newspaper headlines screaming vengeance against paedophiles. Name and shame.

The bartender looked over at him, making a mental note of Jeff's make, model and license plate number. No, thought Jeff, they wouldn't send the pretty ones to deal with the ritual inhabitants of the insomniac booths. That's fine, though, he mused, swilling his brandy round in his glass. Age is immaterial. No, let's get it right, their age is immaterial. My age is entirely material to the case. Anyway, the young ones look right through me these days.

That was the point at which Jeff felt a sudden craving for nicotine. Three months on the straight and narrow. He'd tried before with a total lack of success, but this time it was working. Cold turkey. The day after the ban on smoking in public places he'd been thrown out of a bar for absentmindedly lighting up. Something had to give and Jeff had made his choice. When it came right down to it he needed the low light comfort of the booth more than he needed a hit of tobacco. He reached into his jacket pocket, snapped the foil backing off a tab of nicotine gum and popped four milligrams into his mouth.

Girls. Once upon a time it had been different, they had been different, subtle and alive. Was that right? Maybe it was he who had once been alive. Too much thinking at this time of night was bad for you. He had vague images in his head of eyes meeting sometime in the way back, images of the way women used to look at him. The edges of his inner vision blurred as the slide in time took hold. He couldn't put his finger on it, on the pulse. They used to look at him. Then they smiled but looked passed him, which he'd somehow missed at the time.

My God, he thought, is that what they mean when they say someone looks like an eager puppy. He could see spreading waistlines and floppy ears in the reflections sparkling on the upturned wine glasses hanging by their stems from the shelf above the bar. He shivered. Early onset middle age makes men hopelessly optimistic.

Now, though, even the older ones treated him with disinterest. They didn't even make the effort to look passed him anymore. He took another sip from his tumbler, the last of the night, and decided to buy a cigar from the tin behind the bar. The thin end of the wedge? Perhaps, he thought, but who cares. That's the question. Who cares that my DNA is following the rest of the traffic down a one way street, unravelling, turning me invisible?

Then again, maybe, just maybe he'd come back and order another unpalatable meal. Frankie and Johnny. It had to be worth a shot before he became as washed out as the glass in his hand. Jeff wrapped the knife and fork up in the red napkin and put them with the empty tumblers in the middle of the table. Then he put a five pound note on the table and placed his empty glass on it. It was a small gesture, a token of recognition, from one insomniac to another.

Beginning with Smith

TALES OF CREATION VARY according to time and place in any given universe, and yet, when you hear those dusty tales it is the similarities between them that strike you the most, and from these similarities we assume that there must at least be a grain of truth shared amongst our stories of beginning. For example, most such tales share an idea or thought of conception that is usually expressed as an action of some form of anthropomorphic being. The lists of creators are legion.

In the Bakuba account the Earth was originally nothing but water and darkness, ruled by the giant Mbombo. This giant, after feeling an intense pain in his stomach one day, vomited up the sun, moon, and stars. For the Maasai of Kenya humanity was fashioned by the creator from a single tree or leg which split into three pieces. Beyond the rising Maasai sun the Ainu people of Hokkaidō tell of six heavens and six hells where gods, demons, and animals lived. In the highest of these heavens lived Kamui, the creator god, and his servants. In the bloody annals of Aztec narratives creation proceeds with an Earth mother, Coatlique, the Lady of the Skirt of Snakes.

Not all tales of creation begin with the action or thought of some vaguely familiar being. Although some philosophers of origin may hear such abstracts as nothing more than a little local dissent or muddled thinking, nonetheless these different tales can be just as powerful. In earlier Vedic pondering on origin, the universe emanated from a cosmic egg, while some Daoists interpreted creation as a series of philosophical steps; The Way gave birth to Unity, Unity gave birth to Duality, Duality gave birth to Trinity, and Trinity gave birth to the myriad creatures.

Buddhism, however, largely ignores the question. The Buddha is quoted as saying something like, "Conjecture about the world is an unconjecturable that is not to be conjectured about, that would bring madness & vexation to anyone who conjectured about it."

Allowing for the unknowable and the agnostic, tolerating the conflict between the absolute void and the essential necessity of beginning, and forgetting for a moment the clamour of insistent insanity that underpins all of our attempts to understand anything beyond the obvious demarcation lines of our own fragile and brief existence, the tale that follows may also turn out to be as much a truth about creation as any other...

It is a commonly held belief that where there is light there must be darkness, that forces of life are matched by those of death and that in all things there is a balanced equation of equals and opposites. It stands to basic human reasoning given that we as conscious beings experience everything through a beginning and an end. A human child is born, erupts through puberty, mellows in maturity, fades with age, and eventually returns to the dust of death. A washing machine rises bright and shining from its packaging, suffers a decade of high-speed revolutions and hot water calcification, and finally returns back to its constituent elements through recycling or decomposition deep beneath the gull strewn summits of landfill.

This limitation to life is, of course, entirely human-centric and bears no real scrutiny when we consider the true faith inherent in origin. What was out there before Big Bang? The question is answerable only by an apparently endless circling of the square root of our own experience or by accepting that there is an absolute version of an almost impossible conceptual device; nothing.

The deity in question in this story was and is a small God. He, She or It has by simply existing removed the possibility of nothing, but equally none of the fundamental questions about beginning are answered by this God's existence. We have to face the simple fact that there was, all along, something.

In this particular beginning there was darkness, an almost void, an incomplete essence, and, for the sake of simplicity, Smith, our quietly drifting creator, really rather liked the darkness. Smith was the way and the meaning of nothing. Smith was thought without action, the procrastination at the very start of things. Smith liked to drift in the great expanse of un-place, whiling away the immeasurable aeons of non-time by contemplating the vagueness at the heart of all things. Smith thought about nothing.

Smith was not by nature solitary, rather it was simply the case that He had always been alone. Smith had what we might recognise as thoughts, but He had no shapes upon which to hang them. Smith was unable to fashion physical angels and demons as companions because Smith had never imagined imagination. In effect Smith could draw like an eighteen month old infant. He had no control over the heavenly pencil. All that Smith was aware of was the equivalent of a cosmic itch, and he endured the madness of the itch because he was impotence personified, that impotence inherent in not quite understanding the concept of the scratch, Smith unwittingly agreed with the future earthly Buddha in that He found the unformulated conjecture of eternal peace to be vexatious and maddening.

There is a moment in every natural state, a moment before the reaction, when forces are marshalled, reach a critical point and then tip towards change. Across the far flung boundaries of the void Smith finally determined that the endlessly irritating sensation that underlay the void was deserving of a name. Smith thought through the very fabric of time and finally, in a moment of naturally divine inspiration, He invented the word. Smith called the itch Silence.

Silence was the first form, the first shape upon which Smith could hang an idea, and He marvelled at the universe that crept into view with the naming of this first idea. Silence was a perfection of void and nothing. Smith, using a modern colloquial term, loved silence but with love comes an inevitable discontent. Even in the vast emptiness of Smith-time the itch eventually returned, and Smith was forced to concede a fundamental philosophical point.

In order that Smith might truly enjoy the silence, in the same way that a man might enjoy the silence of a house in the early morning before the space in the world is filled with voices, He had to accept the fact that He, She or It was conceptually awake. To love silence, Smith realised, meant that as the creator He had become aware of self and place and time, and of the difference between places and times and selves, none of which could ever have existed in a true void.

Smith thought, and in thinking proved Descartes right, and therein lay a problem. He was alone. He saw darkness. He experienced silence. He felt need. Smith wanted something but had no means to express such things in any sense other than silence and darkness, and so Smith thought un-shapes out of the fraying circular chords of absolute tranquillity.

Beyond the confines of earth-time, way out beyond the fringes of the universe where dark matter falls forever, Smith thought about nothing, taking slow but gigantic steps towards origin, and in thinking, even on a universal scale, Smith began to acquire the very first trappings of personality. Universal silence had a shape and the simple fact that Smith could hang thoughts from this shape inevitably lead Him to choose particular ways of thinking. Smith preferred those thought-shapes that pleased, that scratched the cosmic itch most effectively, and so He expressed thought in a set of patterned, reactive ways. Smith started to become predictable.

Predictability was, thought Smith in a broad and universal manner, a good thing. Smith preferred to consider a thought from a familiar set of viewpoints, rolling it across the heavens like thunder, looking at all those aspects of silence and darkness that reinforced the heavens as imagined by a responsible God. No matter how hard He tried to order creation, however, he continually discovered unwelcome shades of black within the unlimited spaces of the void, and in so doing He revealed even more of a personality. Smith liked some shades of nothing more than others. Smith put away the shades that displeased, and so came the formation of ideas that later we would call Good and Bad.

Unlike our earthly translators of the divine, unlike our latter day messengers of God, who know the way and speak the truth in our narrowly confined little world, Smith continually refashioned His likes and dislikes. With every turn of thought, as the shades of dark void rippled in the non-light, Smith found that His tastes changed. What had once been a Good shade now became a Bad tone and vice versa. Smith discovered choice.

Silence has a shape and upon that shape hang thoughts, and thoughts ripple, and Smith's universal mind grappled with the meanings of things without words or explanation. Faced with an endlessly moving target of certainty it is probably little wonder that across the gulf of time and space Smith became a little indecisive. With such unlimited options within His darkness how could a simple, artisan, pubescent God make a choice?

We, the readers of books and tales, find it difficult enough to answer questions even when our reading is wide and our thinking deep. For Smith, without access to heaven's as yet empty libraries, the darkness was beauty beyond description, solitude was a cruel mistress who only ever tasked without instruction, and silence was the wonder, the brilliance, the radiance of an eternal symphony half remembered. Smith could never quite be sure of anything. Silence was bliss, was the summation of every force and vitality known to the universal mind, but the inevitably subtle tonal difference within the quietude, as with the spectral shades of the void, caused Smith to vacillate.

In human terms, Smith listened to silence like we listen to Mozart on a Tuesday. We love Mozart the best. Then we listen to Beethoven on a Thursday and love Beethoven the best. Smith loved the Universal Light Programme that fizzed across the unseen radiation waves of His thought, but He loved each and every aspect of silence as if, for a fleeting moment, it was the only silence He had ever heard. Smith took the melody and the rhythm of the void into the soul of creation, swinging in allegiance from every note to every other note in a crescendo of perfect solitude, until it began to dawn on Smith that there was simply no way to settle on a universal truth in un-sound. Basically, Smith could no more organise a cosmic booze-up in an entire star field of breweries than could an ant recite the works of Rabbie Burns across the vast glens of Whisky sodden Scotland.

And so, it came to pass – always a sign of an author who can't quite grasp the deepest philosophical foundations, let alone be bothered to write it all down – that Smith, in the madness of endless conjecture, decided to stick a virtual pin into the dark hide of the universal donkey. Smith drew a metaphorical line in the cosmic sand and, breaking with every one of the unbidden traditions that had as yet underpinned the universe, thought-spoke to the void.

"LET THERE BE LIGHT".

Smith allowed the melody of sudden voice to flood through the vacuum of the void, combining it with the driving base line of fundamental creation that beat at His breast, and in so doing the stars shone suddenly like notes upon a black stave. Smith squinted in the bursting light, rubbed the black holes at the heart of his consciousness and grinned. The music of the heavens filled Smith with delight and He swooned with every rising phrase, letting the maelstrom notes burn through the universe. Had the universe contained any concept as simple as song, you would have heard Smith sing with a booming voice.

"LET THERE BE GALAXIES...LET THERE BE GASES...LET THERE BE COLLISIONS BETWEEN

HEAVENLY BODIES...LET THERE BE STRANGE AND SQUIGGLY CHEMICAL CHAIN REACTIONS..."

This is how the heavens broke forth into starlight, how the suns began to burn and how the cosmic gas and dust coalesced to form the planets. This is how a primordial soup was brewed, how tectonic shifts came to be and how the rocks and the heaving skies settled down to their endless game of birth and erosion. Smith looked out across these symphonic landscapes and grinned ever wider, and it was good.

Except, of course, for the unbending equation, for the balancing highs and lows in the song of Smith's stars. For things to be good, for Smith to feel the warmth of a billion, billion nuclear suns, there also had to be things that were bad. There had to be the absolute cold that allowed Smith to feel the warmth, and the inevitable balancing factor in the equation was Smith. In the primordial soup of creation a chemical chain might have a lifetime of a second, or it might exist in an unbroken sequence that lasted for millennia, but for Smith that moment of absolute happiness in the melody of life was nothing but a blink of an eye. Smith looked down upon one small star and upon one totally insignificant rocky ball at the outer edge of a tiny spiral galaxy of stars, and there He heard the very first bum note.

If, along with suns, molten planet cores and gas nebulae, Smith had invented teeth then he would have understood the problem instinctively. This single second of discord in act three of the universal symphony effectively scratched a single fingernail of blackboard agony across Smith's infant mind, and He knew in that instant of molar grinding pain that the equation must have balance. Good requires Bad.

Smith looked down upon the third rock out from a brightly burning star at the edge of an insignificant spiral galaxy and beheld friction. The elemental soup eroded the rock. Skies billowed and poured acid rain into fissures in those rocks, fissures that cracked and split ever wider, and spellbound by the fascination that makes a B-movie actress in a horror film go forth to see what it is that makes such an unusual noise, Smith made His first fundamental mistake.

Gods, even small ones, should never delegate, but if you read the stories in any one of a thousand books you will find that pretty well every single one of these creative types has taken the odd short cut or two. Smith thought about the Bad, considered the symphonic disagreement at the edge of the universe and, after a millennium or two of orbital time Smith arrived at a conclusion. The solution was simple and elegant; take a galactic eraser, rub out the errant note, and write down a simple harmonic improvement.

However, feeling the pull of a billion, billion stars, feeling the weight of mass and time upon His shoulders, succumbing to the myriad energies of relative balance flexing across the void, Smith put away the cosmic HB pencil with the little pink tip, washed his hands in the ethereal mists of space and willed the skies to peace. Smith brushed the primordial broth with a thought, dismissing this disappointing, barren little rock with a shrug, and left the madly sparking chemical squiggles to their own peculiar frenzy of oxygenated radicalism.

Almost as an afterthought Smith allocated a small portion of his dream time as the equivalent of a galactic closed circuit television system. That part of his ethereal mind that bore the as yet unnamed form of Conscience added just a hint of chiding harmonic resonance to the song of the universe, and thus was born the conduit between God and the third rock out from an insignificant little star. Smith turned his gaze away from the chemical and physical experiment at the edge of what we now call the Milky Way, but he left the monitors on and the tapes running just in case he ever needed to put a face to a crime.

In doing this, in leaving the cameras on constant surveillance, Smith also effected a process of change and evolution. As Smith dreamed and experimented and changed the fabric of time and space, as He formulated infinite varieties of life and death across the vast expanse of the void, small packages of His thought leaked out from beyond the horizon of Smith's dreaming and drifted through the aeons and along the canals and wires that connect the universal whole. Some of these rogue thoughts leaked into the here and now, drifting all the way out to Smith's now forgotten song of the Earth.

In dreaming of a peacock sky on some far distant world, Smith allowed a feather to fall upon the barren rocks of our world. Cells coalesced as notes in the song combined, water formed as notes tumbled over cosmic cliff edges, and proverbial butterfly wings fluttered in their thousands over the future-distant space of Beijing. Amphibians croaked a tenor's song of night. The Unicorn fluttered into the world for an instant before the nightmare broke its back upon the anvil of impossibility. Clouds billowed. Rain fell. Mountains rose and rivers cut deep scars into the surface of the planet. Ferns uncurled their leaves, morphosing into a billion species of tree and bush and flower. A flood of marine shapes colonised the roaring seas, monsters roamed the earth, shaking the foundations of the world to rubble, and finally, in the heart of blackness that was a shallow echo of Smith's loneliness, there was a dream of companionship. The mammals came and one of them, born of just a single microscopic moment in the great dream, stood up and walked out from the crowd.

Through the long ages of Smith's indifference the madly spinning Earth flourished, blooming on the edge of the void like a tiny fungal spore at the heart of a vast, immeasurable forest, and in that paradisiacal garden the ape walked, simply and silently, embodying the dream of Smith, becoming the ultimate, if yet unknown, companion.

Birdsong joined with the universal melody. Volcanoes added deep resonance to the bass lines underpinning the twinkling of the stars. Whales sang in the deeps of the ocean. Life itself upon, within and underneath the good, damp soil blew a fanfare to the heavens far beyond the measure of any single organism. The song was Good and Smith, even though he heard none of the individual songs sung by the flora and fauna of this long forgotten refrain at the edge of all things, found contentment in the straightforward knowledge that the song continued, a fulfilment sufficient for Him to think the work of creation a noble thing. But as always with the rhythm of the universe a discordant note took its inevitable place in the skirl of creation.

Smith batted the discord away like a fly on a hot summer day, but no matter how swift or firm Smith's vast and unimaginable hand, the fly continually evaded the swatter and buzzed back and forth at the edge of His perception. Eventually Smith turned towards the high pitched whine of gossamer winged song and, looking behind the metaphorical net curtain that hid the outer reaches of the old melodies from His hearing, Smith focussed his universal ear upon the sound of this disharmony.

Out at the edge of an insignificantly flat spiral galaxy, by a minute speck of light that shone almost below the visible spectrum, Smith heard a plaintive howling. He looked down upon the bright and savage earth for the first time in countless measures of eternity and there Smith saw something quite unexpected; the utterly familiar shape of loneliness embodied in the outlandish shell of the hairless ape who dared to contemplate creation, baying at the stars, calling out in utter desperation for the companionship that comes with that first sparkling moment of harmony within the song of songs.

Heirs and Graces

(Loosely based on Grimm's King Grisly Beard)

THE WORLD SEEMS TO grow ever smaller, with the grandeur of sheer distance made into a commonplace game of skipping by the advent of more efficient means of travel and the communications revolution that has blossomed in the bright sunshine of this digital spring. England's green and pleasant land is no exception, with every home an entertainment gin palace, where businesses thrive and prosper in the information age, and where the electronically dispossessed watch the valves and fuses of their analogue existence slowly burn down towards a state of mass extinction. London boasts at least seven Interweb billionaires amongst its fabled glitterati, but not one of them can begin to measure their fortune or their white-hot technological status against that of old Jimmy Cameron, the founder, chief executive and principle shareholder of NanoGoo International. Mister Cameron is blessed with the sort of fortune that, in fables and fairy stories at least, has only ever been granted to mere mortals in return for a lien on their soul. Jimmy, of course, puts it all down to a combination of hard work and inspiration.

Before his recent retirement James Cameron's octopine good fortune reached its happy tentacles out to touch every aspect of his life, not the least part of which was his stunningly beautiful eldest daughter, the delightfully named Cyberia. In every facet and viewed from every aspect old Jimmy's business life, his family life and his charitable works, underpinned as they were by an income that was the envy of many developing nations, were beyond reproach. Jimmy Cameron's world was a veritable treasure trove of goodness and sparkling happiness, except for one thing. Cyberia was quite possibly the most haughty, proud and conceited young lady to have ever shopped and lunched in the fabulously gold plated arcades and streets of London Town.

In spite of every advantage in life, including a fabulous education and a family ethos of good works and humble gratitude for the largesse granted by fate, this young lady rarely had a good word to say for anyone. Her sole purpose in life seemed to be dedicated to looking down her nose at people, and nowhere was this alarming personality trait more obviously demonstrated than in her reaction to possible suitors. She was famed throughout the elite echelons of London's highest society for humping and dumping the most eligible young men, and all of it was done in the blaze of paparazzi flashbulbs and on the glossy pages of celebrity gossip magazines. Cyberia was an Olympian in making a sport out of rudeness.

The regularly played out scenes of Cyberia's drunken wantonness eventually became too much for old Jimmy to bear and he finally decided to do something about his wayward daughter. Together with his wife he planned a great party, to which he invited the country's great and good, including every single unattached young man who either possessed or was heir to a significant wedge. Come the day of the party, each of these potential suitors was made to sit in a row, ranged according to their social rank and family wealth. Cyberia, under the gentle but determined guidance of her despairing father, was made fully aware of the fact that her allowances, party frocks and charge card accounts would be summarily discontinued if she failed to choose a husband and settle down into a life of domestic contentment and suitably directed good works.

The young lady was somewhat less than impressed by the situation. It was only under the severest of admonishments that she had ceased to throw plates, crystal knickknacks and sundry items of cutlery at her parents. Come the evening of the party, and even with a substantial layer of foundation on her face, the guests could still see red rings under her eyes from all of her screaming, bawling and crying. Needless to say, and despite the threat of imminent penury, she could hardly contain her contempt for the men displayed before her. As she walked along the line of potential suitors she spat out insults at every one of them.

The first was too fat. "Euk! Mister bloaty or what?" she bellowed.

The next young man was far too tall and lanky. Pinching her nose and turning to the other guests she exclaimed in a nasal tone, "Smells of wee-wee!"

The next young man, while muscular and neither too fat nor too thin, was far too short. Cyberia refrained from speaking to him at all, and simply put her empty glass down on the top of his head.

The fourth young man was too pale and she called him a lungfish, and so it went on. She cracked wicked jokes or made spiteful personal observations at the expense of almost every single one of the young men at the party, until coming face to face with the last of the line she burst out into raucous laughter. It took two security guards to hold her down and a good ten minutes before the sobbing, giggling young woman could regain any semblance of composure.

"Look at him", she said, choking back tears, "his teeth are all crooked and those glasses, that moustache… what a minger!"

And that is how Captain "Rocky" Flashman-Pebble, a company commander in the Royal Horse Guards and heir to the fourteenth Duke of Stackton, got the new nickname of "Minge-face".

Old Jimmy Cameron was furious when he witnessed at first-hand how his daughter treated his guests and friends. Her behaviour was quite beyond the pale and he took all available legal steps to ensure that every one of her lines of income and credit were suspended with immediate effect. He also made a solemn vow to his wife later that evening that, willing or not, Cyberia would marry the very first man, be he prince or pauper, that pressed the buzzer on the security gates that separated the family mansion from the mean streets that housed the capital's hoi-polloi.

All was quiet in the Cameron household on the day after the party. A combination of hangovers, of both the alcoholic and emotional varieties, served to keep father and daughter well out of each other's way. On the second morning after the party, however, there was a loud bleep on the intercom that connected the house with the electronic gates. Jimmy buzzed back and heard a young man's strangely colloquialised voice ask, "Sorry to bother you, guv, but I'm a bit down on my luck. Tenner for a song?"

The busker was granted admittance to the Cameron estate and proceeded to play a very rough rendition of a then popular chart tune as he stood on the front doorstep. When he finished murdering the melody, the clean shaven young man asked for a few pounds to keep hunger at bay, at which point old Jimmy asked him if he would like to come in for a cup of coffee and a bun. Over a mid-morning snack in the kitchen, with Cyberia watching from a safely curious distance, her father turned to the young vagrant and said, "Tell you what, you've sung so…erm…beautifully for us this morning that I'm going to give you my daughter for a wife!'

Cyberia stood transfixed for a long, fecund moment, quite unable to believe her ears. Her father had often threatened her with punishments when she was naughty, but he had never actually carried them out. She was his little princess, his little starlet, and he simply couldn't mean to go through with his threat from the party. Cyberia looked at her father and saw in his eyes something that she had never seen there before, namely hard, cold, blue steel. The poor little rich girl sank to her knees and begged her father for forgiveness. She promised, swearing blue and blind to every saint and deity that she could think of, that she would be good from now on, but no matter how much she pleaded and cried, her father would not to be moved.

"I swore the other night that I'd be rid of you. I'm going to teach you a lesson, and this fine young man is the first to knock on our door. This time I will keep my word!"

The car was called for and Jimmy Cameron, his wife, his daughter and the young busker were whisked through town to the 'Elvis, "The King", Wedding Chapel', where, by twelve noon, the young man and his reluctant bride were duly wed by a fully shell-suited, coiffured and qualified registrar. Once the ceremony was over, old Jimmy poked his head out of the car window and looked at the newlyweds. Cyberia stood dumbly next to her beau.

Jimmy smiled at the happy couple and said, "Well, my girl, you're on your own now. I've stopped your allowances and cards and given this young man a small bung to see you through for a day or two, but it's up to you now. Don't come back to the house".

With that the black tinted window glided back up and the car purred its silent, luxurious way into the teeming lunch time streets of London's hustling West End.

"Well, doll, time to be on our way", said the young busker and he lead his bride by the hand through the crowded and dusty city streets.

Cyberia, unaccustomed as she was to seeing the metropolis in its daytime apparel, walked open-mouthed past dingy basement flat windows, down long, dark alleyways and visibly felt herself shrink before the impressive, classically styled porticos of ancient institutional temples. Eventually, as she and her new spouse walked down one of the leafier boulevards of the city near the diplomatic quarter, she saw a mansion house of the most ornately carved variety. Stopping and pulling the young man back towards her she asked, "Please wait. Do you know who lives in that marvellous house over there?"

The young man looked at the house that Cyberia was pointing at and replied, "Oh yeah, that's Stackton House, owned by the fourteenth duke. I think his son, Minge-face, lives there at the moment. If you'd behaved properly, all that could've been yours".

Cyberia felt a long, hollow pain swell up in her chest as she gazed on the magnificent residence and sighed, "It's not fair…if only I'd been nicer to Minge-face…"

The unhappy couple continued their foot slogging journey across the Smoke, heading for the river and the poor busker's home territory in one of the poorer southern suburbs. As they crossed the river on one of the city's famous bridges Cyberia caught sight of a huge, enclosed park and wished for all the world that she could sip some cool lemonade and rest her weary legs under the shade of a great oak tree.

She stopped the young man once again and asked, "That park looks lovely in the sunlight. Who owns it?"

The young man shielded his eyes and looked across the diamond-encrusted water. "That place? Lovely isn't it. Belongs to the Duke of Stackton, part of his extensive estate here in the city. You see, if you'd been a good girl you could've enjoyed all your summer afternoons in there."

Once again the shattered young lady felt great pangs of regret well up in her throat. "Shit", she muttered, "if only I'd listened to the old man".

Cyberia turned to look once again at London's more fashionable districts that towered above her on the northern bank of the river Thames. Never again would she see the inside of a five-star restaurant or dance the night away to the latest drum n' bass beats in the Department of Tunes nightclub. As she gazed on her former life for the last time she found her eyes drawn to the tallest glass tower on the city skyline, on the windows of which the brilliant afternoon sun was conducting a symphony of light.

"Oh", she sighed, "how beautiful. Who owns that skyscraper?" The young man didn't bother to turn and look, but continued to drag the reluctant young girl towards his home as he spoke.

"Stackton family", he said. "Actually, it's called the Flashman-Pebble Tower and it's owned by old Minge-Face's property development company. Part of his long term plans, so they say, for when he leaves the cavalry and becomes a city gent."

Words could never convey the utter despair and horror that Cyberia felt as the full force and consequence of her past life fluttered down to roost on the parrot cage perch in her brain. As she stumbled blindly after her new husband towards a life of disappointment and endless drudgery, the brightly coloured bird of regret that now inhabited her waking mind squawked repeatedly, "Told you so! Told you so!"

The newly spliced couple tramped onto the dirty soil of the young man's home manor, and as the young woman became visibly cowed and burdened by her fate, the young busker made one final observation.

"No point crying over spilt milk, love. No point wishing you'd married someone else. We're done and dusted, all legal, and you'll find I'm perfectly good enough for you."

At last they came to a very down at heel street, where most of the back-to-back terraced houses were either boarded up or bare boned skeletons. The man stopped outside the only house in the road with glass in its windows.

"What a dismal place", said Cyberia. "Who on earth would live in a place…?" She didn't need to finish the sentence. She knew in her heart of hearts that this was now her home. The young man opened the front door and ushered her into a world of bachelor squalor, where dust hung in the air permanently because it refused to fall on flat surfaces that had already accumulated too many years' worth of grime and flaked skin.

"I don't suppose we have a cleaner?" asked Cyberia in a flat, monotone voice.

"We do now", replied her husband. "You'll find the kitchen down the end of the hall. There's a mop and a bucket and stuff. There's also a kettle and a cooker, although that'll need some elbow grease on it. Be a love and make a cup of tea".

A cup of tea was one thing, but when it came to domestic chores, cooking and the generality of tasks that comprise sound household management, Cyberia was a complete novice. For two days the blissful romance that should be the ambrosia of all newlyweds was forced to give way to lessons in using the Hoover, heating up baked beans and loading the washing machine in such a way that the clothes didn't all come out shit colour drab.

When the small pile of cash that Jimmy Cameron had given to the young man had been exhausted on take-away curries and some cheap red plonk, the young busker turned to his new wife and said, "Right, time for you to earn your keep. You're to look after the house and cook meals, and you've also got to earn cash. I'll put an advert in shop windows telling people you take in ironing.

Over the next three or four days a succession of busy city types, who had invested in this run down part of the city in an attempt to make a killing on property prices in a rising market, brought around baskets full of striped shirts, frilly blouses and flimsy briefs to be ironed. During the day the young man went off to commit his musical crimes in shopping malls and bus stations, only to find that he had to hand over most of his meagre gains to blustering brokers and flustered financial advisers because Cyberia had scorched their whites. Eventually, over a bowl of thinly disguised gruel, he said, "Look, love, this won't do. I can see ironing's not your strong suit, so from tomorrow you'll do piece work. There's three hundred greeting cards a day for you to paint and stick. I've arranged for someone to drop them in of a morning".

True to her husband's word, a man arrived on the doorstep early the next morning and deposited a number of cardboard boxes in the hallway. He told Cyberia that there were some instructions in an envelope in one of the boxes and that he would be back that evening to pick up the first three hundred cards. All she had to do was colour in the flower petals and stick paper leaves to the front of each card. Having spent her first week of married life struggling with piles of creased cotton and Lycra, Cyberia felt much happier about her revised career prospects.

"After all," she said to herself as she unpacked the boxes and made neat piles of the cards and the packets of paper leaves, "I always enjoyed art classes at school and it can't be that hard to make a few hundred of them".

Unfortunately, Cyberia's appreciation of art and craft was based on the experience gained at her finishing school, where she had spent relaxed Wednesday afternoons fiddling with watercolours and making decoupage kittens out of old socks and yoghurt pot lids. Nothing, however, on her curriculum vitae included the term 'industrialised'. When her husband returned home after another hard day performing for London's musical cognoscenti he found the poor girl buried up to her armpits in smudged sheets of thin cardboard. Her arms, her nose and her hair were covered in glue and disintegrating paper leaves. She was in such a frustrated lather that her mascara had run right down her cheeks and lay in a sludgy grey puddle on the kitchen table.

"What the bloody… you're crap at cards as well!" he exclaimed, sweeping the mess of celebratory messages into a big black bin liner. "Right, plan C. It's Saturday tomorrow. There's a load of old rubbish in the lock up I nicked from outside charity shops, you know, dead men's suits and dog eared paperbacks. I want you down at the car boot sale at six tomorrow morning flogging the lot. One way or another you'll earn your keep, girl!"

Clothes, of course, were something that Cyberia did know about and despite the unearthly hour of her rising and the wonky wheels on the shopping trolley that she had to use to transport her uncharitable apparel down to the local football club's car park, she made a good fist of the first hour. By arranging the suits, shirts, blouses and skirts by label, size and colour she managed to shift most of the better items to middle class bargain hunters and a good deal of the less fashionable items to the local student population. By nine o'clock Cyberia had nearly sold out her stock and was looking forward to the little luxury that might be afforded by way of a bacon butty and a polystyrene mug of tea, when her husband arrived pushing an old pram full of soiled tee-shirts and builders' low slung jeans. He forbade her to take a break until the whole wardrobe had been disposed of and it wasn't until nearly four o'clock that afternoon that Cyberia managed to trudge home wearily, smelling of sweat, fried burgers and other people's loose change.

Nonetheless the day had been something of a success. From the takings her husband was able to recompense his mate for the ruined cards, put enough cash in his pocket for a good night in the pub and leave Cyberia with enough housekeeping to keep them going for nearly a whole week, providing, of course, that she shopped frugally and avoided anything expensive like fresh bread and real butter. During the week Cyberia cleaned the house, cooked meals and performed a range of other wifely duties while her husband, under the guise of bringing euphonic enlightenment to the masses, rescued black bin liners full of old clothes, books and partially complete jigsaw sets from the doorways of London's charitable retail outlets. On Saturday and Sunday mornings for the rest of that summer you would have found Cyberia pushing shopping trolleys full of used clothing in the direction of car boot sales full of eager, budget priced consumers.

In relative terms everything seemed to be going well for the young woman until she encountered a group of local youths one Saturday afternoon. She had seen them hanging around the car boot sale all morning but thought nothing much about their presence other than that they exuded the normally confused menace of seventeen year old boys. They had, however, been scouting out a likely target and had chosen the slightly built young lady with the bulging money belt as the best source of the filthy lucre that they needed to maintain their lighter fuel and crack cocaine habits. Cyberia soon realised that the normally confused menace presented by a group of teenagers in a crowded car park was nothing like the real, in your face, blade wielding menace that they could deliver on the corner of a quiet, backwater city street. Her husband was not impressed when she eventually returned home minus the shopping trolley, without any money and too scared to make amends for her failings by popping down to the off-licence for him.

"I mean…it's not as though you're a child", he admonished her. "They're only kids but you're a grown up and with all the work you've been doing around here you've got muscles on your muscles. If you're going to make your way in this part of London you've really got to learn to stand up for yourself".

Cyberia tried to be brave but the trauma of the robbery combined with the endless trials of her new life had worn her out. As she sat on a kitchen chair and quietly sobbed to herself, her husband decided that he had, perhaps, been a little harsh. He made her a nice cup of tea, sat down opposite her and suggested an alternative way in which she could contribute to family life.

"OK, darling, what about this? I've got a mate, well, a contact really, up in the city who's always looking for a nice girl to do a bit of work for him. It means working at night, but the pay's not bad if you don't mind a bit of scrubbing. Shall I tell him you're interested in a bit of office cleaning?"

And so Cyberia became one of London's army of night cleaners helping to keep the wheels of commerce running on well-oiled bearings, and by combining her weekly wage packet with her husband's musical royalties the couple managed to earn enough to keep the wolf and the bailiffs from the door. After a few weeks Cyberia was even asked to become a cleaning team supervisor and, accepting the increase in wages without a second thought, took command of the cleaners on the executive floor at the NanoGoo International headquarters building.

A few evenings later, as Cyberia was preparing to dust the huge, polished wood boardroom table, an officious looking woman in a bright red power-shouldered suit came into the room and buttonholed her.

"Can you make a bit more of an effort today, dear. We're holding a party here tomorrow afternoon to welcome Captain Flashman-Pebble onto the board. I want you to make sure you can see your face in the table, that the bins are all emptied properly and that you run the Hoover under the chairs and not just around them. Understood?"

Cyberia just looked at the woman.

"Hello? Speakie English?" asked Jimmy Cameron's personal assistant, before pointing at the table and making grunting noises. She turned on her heel and muttered something about employing immigrants.

Left alone with her thoughts, Cyberia collapsed in on herself and slumped down into one of the big leather boardroom chairs. After all of the hardships of the last few months, this was the final straw. She cried and cried and cried, grieving for the pride and the utter folly of her previous existence that had now laid her down so low. The teams of cleaners finished their work and, wondering where their supervisor had disappeared to, signed themselves out of the building and evaporated back into the teeming maelstrom of the city from whence they had come. Left alone in the boardroom, Cyberia lost all sense of time as she sobbed her heart out for her foolishness.

Time passed in a blur of wet eyes and convulsive sobs, and it was late into the evening before Cyberia realised that she was not alone in the boardroom, and through her tears she could barely make out the shape of the person standing by the door. She waved her hand at the figure, desperate to shoo the person away, and continued to spill bitter tears upon her red flushed cheeks, but the figure came towards her, knelt at her feet and held her hands. She felt the rough calloused fingers of someone she had come to know well in recent weeks and her shoulders immediately began to heave in a great, heartfelt wail. He would only make fun of her, she thought, and pulling away from her husband she tried to rise from her chair and run for the door.

Her husband refused to let go and pulled her back into his arms, where he held her close and tight to his chest until her anger, fear, frustration and wretchedness dissipated and she fell into a gentle half swoon. Quietly and softly he lifted her head up so that she could look him in the eye.

"Aaaarrrgggghhh!" she screamed, desperately trying to push him away. "It's…it can't be…Minge-face?"

"I prefer Rocky, or Captain", he said tenderly, taking off the milk bottle glasses, pulling a set of theatrical teeth out of his mouth and ripping off his fake moustache. "Don't be afraid, my darling. It's always been me. I fell in love with you ages ago, but you were always so rude. Your father and I cooked up the whole plan. All of the other girls are sweet but so utterly boring. To be a real member of Albion's aristocracy you have to have some spunk in your soul, but you we're something else. I had to cure you of your pride before you met Mummy and Daddy".

Cyberia flung her arms around her handsome, landed busker and hugged him so tightly that he thought he would burst. Just then the doors to the boardroom crashed open and the combined weight and wealth of the Cameron and Flashman-Pebble clans surged into the room, waving glasses of bubbly and cheering loudly as they celebrated the perfect society couple locked in true love's wonderful embrace.

Fergus on A Bridge

THERE WAS A CERTAIN immature swagger in their collective step. Four young men on the still industrially stained streets of an as yet unregenerated city. Leeds. Nineteen eighty-one or thereabouts. Drainpipes and frayed surplus army jackets. An overcoat, a white button down shirt and a bootlace tie. Students. An Arafat scarf. Pixie boots. Baggies. Boot cuts and plaid shirts. Vaguely stubbled chins. One of the boys was brave enough to wear mascara. Broad grins and urgent laughter. An early eighties twitch away from punk towards Smithian Cures and McCulloch's Bunnies. In the wild and wuthering Yorkshire heathlands superimposed on the otherwise blank landscapes in their heads these boys never cried when they were on a promise.

They were, though, still gentling boys, most of them, breathing the sweet airs of a spring evening on the trek down from Burley towards the Arndale and then along the Headrow to The Warehouse. Sweet airs upon sweet air and all just a wheeze away from their digs and fetid piles of washing lurking in corners by desks laden with every accoutrement known to a Maggie Thatcher-era student except essays and assignments. The unwashed waited stiffly and stoically together for the placcy-bag haul back home on the train, for a long weekend of proper food, for a mother's indefatigable love and a twenty on the paternal bung.

Tonight, though, it was rumoured that Heaven 17 would be making a late, choreographed, tape machine backed appearance on The Warehouse's postage stamp of a stage. Fascists and Groove Thangs. The stuff of boyish nights and childishly exaggerated Friday morning hangovers. The four of them had abandoned their varied attempts at academe for the week and had already spent an hour in Dick's flat watching The Munsters, drinking Bulls Blood, smoking a spliff or three and had then livened themselves up with a line of something worryingly but whizzingly speckled blue. Dick swore that he knew the bloke who knew the bloke who had driven over to Chapeltown so that made everything just fine.

The chemical order of things dictated that they head now for the chippy opposite the old Uni clock tower steps, kill the munchies, find a pub, drink beer and then dance until they dropped or the lure of a fragrant smoko on the town hall steps called them out into the wee small hours. They might try to nick another digger from the building site down by the Engineering Department. They might just walk. Fergie was the king of the walk. Fergie was the king of the bridge. Secretly they were all slightly infatuated with Fergus Patrick McGoldrick.

In the beginning there was Fergus. Twenty-four. A mature student. The one who had remained in halls for two years and only moved into digs when the new crop of first year boys begged him to. Fergus was the one with the weird and unfathomable background. In Fergie's case it was an Irish thing, northern, and never really explained or asked about. One mention of Troubles with a capital "T" gummed the English lads right up. Fergie was studying English Literature. Faerie Queens and peering ploughmen. Fergie laughed freely and tested the boys whenever he got bored. He introduced them to the craic. He drank too much but never got drunk. Same with the smokes. It never seemed to matter how much he took, he could always, always shoot straight on the black for winner-stays-on in the Skyrack.

Then there was Dick. Lovejoy duffled and scarved as often as not. Thick short browns and heavy boots. Public school. The actor. Feigned drawls, mock candours and fantastically flawed relations. Dick was the provider of Thursday evening dossery. Allegedly Dick had a girlfriend but as yet the boys had only caught glimpses of something feminine in the creases of his turn-ups. Unlike Fergie, Dick got royally drunk pretty much whenever he could. He was an anthropologist. He got drunk on the back of a ten hour working week.

Dick had it hard. Mick was the obligatory history wonk. Four hours of lectures and two in tutorial. The rest of the week was library time. Barring an occasional spin on the hockey pitch, library time was mostly spent reading the signs on hand-pumps in The Skyrack, The Original Oak, The Haddon, The Queen, The Eldon, The Hyde Park and the Union Bar. He could also read a snooker scoreboard, although a teenage onset myopia meant that he mostly recorded the results of his own foul shots. Once in a while he rushed madly to finish an essay. He was the grammar school rebel. Essentially off the rails except when the work ethic actually mattered. He claimed that his favourite historical character was Yosemite Sam.

And then there was Dave. The compo genius. The one who should have gone to Oxbridge. The one who really did have to deal with issues but mostly covered them up. Dave was a fosterling. Dave went home to people who were essentially friends of the family once removed. Dave deserved better. Dave worked bloody hard to compensate, and then somehow managed to screw it up on the point of each and every victory. Every time. Without fail. Dave was jeans and plaid. He owned and actually wore a grey check sports jacket. In public.

Four boys. Four young men. Russell Group red-bricks. Three of them not yet twenty and oblivious to their privilege. Four of them telling the world that they did not care. Three of them liars. Four of them out on the craic.

*

The wired little gang of four on the lash reached the university clock tower opposite the now closed Islamabad restaurant. They were culturally closer to Blyton than they were to Missus Mao's revolutionary brotherhood so recently deposed in the far Orient. The boys had been genuinely shocked and then thoroughly delighted by the latest rumours. German Shepherd in the lamb Madras. Collie in the cauliflower bhaji. The Islamabad had been closed for nearly a week. It was, to the day, precisely one week since their last two-in-the-morning stopover for something brown and spicy on their trudge home from the previous week's Indie night at The warehouse. A Doggie Dhansak?

Just as they passed in front of the last of the restaurant's four plate glass windows, the one with the green and yellow palm trees painted on it, Fergus stopped in mid walk, leaned over the kerb and vomited. Bile. A trick he had for the boys. Faint disgust and fascination. Assumptions. An ironic commentary on the state of take-away culture? One too many Bulls? Fergus being Fergus? None of them yet suffered like he did from chronic reflux.

"Better out..." A clearly and flatly intoned brogue. That harsh drive through the vowels that marked the Ulsterman.

Being typically English the boys kept walking. They said nothing, as though it was all just a commonplace. It was just a commonplace. They exercised that age old English oxymoron that is hurried and consciously applied nonchalance. It was not until the Arndale swung into view and concrete shadows engulfed them that the boys' shoulders visibly relaxed. They had been dismissed from their parade ground drill by the sight of The Haddon. The first pub of the night. The long walk done. Now they could relax into the drifting rounds that marked the hours between nine and eleven. Just enough time and booze to feign wasted but not enough to be denied entry by the bulldozers on The Warehouse door. Darts and Timmy Taylors and Tetley and thick tar stains on fingers and heavily paint crusted wallpaper.

*

And so to Heaven 17. Martyn, Ian and blonde shocked Glenn. Synchro-synthotechnics. Almost clockwork. Loud and bright and brown and black and bass lines driven on for stylised boys and girls on the beer soaked dance floor. Drifts of weed floating under a heavy Silk Cut pall. That strange angular, sideways jog that passed for new-wave-indie dancing in the early nineteen-eighties. Mullets and Mohicans. That slight tinge of tinnitus swelling as the evening wore on.

These were the days before craft beer and imported lagers.

Tetleys and Harp and an exotic Fosters XXXX for the brave. Four songs, one of which was a popular reprise of Fascist and then the tape machine broke down. Boos and laughter and a rock star on the dance floor trying to find a groove to Typical Girls. These were the things that Fergus, Dick, Mick and Dave chattered and laughed about as they straggled along back-to-back lanes on the homeward Burley trek, up past Jimmy's and all those resting patients on Victorian wards a-screaming where one James Saville esquire worked shell-suited devilry in the name of sweet charity.

They fetched up down by the Engineering department. Déjà vu. A rerun of a scene from The Great Digger Heist. Streetlights burning sodium orange. Stopping to light up. Coughs and rollies and matches shielded in cupped hands against the night breezes. Footsteps dragging, the pace slow and meandering. Beer on breath. The way seemed dark and long when the walk was on the up. Collars pulled up. Heads were starting to ache and cheeks to burn.

And so to the bridge over the inner ring road. Woodhouse Lane. Two o'clock quiet. A thirty foot drop to the rumbling tarmacadam below. Busy down there. Clubbers in cabs. Mums and Dads grumbling about free bloody taxi services but nonetheless relieved that the kids were alright. A sudden burst of blues and twos. The siren wailings echoed off the ring road walls as they rose up towards the Woodhouse Lane bridge.

A siren call. Three of the boys began to chant. They egged each other on. Fascination and dread. An almost messianic admiration of the doomed saviour. That one might die to save all others…

"Bridge..! Bridge..! Bridge..!"

Fergus waited and watched. The boys baited and panted. They

felt like lords of the night and as happy as flies on a dung hill. Fergus shut his eyes for a moment. He let the chants fade to laughter. He waited just long enough for the derision to start, for the nerves to jangle and for childish taunts to pitter-patter across the pavement.

"Really?" he asked archly.

And so to the walk. Fergus took off his pale green army surplus and rolled up the sleeves of his red cotton shirt. He took off his shoes and socks and handed the bundle to Dave, who almost bowed in supplication. Breathing quickened around him, but Fergus remained calm. He stood silently for a moment and then, at a point where the road bridge was still firmly tethered to the land he climbed slowly onto the top of the side wall so that he ended up in a crouched position, one foot behind the other, with his hands on each side of the top rail while he groped for and then sensed and finally felt his whole being slide into this new elevation.

A small part of the man wanted to be sick. Another chink, a sliver, wanted to cut and run. Around him he could sense that same mixture of revulsion and fascination and fear rise, but it was in the doing of this thing that Fergus gained true control and mastery. He stood and wobbled. He heard gasps and giggles. He heard the rise in pitch and tone as the boys shifted towards discomfort. It was time to up the stakes. Fergus slowly turned atop the rail so that he would have to walk backwards.

"No fucking way…" Dick.

"Jesus, Ferg. You sure, mate?" Mick

The sound of beer and bile on a paving slab. Dave.

Fergus moved both arms out to the horizontal. He closed his eyes. Left foot backwards. He held that moment. He measured the fabric of the universe. He could feel the cold metal on his heel and his ball and his toes. He could feel alcohol in his bloodstream. He could see a shining path behind him, as wide as a boulevard. Right foot backwards. He adjusted. He flexed and waved his right arm out towards the ring road thirty feet below. It was, he mused, calculated insanity.

"Shit!" Mick.

"No, Ferg… Come on mate. No need. Just kidding." Dick. Panic. Really bricking.

The sound of a grey check sports jacket sleeve being rubbed across slickly sickly stubble. Dave.

One foot after another. At his feet Fergus imagined the scene; a hesitant, fidgeting gaggle of three spooked kids waiting for the crack of a skull on concrete. Fergus reached the middle of the bridge. The point of no return. The boys hovered in some vague reverie, assuming that if Fergus fell then they would be able to defy the perceived slow motion reality of gravity and haul their Messiah back to safety. They knew in their hearts, of course, that they would grab at thin air. This was all about faith. That was the thrill of it. That and the cackle and the full on tongue-lashing that they got if they moved too close to the tightrope walker extraordinaire. This was full bore road-kill obsession.

Fergus had, however, no intention of ending his days with his head beneath the wheels of a thirty-two tonne pantechnicon. Fergus was in control. Each step was an act of defiance and an act of compliance. At times like this he felt at one with the world, with this starscape, with this wonderful chaos. For Fergus those long days and nights in between bridges was an endless falling. Up here on this railing was precisely where and when he truly fitted into an otherwise alien universe. He was halfway across. He kept his eyes closed. He saw the hovering boys as deeper shades upon the grey tones of an otherwise bland night. The shades moved a little closer. Fergus took a long stride backwards and started to twist spirals on the night sky with his outstretched arms. He was finally going to fall. He whooped with delight and cracked a huge smile.

"F…" was all that he heard.

Fergus laughed out loud. He turned round to face the rest of the unconquered bridge, still laughing. "Fuck off," he shouted out loud. "All you's just fuck off. Did you think…?" Roaring laughter. Fergus ran along the second half of the bridge in a semi-controlled staggering, felt his foot slide at the last step and launched himself onto Woodhouse Lane, landing and rolling and ending back in the crouch position. He did not look back. He was, for a magical moment, king of the world. The boys tried to saunter. Their hearts hammered in their chests.

"Socks and shoes" Fergus demanded softly. Confused shufflings. The sound of Dave being sick again. A cigarette being lit. Fergie's bundle of clothes was dropped to the floor at his feet. The cigarette appeared in Dick's disembodied hand, the butt proffered first for Fergus to take. The disciples backed away and waited, giving the walker space and time to adjust to a life that was again merely mortal and temporal.

"Shit, Ferg", whispered Dick when he could bear the silence no longer. "I mean… you don't…"

"It's just for the craic" grinned Fergus as he pulled on his socks and shoes. "Nothing else." He paused as he tied a shoelace, blowing smoke streams through his nostrils. "When's one of you's gonna give it a go? Can you answer me that one?"

Nervous laughter. Hearts in mouths. Three year contracts signed on the mild side of wild was all that the English boys had ever committed to. Silence. A brisk and sober walk back to Burley digs. Admiration and fear. Fergus was a madman. He terrified them one and all. They loved him for it.

Fergus wondered whether these boys really understood what or who it was that they loved. The trick was being in control. The magic lay in balancing the weight of his possibilities against their lack of imagination. He did not want to explain that to them. He rather liked their fickle love and fascination. He knew as well that such things do not last. These boys would get their tickets of leave and return to a craicless world painted in dulls and duffs. He too would one day soon get bored. One day, one day soon enough, he would look for a much bigger bridge.

The Starving Wolf

THERE ARE STILL, EVEN in these most enlightened of times, some people who believe that wolves only exist in children's stories. There are others for whom the sight of a shaggy, grey-coated creature prowling around a wildlife park enclosure warrants little more than a photograph and a half-stifled yawn. But all of these people are wrong to think like this, for wolves come in many forms and their ways are rarely simple and benign.

A short while ago, in days much like our own, there lived in a busy country market town the prettiest little girl that you could ever have seen. Her hair fell about her shoulders in free flowing cascades of black, liquid motion. Her face was as serene and quietly beautiful as that of the fairest fairy tale princess.

This little girl's mother was excessively fond of her, as were the whole of her family, but no one was prouder of the little girl than her dear old grandmother. In fact, and much to the little girl's delight, her grandmother made a bright red hoodie for her with the words 'Shooting Star' emblazoned upon its chest in gold lamé lettering. The little girl doted upon her grandmother, and because she wore her lovely red hoodie every day, everybody in the neighbourhood called her Little Red Gangsta.

One day, just as Little Red Gangsta was about to set off to meet her chums at the local park, her mother called out to her. "Dova, love, be a dear and take this packet of Writher's Uniques to your Granny's house. She's not been at her best lately and you know how she loves a nice suck on something tasty and hard boiled".

Little Red Gangsta's real name was, indeed, Dova. Her mother gave her this name because it was fashionable at the time to call a child after the place of his or her conception and little Dova had been conceived during a pre-Christmas booze-cruise. Needless to say, Dova's mother had not done well at school.

Little Red Gangsta thought about complaining, but then she decided that enjoying a packet of hard-boiled sweets with her darling Granny might be just as much fun as hanging about on the swings with her girlfriends and talking about boys.

"Of course, mummy", she replied as she took the bumper pack of sweets from her mother and set off immediately towards her grandmother's house. She skipped and sang her way along the city streets, waving to her grown up friends and schoolmates as she went happily on her way.

By the local convenience store Little Red Gangsta turned into an alleyway that she used as a shortcut on her way to Granny's house. The alleyway passed around and behind the corner shop and as Little Red Gangsta idly kicked a half-squashed fizzy cola can along in front of her, she suddenly caught sight of a whole row of overturned dustbins. The pavement was littered with gnawed chicken bones, chewed up burger cartons and masticated carrot peelings. It was a terrible mess and Little Red Gangsta thought it was appalling. Her outrage at this wanton vandalism turned to shock and then to fear when she saw a thin ribbed, spare and shabby looking dog nuzzling his way though some greasy chilli kebab wrappers.

The poor dog was so pre-occupied with his desperate search for nourishment that it was he who recoiled in fear and terror when Little Red Gangsta shouted at the top of her delicate young voice, "Oi, scram!"

The dog sprang backwards and landed bottom first against the alleyway fence. He squatted there, trembling from the tip of his jet-black nose all the way to the end of his scrawny grey tail. He cringed and whined as he hunkered down on his belly in abject supplication to this menacing phantom dressed in red.

Little Red Gangsta's initial feelings of fear gave way to a sense of disbelief. The dog looked so pathetic as he cowered there in front of her that her initial feelings of disgust and revulsion gave way to the strongest feelings of pity. She was so overwhelmed by her feelings of compassion for this desperate creature that she quite forgot to be amazed when the dog spoke to her.

"Don't...don't hurt me, please", whimpered the dog. "Just...want...food, yeah, yeah, yeah"

"Well, you won't get much of a meal out of those bins", said Little Red Gangsta. "What you need is some nice steak or some sausages".

The dog continued to cringe and whine, although he was starting to eye up the rather large bag of sweets sticking out of Little Red Gangsta's hoodie pocket. She continued to talk to the dog in a quite matter-of-fact way.

"You look so sorry for yourself, dog. I think you need some help.

Oh, and by the way, you're not having any of Granny's sweeties".

"Dog!" growled the pathetic beast and he rose up to his full height. Despite his trembling and the rumbling of his stomach, he barked as fiercely as he could. "I'm no dog. I am Wolf, proud master of the wilderness, spirit lord of the north lands and of the mountain slopes!"

This momentary act of bravado was all that the wolf could manage. He slouched back onto his hind legs as the hunger pangs took hold again and he whimpered, "I'm lost and alone here in this horrible place. Help me, please, help me".

Little Red Gangsta remembered the tales that her Granny had told her when she was very little. Before she considered helping further she asked the wolf, "You're not going to eat me or my Granny, are you?"

"Haven't got the energy", the wolf said forlornly, "and I'm far too frightened of this terrible city. I promise to be good if only you'll help me find some shelter and something to eat".

Little Red Gangsta was so touched by the plight of this bedraggled lord of the wilderness that she agreed to help him straight away. He explained that he'd escaped from the city zoo a few days previously and now rather wished he'd ignored the call of the wild. After some discussion it was decided that the wolf should go to Granny's house for the time being. Little Red Gangsta was sure her lovely Granny would be only too willing to help such a poor and lonely creature. Granny was, after all, such a dear old bat and she had a heart of gold.

"Right, Mister Wolf, if you're sure you can follow my directions to Granny's house, I'll be off to find some sausages for you", said Little Red Gangsta.

"No problem", said the wolf and off he slunk into the shadows, heading towards the west, where Granny lived in a little red brick, terraced cottage.

The wolf made his way to Granny's cottage with as much speed as his four tired and scrawny legs could muster. Little Red Gangsta worked methodically and quietly, the way that she'd been taught by the big girls who hung out with her at the park. She managed to relieve the local branch of a national supermarket chain of two pork joints, a pack of minted lamb sausages and a box of turkey wrigglers. It was amazing just how much contraband she could hide underneath her big red hoodie. She knew not to hurry, because that's how mistakes are made, and so, at last, she set off for Granny's house carrying all of poor Mr. Wolf's rations.

Meanwhile, upon reaching the house where Granny lived, the wolf checked to see that no one was about, put on his bravest, most charming smile and knocked on Granny's front door.

"Who's there?" asked Granny, peering through the little spy hole in the middle of her front door. All that she could see were the tips of two very furry ears and the tip of gently swishing tail.

"I'm...I'm a friend of Little Red Gangsta", replied the wolf, trying to sound as warm and as cuddly as he could. "She found me wandering the streets and she befriended me. She told me to come here and to wait with you while she gets me some food. She said you're kind and caring and you have a heart of gold".

"But I'm not a fool", muttered Granny behind her door, for although she was old and frail, for although she did have a heart of gold where her family was concerned, she also remembered the olden days, when wolves were wolves and vicious brutes to boot.

"Hold on a minute, please", said Granny as she lifted a cast iron fire poker out of her elephant's foot umbrella stand.

Granny flung open her front door and brought the cast iron fire poker crashing down on the wolf's head with all the strength that she could muster, which was, alarmingly, quite considerable for someone of Granny's age and general physical condition. Being as weak and feeble as he was, and having led a relatively unferocious life at the city zoo, the wolf was totally unprepared for an assault by a Granny using extreme force. It was all that the poor creature could do to roll over and die as quickly as he possibly could.

It took Little Red Gangsta nearly two hours to purloin Mr. Wolf's luncheon and to trek all the way over to Granny's house. When Granny opened the door to Little Red Gangsta she was so relieved to see that her grandchild was still in one piece, having spent the last hour or so wondering whether she had become dog food. She really did think the wolf had eaten her grandchild and she'd been getting into a real state trying to work out how best to tell Little Red Gangsta's mother.

"Oh, my lovely, lovely girl", cried Granny, quite overcome with emotion, and she hugged the little girl tightly to her ample breast. Little Red Gangsta loved her Granny very much and didn't think anything was at all wrong with this welcome. She accompanied Granny into the kitchen, where she gave her the pork joints, the minted sausages, the turkey wrigglers and the very large packet of sweets.

"How very thoughtful", said Granny, beaming, "and all for me?"

"Not exactly", replied Little Red Gangsta. "You see, the meat is for a poor, starving wolf I met in town. I told him to come over here and wait for me. Have you seen him, Granny?"

Granny sat Little Red Gangsta down on a stool and looked at her sternly. "I know you meant well", she said, "but you can never trust wolves. Promise me that you'll remember that in future. No matter how sad or cuddly or playful they might appear on the outside, remember, my darling girl, remember this; a wolf is always a wolf, in the same way that a boy is always a boy. Neither of them can ever be trusted."

Granny and Little Red Gangsta both looked over at the cooker. Boiling and bubbling away on the hob was Granny's huge old stockpot and even though the pot lid was rammed down as hard as possible, poor Mr. Wolf's head, bleached right down to the bone, could still be seen looking right back at them.

Little Red Gangsta started with fright and she looked into Granny's lovely face for some reassurance. Granny looked back at her and smiled what she hoped would be a big and comforting smile.

"Good gracious, Granny", said Little Red Gangsta, "what very big teeth you have…"

Fancy and the Flutter

"BLOODY TESCO. BLOODY RAIN. Bloody, bloody, bloody…"

November's dim witted cudgel was flailing at the world with all its might, smothering life and expectation under a blanket of grey cloud. The world existed only as a collection of cold, dank, fetid streets. This was the inevitable killing time in the gardens, the woods and the fields of this watery land, the dreaded days that heralded the arrival of Christmas.

Goodwill to all men? Not as far as Cat was concerned. It was pissing down, she couldn't find a space anywhere near the covered walkway, and that meant the place would be heaving, and worst of all, heaving with angry, frustrated, miseries being induced to enjoy the miracle of marketing. The immaculate conception had nothing to do with any God. It was something dreamed up by the Devils of this world - the run up to Christmas. Cat hated the whole thing with a vengeance.

Cat reached over into the littered passenger side foot well of her battered blue Ford hatchback to fish out her trusty little fold-away umbrella but a sudden, unwelcome and chilling realisation hit her squarely in the chest. She'd used it this morning when she'd brought the bins in and it was still sitting, dripping puddles onto the parquet in the back lobby of her compact stone cottage in the outer, now leafless suburb of Cheltenham where she lived. Cat screamed internally. She took a breath and with seemingly nothing left to fume about Cat opened the door, pulled the collar of her jacket tight around her neck and prepared to brave the elements. Right foot first. Splash. Ankle deep water, cold and oozing November's scum of oil and decaying vegetation, soaked through the sole of her boot.

"Fuck!"

The rain fell in a curtain drizzle, neither hard enough to be impressive nor light enough to be shrugged off as a minor inconvenience. This sort of rain persisted, becoming an oppressive shroud on the world, especially in the late afternoon dusk, when Cat felt like a caged mouse. She scurried across the car park as if it were the exposed wood shaving floor of her tin cell yard, feeling as though she ran under the baleful yellow eyes of a thousand feline predators all lined up just beyond the bars, waiting for the catch to drop, for the cage door to spring open, and for dinner to be playfully served. By the time she reached the covered area by the main doors she was drenched and bedraggled. Her hair, always long and black and quietly coiffured, now curled impossibly and stuck to her forehead and cheek. Her right foot felt cold and clammy from the puddle by the car. The first shopping trolley that she womanfully tried to haul towards the bright inner sanctum of the modern retail experience was, of course, buggered. Cat mouthed another expletive, using the unmentionable word with a venom that would have turned hearts instantly to stone had she dared to say it out loud. Things could not get any worse.

No worse that is until having found a trolley without a wonky wheel, having negotiated the log jam of the entrance, and having pushed her way into the aisle with the stationery, books, CDs and housewares just to escape the murderous melee taking place around the vegetable racks, Cat found herself pushing her empty trolley towards a grinning man dressed up like a riverboat gambler. The dreaded promotional geek. It was most definitely time to turn and flee, to dive deep beneath the turgid sea of morose fathers and screaming brats down by the frozen ready meals.

Except that she couldn't. From nowhere a mother and daughter combination, two trolleys strong, laden to the gunwales with Christmas crackers, wreaths of tinsel and a thousand other essentials for the great day, had blocked her only escape route. To cap it all they appeared to have stopped mid aisle for a chat about Dad's forthcoming bunion procedure. The riverboat Dapper-Dan could not be avoided. Cat steeled herself for the moment, for the delivery of her cold impregnable stare towards the far end of the aisle, and set off towards her nemesis. He stood quite still, letting the grin fade to a thin, charming little smile, then cocking his head slightly as if to say, "I know, I know", and slowly he moved aside.

Cat looked into his eyes. It is always a mistake to do that, she thought, remembering the weekend before and the chap in the bar with the rugby pectorals and the deep brown smoulder that, by the end of the evening, turned into nothing more than a misguided drunken fumble. Leopards and spots came to mind. Once again she was lost in the jungle undergrowth where you only see the predator's eyes for what they really are in that instant before the beast leaps towards you. As ever, the first words were both inane and laced with hidden undercurrents, suffused with that sparkle in the eyes of the hunter and the hunted.

"If you've got a moment", he said softly, smiling again to reveal perfect white teeth.

"Not really. Very pushed for time." replied Cat summoning up her finest hard-pressed housewife look.

Still he smiled, ignoring her attempt to fend him off.

"It's just that we've got a little promotion going on. It might interest you. Certainly better than this Hell".

He looked over Cat's shoulder at the mother and daughter combination further down the aisle.

"That's what it's about, really, changing the shopping experience. Changing you and the shopping experience. It doesn't cost a penny, just a few club card points, but in return you get…well…heaven, really."

"Heaven?" Cat asked, incredulously. The man was clearly stark raving mad. "Heaven in Tesco? I know the buggers are taking over the world but that's just a little far-fetched, isn't it?"

She had broken cardinal rule number one. Instead of smiling sweetly, staring at the far wall and pushing on past the gambling man, she had responded. The hook had been taken and Cat knew instinctively that he was about to play the line.

"I don't mean Heaven and Hell, not in the biblical sense". He rested one hand on Cat's trolley. That smile again. She melted just a little. Such a warm and forgiving smile.

"I mean", he continued, "we all know that's a load of hocus-pocus dreamed up by our less than bright cave dwelling ancestors, don't we?"

Was that a wink?

"Truth is, Heaven and Hell are entirely human things. And I could tell by the look on your face when you walked in here that this may well be Hell for you. And think of those starving kids in Africa or the poor maimed sods in war zones. That's human Hell. Nothing beats it, not even Old Nick. No, what I'm talking about is heaven with a small h. The real thing. Or hell with a small h, of course. Small print and all that."

"Yeah…" Cat mumbled, more to herself than anyone else. The feral air amongst the shoppers seemed too thin around her. She didn't quite understand. The pitch was interesting but hardly your average bit of foreign cheese on a cocktail stick. She focussed on the situation. He edged a little closer along the trolley, brushing a display of disgustingly twee kiddie birthday cards with his shoulder and knocking both cards and envelopes to the floor. They fell in slow motion.

"You're for real?" she asked. "I mean working for Tesco? Not just some chancer with a bit of patter?"

The smile faded. Hang dog. Big eyes and a slightly mocking downwards curl of the mouth.

"Pretty much. They know I'm here, let's put it that way. Can't really miss a bloke dressed up like Fort Laramie, can you. You certainly didn't."

His hand moved to Cat's elbow. He gently pushed the trolley away and she let go. She ought, she thought, to be banging on about invasion of her private space. She ought to be calling security, but none of that mattered. He was close. She could smell his male musk. Those eyes of his were so bright, dancing almost, rich and dark and endless. He moved her with a firm but gentle pressure out of the aisle with the still falling cards into a section with row upon row of discounted DVDs. He was close and hot and fecund. This was no Saturday fiddler. Cat felt as though she was being lifted out of time itself.

He paused, looked directly into her eyes, and said earnestly, "It's about choices. Taking a bit of a risk. Having a flutter, as it were. Walk away now and you stay in Hell. Stay with me, take a moment to dance with me down these aisles, and I guarantee that shopping will never be the same again. Whenever you walk into a supermarket your heart will lift. Raindrops will be your dancing partners, puddles will become oceans for paper boats again, just like they were when you were little. It's a simple question. If you believe that Heaven and Hell are here on earth, what have you got to lose? What do you say?"

Cat had never sailed paper boats in puddles, but she got the gist of it.

"It's not like any promotion I've seen before. And why club card points? What do you get for those? How many do you want?"

That smile again, burning a thousand fold. "Actually, I lied about the points. I don't want them. This is about you. Instead of grumbling about the world, instead of living with continual resentment, rather than looking at the old man most of the time as though he's a moron, why not lighten the load, free your mind and spirit, let loose your soul? One dance is all it takes."

As Cat pondered on that last statement, the noise of twenty-four hour bustle under the ever ticking clock-face of consumer excess faded out completely. There was no old man at home, anyway, only the dog, and Cat never thought of her as a moron. Actually, she did, but in a sweet way. Now the aisles were suddenly and miraculously clear of traffic. The cavernous roof with its harsh strip lights folded into starry night. There were palm trees over by where the wine used to be and Cat was sure that she could hear the gentle break of surf on golden sand. The shelves and racks were dotted with candelabra, and on their vast, open surfaces were displayed sweetmeats, butter biscuits, tarts dusted with cinnamon and so, so many other sugary trifles and temptations. Over the public address system there came the first strains of a waltz, low and hazy to begin with but building slowly and surely to the point where Cat would have to dance.

Cat stopped in front of a long oval mirror that had suddenly plopped into existence. She felt, then heard and finally saw the metamorphosis. She was dressed in the most fabulous red velvet ball gown, suffused with diamonds and adorning her neck, ears and head were jewels beyond the imagination even of Tiffany or Faberge. She was tripping. She had to be on some mad hallucinatory spree. The gambling man was standing in front of her now in a Fred Astaire pose, arm outstretched, calling her into the rhythm and the pulse of the dance. Cat tried to think. What had she eaten? Tinned soup for lunch. It couldn't be that, could it? She felt hot and faint and exhilarated all at the same time. The music was in her bones, was in her blood, cascading around her mind like a red-hot fury.

"I don't even know your name", she gasped, as she took his hand and was twirled into his firm embrace. His mouth was inches away from hers. His breath was almost feverish. She melted once again into his gaze.

"I'll be whoever you want me to be", he whispered. "Just dance."

He spun her round, stepped towards her, took the lead, and off they sped, twisting and shimmering in brilliantly mellow candlelight. He was divine, a gazelle, lithe and firm. For Cat, who had never accumulated any sort of ballroom skill in her thirty years on the planet, the spiral and the vortex were all consuming. Her feet and body moved of their own volition in perfect time with her beaming beau. With every step, with every heartbeat, through shampoos, down cat food lane, up to where the toilet rolls should be, they skipped and floated on the very fabric of the universe. The cares of the mortal world simply fell away, and all that Cat could feel now was the unending cycle of life portrayed in the music. She thrilled at the touch of this creature who could charm the stars into existence as though he were dressing a Christmas tree. She felt utterly and divinely fantastical. Her heart raced with the pure emotion of this wondrous and amazing gift from a stranger for whom, right at this moment, she would give her life.

Minutes sped by. The waltz continued without time, almost without end, but as with all perfection, it can only ever last for the briefest moment. The gambling man slowed his pace, drew close, pressing his body into hers and as the music faded he kissed her. There was no blinding display of fireworks. There were no marching bands, no ticker tape parades, no gushing fountains of love. There was just the warmth of his lips on hers and the definite imprint of his being there.

Slowly Cat unwound herself from his embrace and stepped back a little from him. The stars twinkled out one by one to be replaced by a flimsy, whimsy of strip light. The aisles filled again with every kind of produce. The hustle and bustle of the two-for-one offer resumed, and through it all Cat breathed hard and fast. Her dress faded back into her everyday clothes and the jewels sparkled once more, briefly, before drifting out of this world. Only he remained, holding her hand, squeezing her fingers gently to ease the pain of the parting.

"Oh my God…Oh my God," panted Cat. She could say no more. Behind her the mother and daughter were carrying on the bunion conversation as if nothing at all had happened.

The gambling man released her hand and quietly but firmly manoeuvred Cat's shopping trolley back into position in front of her. He smiled and then frowned, shaking his head as he said, "See what I mean. You found Heaven. Shopping will never be a chore again. There is one little thing, though."

Now he looked ever so slightly apologetic.

"The small print and all that. I probably should've mentioned this at the outset but, well, you know how it is. You get a bit carried away with it all, and you being so lovely."

That million candle smile.

"The price. This is Tesco, after all. We never discussed the price, did we?"

Cat tried to think, but she really couldn't remember. Her head was still spinning with the waltz, her blood still racing with his touch. She looked at him blankly but happily.

"No…no, I don't think we did", she whispered.

"Not much, a trifle really", he said as he backed away towards the aisle with the potions, lotions and vitamins. He turned to walk away, looking back over his shoulder and grinned again as he said, "A soul. Just one tiny little soul."

With that he was gone. Cat tried to make sense of his words. Did he mean her soul? That couldn't be right. She pushed her trolley down the aisle and turned into the one that he had disappeared down but there was no Clark Gable look-a-like perusing the ginseng. Her soul. She felt a moment of terror flood through her, but then, just as quickly she thought about their conversation, thought about what he had said to her at the beginning. Heaven and Hell were human. What on earth could a soul cost, then?

She began to laugh, quietly at first but with every tremor, with every rib tickled, the laugh grew until she let forth a cannonade of mirth right in the middle of a knot of grim faced mothers. It was worth it after all, she thought, as she pushed her trolley at the lead woman of the pack, turned on her heel and marched out of the store. She was going to the pub.

"Why the bloody hell not!" she said out loud to a sour faced septuagenarian by the entrance, and as she did so the public address system roared into life. Against a soundscape of Johannes Sebastian's finest Viennese swirls she heard a familiar voice.

"And just to say a real thank you, Cat, my darling, I'll make Dad's bunion operation really, really painful. Be seeing you, babe…"

Towering Dreams

A GOOD MOMENT? THAT'S what the girl called them. Good moments, little spells when faces fitted names.

Deaf in one ear, Edie sat watching the television side on, her armchair backed up against an old utility dining table in the living room of a one bedroom flat up on the fourteenth floor of Balmoral House. She looked at the reporter's notebook on the arm of the chair. Bold black letters. A child's capitalised script; times and names; two o'clock, Ruth. Her daughter. It was odd seeing Ruth in the good moments. She was much older than Edie remembered. She seemed worn down and she definitely had a limp. Her hip. That's right, Edie remembered, her daughter's hip was crumbling and she needed a replacement but couldn't face the thought of all that fuss.

"Doctors aren't a fuss", she told Eamon. "Silly girl".

Eamon was rattling through general knowledge questions on a lunch time television quiz show. She knew that last one. The answer was Doodlebug. Bloody Hitler. Sodding Goering. She could remember them all right. They bombed her out of the house on Whitestyle Road. Glass everywhere when they went back. Rubble and dust. Her best tablecloth in tatters, its ragged edge flapping in the breeze from under a slab of brick work.

He used to come home then. What was his name? Always asking for dinner at breakfast time. The world was crazy back then. It was different now, but still crazy. Smaller. The world, these days, was made of walls and ceilings. Back then there was grass and sky. He had big, heavy boots, she remembered, and a boiler suit under an old double-breasted jacket. She could hear the rumble of underground trains, could feel the rush of warm air as they approached the platform. That's where they went when bloody Hitler and sodding Goering came calling.

"Funny", she told Eamon and chuckled to herself. "Can't see his face anymore, dear, just his boots. He went out at teatime and came back with the lark. Regular as clockwork. Worked on the trains. He was a reserve for something or other. Sometimes, his boots were under my bed. Fancy that."

The window onto the balcony of the flat was open and the net curtains caught on the backdraft from lorries hurtling along the expressway that gouged its way into London's West End. Up West. Those were the days. She worked in the bakery then, just like her Dad. Before that she helped her mother with the youngsters. Was it eleven or twelve of them?

Edie was the eldest. Responsible. She could cook a Sunday dinner by the time she was ten. She had to. After her Dad went, her Mother disappeared down the pub on a Sunday lunch and you never did know when she'd pitch up again. Edie usually had to set another place, that or risk the back of her mother's hand for being rude to that week's beau.

Up West. The man with the boots walked across a crowded dance floor, the Palais, and asked her to dance, only he was wearing brown brogues this time. She'd recognise the weight of his walk anywhere.

"Don't mind if I do", she giggled at Eamon, leaving her posh, her only handbag in the hands of her imagined girlfriends for safe keeping.

They were always asking her questions. Ruth and the boy. They were always asking her if she remembered names. Well of course she did. Not theirs, not all of the time, but she remembered the old names well enough. Louis. That was one she remembered. He'd put his hand on her bottom one Sunday teatime when her Mother was in the kitchen brewing up. Children need discipline, she thought. She could make her Ruthie's cheek smart if she needed to. A heavy hand, that's what you need, a heavy hand. They were bad. They made her cry sometimes. Bad Ruthie.

"Cobbles", she muttered as one of the contestants on the television was eliminated from the quiz. "You don't get cobbles like you used to."

There were only the seven of them then, back when the streets were full of cobbles; Mother, Father, Edie and the four boys; Edwin, Charlie, Joe and Syd. Little Syd. Her father would come home all covered in flour, sneaking up on her mother as she was taking in the washing. Edie stood on a box at one end of the line hanging tea towels out to dry, tea towels and swaddling. He would make a playful grab for Mother, using the sheets and his work shirts as cover, and she would cuss him for ruining the wash. The bath used to hang on the wall. That was before boozy Sunday lunch times. A tear caused Eamon to go all blurry.

"Dad? Is that you?" she said as a key slid into the Yale lock in the flat's front door. "You died. Cancer from them baking trays. Dad?"

From the hall, in the act of hanging a damp overcoat on the coat stand, Ruth called out, "Only me!"

Edie recognised the voice. It was the woman who washed her, the woman who spooned food into her mouth, getting in the way of the pictures, breaking the threads of the dream, breaking the line of string that she was following home. Bad child. She would have to put a stop to it, have to let them know who was in charge around here. You can't let the little ones take control, Edie thought, not when she was their big sister, all grown up and could cook dinner at ten years old.

A kiss. She was always being kissed these days, kissed by complete strangers. Manners had gone to pot. Eamon rattled on. Colours shifted and the volume on the television rose a notch or two. Did she want a new sofa? Why would they ask her that at her age?

In the kitchen Edie could hear someone talking but she couldn't make anything out of it. There was no point. The people in the conversation didn't really exist. She'd never known anyone called Sydney. Not like she'd known little Syd. He was always getting into scrapes, never worked a day in his life if he could help it, always down the dogs or bringing his washing round, but he was a good boy. He gave her a share on the odd occasions when he won.

"A little something for looking after me, Ede", he used to say.

She used to wear a pinafore. She used to sit by the front door on her father's knee. It was always sunny. He used to feed her off his own plate. Edie grinned at her Father as he placed a napkin at her throat, listened idly as he told her a story about a bright monster of a car hitting a bollard down on the High Street, and felt something hot in her mouth. A car on the High Street!

She was always a good eater. Her Dad always said so. His hand looked pale and thin now, almost girlish, but he was a good man, always had been, and he'd come back after all these years. He lifted the corner of the napkin and wiped gravy from her chin.

"Thanks, Dad", Edie said and shifted sideways in her seat. She liked watching programmes about Doctors. Sometimes they reminded her of silly-billy Ruth and her funny bones.

Do Unto Others

(Loosely based on Charles Perrault's Toads & Diamonds)

A BROKEN HOME IS RARELY anything other than a trial for all those who have to live within its walls. Apart from the trauma caused by the breaking up of a previously coherent family unit, subsequent actions and hardships often make life extremely difficult and taxing for each and every one of the unhappy participants in these events. The time when and the place where lives are squeezed and wrung out under such circumstances is, in the great scheme of things, immaterial, but for one such family, living in a small village in one of England's elm-folded western valleys, the struggle for a good life was particularly hard.

Mrs. Milligan and her two daughters, Estelle and Hazel, lived in a small redbrick cottage that stood in a forlorn and lonely spot at the far end of a shabby and dusty village high street. Where there had once been rows of vegetables growing in the front garden and a pretty orchard of neatly pruned and espaliered fruit trees in the back garden, there was now nothing more than a choking of weeds and ivy smothered, skeleton branches. Ever since the departure of her husband some years previously, the family had scraped a living by taking in washing and ironing, and doing cleaning jobs for some of the village's more prosperous families. The two girls could remember little other than traipsing around after their mother, visiting house after well-appointed house, in a desperate quest to earn money amid fineries and fripperies that they could never hope to afford for themselves.

Of the two daughters, Estelle was the spitting image of her mother, although blessed, thankfully, with the softness of youth, while Hazel, two years the younger, was the very picture of her father. The similarities between mother and eldest daughter did not end in looks. They were both of a similar personality and disposition, being proud and disagreeable to an extreme, convinced as they were that they were the victims of a cruel and heartless man. Because of this undoubted sin perpetrated against them by the ogre, they both believed the world owed them big time for all of their suffering and undoubted grace under poverty's iron heel. It was no surprise to anyone in the village that Mrs. Milligan had remained single for so many years.

Hazel, on the other hand, was one the sweetest, kindest and most courteous little girls in the whole county. She had a radiant smile that lit her face up with a pure and natural beauty, a beauty that brightened the gloom well beyond the physical limits of light. No matter what the hardship or the provocation, she always tried to see the best in any situation and so, despite the tragic circumstances of her family's life in the closeted world of Upper Risington, she remained a shining beacon of happiness when all around was shadowed in darkness and despondency.

Life in the Milligan household was a bleak affair at the best of times and Mrs. Milligan suffered unaccountably from her nerves due to the continual reminder of her bastard husband that blazed out from her youngest daughter's face every minute of the day. She would have been quite content for the girl to spend her days out of sight and her nights locked in her bedroom had it not been for the fact that Hazel never complained about chapped hands or ironing elbow. Hazel was quite unlike Estelle, who preferred to spend her time, when not pretending to dust someone's knick-knacks, watching daytime television soap operas and reality shows about other people's lives. Mother and eldest daughter doted on each other and regularly shared the little luxuries that came their way when there was a purse full of cash left over from the benefits payments and the hourly wages earned from charring.

Poor Hazel, meanwhile, worked her fingers to the bone in a never-ending cycle of drudgery and domestic slavery, washing other people's clothes and ironing them, cleaning the house, cooking meals and fetching thick, black coal from the back yard bunker. She was never allowed, now that she was blossoming into a beautiful young woman, to leave the house and accompany her mother and sister on their daily errands and cleaning jobs. Her only respite from the drab surroundings of the little redbrick cottage was a weekly trip to visit an aged, one time neighbour, a certain Miss Huddlestone, who had been kind enough to baby sit for the girls in happier times before the family had split asunder.

Miss Huddlestone now lived in a sheltered retirement bungalow in the next village, Lower Risington, and every Wednesday afternoon Hazel popped into the village shop, and, out of the bus fare given to her by her begrudging mother, she bought a large Bakewell tart and a bag of lemon sherbets, and walked, come rain or shine, the two miles to her friend's neat little home.

One Wednesday afternoon, with the sound of her sister's harsh voice still grating in her ears, Hazel put the usual cakes and sweets into a plastic bag and walked all the way to Lower Risington bathed in bright spring sunlight. She was particularly fond of spring, heralding as it did the lengthening of days and the chance to hang the washing outside to dry in good, clean, fresh air. On this particular Wednesday the world was particularly bright and full of goodness, with the hedgerows sparkling in their blossom coats and the birds busy with their nest building songs. Hazel was in a fine mood when she knocked on her friend's door and together they enjoyed quite the happiest afternoon tea they had ever had together.

As Miss Huddlestone drained the last dregs of her Earl Gray and wiped Bakewell tart crumbs from the lightly sprouting beard that covered her withered old chin, she turned to young Hazel, took her hand and whispered, "You are such a lovely girl, my dear, so pretty and kind, and you've never forgotten to come and see me. I want to give you a gift".

Hazel smiled sweetly and protested that visiting her friend was enough of a gift and that she wouldn't think of accepting anything else, but the old woman paid no attention to her whatsoever.

"I think you'll like the gift", continued the old girl, smiling broadly. "You see, I'm not just any dear old bat, dear, I'm a dear old witch, dear!"

Hazel tried very hard not to laugh because she didn't want to appear rude, but she couldn't help smirking slightly behind her hand.

"I know, I know", said the old woman, "it's all very hard to fathom, especially when you're so young and inexperienced. Anyway, I've decided to reward you for all of your kindness and for taking the time and trouble to come all this way every week.

From now on, whenever you smile a real smile, a smile that breaks like sunrise on a clear blue summer morning, you'll find a little pearl or diamond in your pocket!"

Hazel laughed out loud and beamed at the old woman. "Oh go on, Mary, you're so funny", and as she grinned at the old woman with every ounce of her happy, joking little soul, she put her hand into her jeans pocket.

No one in this fair land's long history could ever have been as surprised or delighted as little Hazel. Between her fingers she could feel something small and hard and round, and she was sure that there had been nothing in her pocket just a moment ago. She pulled out her tightly bunched fist and opened her fingers out slowly and nervously. Right there in the palm of her hand was a perfectly round, moonshine pearl of such beauty and radiance that the girl was unable to move or to speak for a full five minutes. As the shock and surprise subsided, Hazel realised that she did believe in witches and fairies and she let out a yelp of joy, hugging Miss Huddlestone so tightly that the old dear thought she would burst her seams.

By the time that Hazel had greeted everyone she met on her way home that evening with a massive smile and wave, by the time that she had expressed her joy to the world a hundred and one times, her pockets were positively bulging with gemstones and pearls. She arrived home a little later than usual to find her mother and her sister waiting impatiently for their tea. As soon as the front door shut they both began to scold her for being so late and so inattentive to their well-being.

"I'm sorry for being late, Mum", replied Hazel, smiling in spite of the hurtful things that were being said. She walked over to the coffee table in the middle of the living room and filled the spaces in between empty cola cans and the overflowing ashtray with a heap of brightly shining diamonds and pearls. "But I can explain…"

"What the bloody hell have you been doing?" screamed her mother as Estelle immediately knelt down by the coffee table and started to pick out all of the biggest diamonds from the pile. "Where the chuffin' hell have they come from?"

Hazel told her mother and her sister the whole story about their mutual friend, about her being a witch and about her wonderful gift. By the end of the story the entire family was beaming. At last their suffering was over and their fortunes assured. Mrs. Milligan cuddled her youngest daughter to her ample bosom for the first time in years and called her things like 'darling' and 'poppet' and 'precious'. Every time that Hazel smiled at her mother or her sister she reached into her jeans pockets and added another sparkling gem to the pile on the coffee table.

By nine o'clock that evening the family had enough booty in their living room to retire from the domestic cleaning and washing business forever more, and Hazel, tired out from smiling so much with all of the love in the house, went to bed to dream happy dreams of a future where neither the bogeyman nor the tallyman would ever come to get her again.

Once Hazel was safely tucked up in the land of dreams, Mrs. Milligan, having allowed her eldest daughter to keep a few of the smaller diamonds, then swept the pile of jewels into a plastic food container. Sharing a bottle of fizzy wine with Estelle, she set about making her own plans for a future far removed from the heartache and stress of her current life.

"Hazel's luck should be yours by right, my girl", she said to Estelle. "From now on we'll keep her here on Wednesdays while you visit that daft old bugger. With a little bit of work you should be able to get her to do the same trick for you. She was half raving when we moved in here and she's obviously gone the whole hog now. Treat her nice for a few weeks and we'll be millionaires by Christmas".

"I'm not visiting the daft crow, ma", replied Estelle with a whine. "She's old and she smells and everything."

Mrs. Milligan looked at daughter number one with a hard ratty stare.

"Do I have to?" whimpered the girl.

"You'll do as you're bloody well told, miss", hissed her mother, and with that, and despite all of the sullen whinnying and misery that Estelle brought to bear, schemes and plans were laid for the following week.

Come the Wednesday afternoon, Mrs. Milligan locked Hazel in the under stairs cupboard and frog marched her eldest daughter to the village shop, where she bought the finest assortment of soft centres that the proprietor had to offer. Then she ordered a taxi to take Estelle to Lower Risington. In no time at all Estelle found herself on Miss Huddlestone's doorstep, box of chocolates in hand, forcing the most wheedling of smiles across her barely cleaned teeth. The taxi parked up at the kerb side, Estelle having told the driver that she'd be no more than ten minutes.

Miss Huddlestone opened the door to her beloved Hazel but found there instead the gum chewing, pony-tailed whine that marked Estelle's presence in the world. She let out a long sigh, but nonetheless she ushered the girl into her home and brought the tray full of tea things through to the front room.

Estelle sloped into one of the armchairs, declining a drink or a biscuit. She chucked the box of chocolates at the old lady and pouted.

"Are you sure you won't have a cup of tea, dear?" asked Miss Huddlestone

"No", grunted the girl.

"Oh well" replied the old woman. She took a sip of Earl Gray and looked at her visitor over the rim of her teacup.

"Would you mind awfully fetching my glasses from the kitchen? I must have left them on the work top and I can barely see anything without them"

"What am I", complained the girl, "you're bleedin' slave or something? I'm not a skivvy, you know!"

Estelle gave the old bat one of her looks, a look that told you to sod off because you were boring and didn't understand anything important. Miss Huddlestone, who was no stranger to angry young women, having spent many years in secondary education before taking up her current line of work as a white witch, returned the look, eyeball to eyeball, pensioner to youth, and won the contest hands down.

"I'll tell you what you are, dear", she said calmly and quietly, as she put her cup down on the tray. "You're a rude and spoilt little hussy, definitely your mother's daughter. You've all the breeding of the pigsty, but despite your ill manners and your attitude I will give you a gift, just like I gave lovely Hazel a gift. Every time you give someone one of those vacuous and disobliging looks you will find a little present in your pocket."

"Vac…what?" muttered Estelle

"Just leave now, dear, before I get really pissed off"

Estelle had her pride. No one had a right to talk to her like that. She gave the old hag her most vicious, drop-dead stare and stormed out of the little house. She slammed the cottage door shut and jumped into the waiting taxi, barking orders to the driver to get her back to Upper Risington pronto.

That might have been the end of Estelle's ordeal, except that Miss Huddlestone's power to grant gifts was unparalleled anywhere in England's green valleys. The car had only gone a few hundred metres down the road when the driver slammed on the brakes and turned to look at the girl on the back seat.

"What the bloody hell is that smell?" he hissed nasally, holding his nose tightly shut between his thumb and forefinger. Estelle pouted, stuck her hands in her pockets and was about to deliver her best ignoring look when she made a dreadful discovery. Her right hand, rather than being thrust into a soft, warm pocket full of dark, tight nothingness, had actually made contact with something altogether more disgusting. She felt something soft and warm all right, but whatever it was it was certainly of some substance.

"Out", yelled the taxi driver, in a horrified, gagging voice, and out the girl got. She was left stranded in the middle of a country lane on a bright and sunny summer afternoon with nothing to show for her effort but a pocket full of dog mess and a smell that seemed to follow her whichever way the wind blew.

When Estelle eventually reached her home, bedraggled and exhausted after her long walk under a baking sun, she hung around in the front garden, not daring to enter the house. As soon as her mother caught sight of her lurking there in the front garden she rushed out to find out how the afternoon had gone.

"Well?" she demanded urgently, before taking a step back and asking, "Have you trodden in something?"

Estelle stood there dumbly, mouthing words but unable to make any sounds, and so, after a few mute moments during which she could feel her mother's anger rising, she pulled her right hand out of her jeans pocket and let little gobbets of half-baked ordure drip from her fingers. At the sight of the awful gift given to her by Miss Huddlestone both mother and daughter wailed like banshees, cursing their ill luck and the name of poor Hazel to hell and back.

"It's all her fault", screamed Mrs. Milligan. "I'll beat her black and blue, I'll tan her, I'll strip that smile of hers from her bones!"

Needless to say, poor little Hazel, who had been locked away in the cupboard for the whole of the hot and sweaty afternoon, had finally come to the end of her own tether. When her mother unlocked and opened the door, Hazel burst through the opening like a small hand grenade and ran out of the house, down the road and far, far away, taking her wonderful gift with her. No one in Upper Risington ever heard from her again, although there were rumours that she ended up in London, where, it was said, she married a prince or a famous footballer and lived happily ever after.

As for Estelle, try as she might, she couldn't break the habit of her early years and she never learned to smile. Eventually, after suffering many years of ridicule and evil odours, she learned to never wear any clothes that had pockets attached, but by then the following wind that had first assailed her one Wednesday afternoon in her teens had saturated her skin. Wherever she went people called her names until, one summer some years later, she took herself off to a remote corner of the Lake District, lay down in a corner of a field and there, as far as anyone knows, she still remains.

Mrs. Milligan, meanwhile, minding the Tupperware tub full of diamonds and pearls taken from Hazel when she had come home from visiting Miss Huddlestone's bungalow, found that a life backed up by a little capital was much more bearable and now lived in genteel respectability in a seaside villa on the south coast with a retired bank manager, which goes to show that happy endings, even with Estelle's tragic and lonely life taken into account, usually have little to do with what some people deserve.

The Mobile Phone

(Loosely based on Andersen's The Tinderbox)

A SOLDIER CAME MARCHING along the road one fine day; left, right, left, right, left, right. He had a kit bag over his shoulder and wore his cap all askew upon his head, because he was coming home from the wars and although not yet formally and officially de-mobbed, he simply didn't feel like complying with dress regulations anymore. He had served his time and was now heading for London, where they said that money grew on trees. He didn't quite believe this, but nonetheless he fancied a change of career and scenery.

On the outskirts of the city he met an old woman with hideous, blotchy skin and a bottom lip that stretched all the way down to her chest. In olden days she would have been called a witch, but the soldier, being thoroughly modern in his outlook, just assumed that she had wandered off from her care home.

As he walked past the old woman she turned to him and said, "My, what a handsome boy you are. What a lovely cap and what a very big kit bag you have". She winked at him suggestively as she continued, "I know where you can find lots of lovely money".

"Sure enough", said the soldier to himself, "she's escaped from the local nut house".

"Do you see that old tree over there?" asked the weathered woman pointing at a gnarled and ancient oak tree that stood in the middle of someone's front garden. "It's quite hollow. If you climb to the top and drop down inside, you'll find three magical money making machines in a great hall lit by a thousand fairy lights".

"Humour her", thought the soldier. He stopped and asked the old woman, "How will I get out of the tree after I've gone down to this hall of lights?"

"Oh, don't worry about that", she said, "I'll tie a rope around your waist and pull you back up".

"Right, of course you will", said the soldier pretending to be interested. You can imagine his surprise when the old woman produced a long length of coiled rope from under her voluminous purple overcoat.

Wide-eyed and somewhat taken aback, the soldier asked, "So, how do these magical money machines work, then?"

"I'll tell you", said the old woman. "You'll see three doors in the hall, all of them unlocked. If you go into the first room you'll find a Northern Bank cash machine guarded by a dog with eyes the size of compact disks. But you needn't worry about him. I'll give you my tartan shopping trolley. Just pop him inside, press one, two, three four and you can take as many ten-pound notes from the machine as you like. Of course, if you'd rather have twenty-pound notes you can go to the second room. There you'll find a dog with eyes the size of saucepan lids. Pop him into the shopping trolley, key in the same numbers and take as many twenty-pound notes as you like from the machine. On the other hand, if you'd prefer fifty-pound notes you should go to the third room. There's another dog, of course, with eyes the size of giant sparkling Catherine Wheels. Now he's a real dog, a real son of a bitch, but don't worry about that. Just pop him into the shopping trolley, key in the magic numbers and take as many fifty-pound notes as you like".

The soldier decided that he'd better do as she said, if only to keep her under surveillance until the search party arrived from the hospital armed with really strong sedatives and a straitjacket.

"Sounds like a good plan", said the soldier. "But I ought to get something for you as well seeing as you've been so kind".

"No, no, no", said the old woman. "I don't need any more money. All I want is my mobile phone, which I dropped the last time I was down there".

"Well, tie the rope around my waist", said the soldier, "and I'll hop up into the tree and take a look".

The old woman did just that and after the soldier climbed the tree and found the hole, she passed the shopping trolley up to him. The soldier then climbed down into the hollow tree, which was made more difficult than it ought to have been by the awkwardness of the trolley. To his amazement he found himself in a great hall lit by a thousand fairy lights and sure enough there were three doors set into the far wall of the hall, all of them slightly ajar. The soldier entered the first room, and sure enough, there sat the dog with eyes as big as compact disks.

"Bugger me, but you're ugly", said the soldier, but he steeled himself and popped the dog into the shopping trolley. Then he keyed the magic numbers into the magical money machine and watched in absolute wonder as the machine spewed out huge great wads of ten-pound notes. Needless to say he stuffed every one of his jacket pockets with the cash. Having filled every pocket the soldier popped the dog back in front of the cash machine and went on his way to the second room.

"Careful", said the soldier to the dog with eyes as big as saucepan lids. "You'll get eyestrain if you keep staring at me like that".

He popped this second dog into his shopping trolley, entered the magic numbers on the cash machine's keypad and proceeded to stuff his trouser legs full of as many twenty-pound notes as he could. With the second dog safely deposited in front of the cash machine the soldier waddled into the third and final room.

Hideous! There sat the dog with eyes as wide as sparkling Catherine Wheels.

"Afternoon", said the soldier, saluting, because he had never seen anything like it before. He looked at the dog. The dog looked straight back at the soldier. After a few seconds the soldier started to feel really freaked out, so he popped the dog into the shopping trolley, pressed the buttons and built the biggest pile of fifty-pound notes he had ever seen by the door. There was enough money in the pile to buy a small army all of his own.

Being thoroughly practical and having been trained to deal with difficult situations, the soldier put the dog back by the cash machine and proceeded to empty all of his pockets and his trouser legs of ten and twenty-pound notes. These he stuffed into the shopping trolley followed by the huge pile of fifty-pound notes. Then he wheeled his heavy load back to the base of the tree and shouted, "Pull me up now, old woman".

A faint voice replied, "Have you got my mobile phone?"

"Bugger", muttered the soldier, "I nearly forgot".

He searched for a while by fairy light and sure enough he found an old mobile phone on the floor in the middle of the hall. He pocketed the phone, called up to the old woman once again and she pulled him and his trolley back up through the hollow tree. Soon he was standing back out in the open air with a tartan shopping trolley full of ready cash.

"What do you need a mobile phone for, old woman?" asked the soldier.

"That's none of your business", the old woman snapped. "You've got your money, so just give me my phone and I'll be off".

"Doesn't seem right to me", said the soldier. "There's something fishy going on here. Tell me what you want that phone for or I'll push you under a bus, you old crone".

"No", shrieked the old woman, making ready to pounce on the soldier like a wounded lioness.

As luck would have it a red double-decker London bus turned the corner of the street at that very moment. Just before the old woman leapt at him with her hands bared like claws, the soldier pushed her under the wheels of the bus and ran off, pulling the tartan shopping trolley behind him like a demented go-cart running in reverse gear.

Later that night, when the coast was clear the suburban hiatus by the oak tree was just a distant memory, the soldier stood on Harrow hill and gazed out across his new world horizon. After his experiences in the dust and heat of war, the soldier looked at the steaming city and saw that it was beautiful.

The busy streets in the centre of the city were full of light and music and pretty young girls, and the soldier paid cash for a suite at the Ritz with room service on call twenty-four hours per day. He sent his old army clothes for dry-cleaning and the cleaners simply couldn't believe that someone so rich could dress so scruffily. The very next day, guided by the hotel concierge, the soldier went to the finest tailors and shirt makers in Saville Row. Overnight he turned into a fine looking gentleman and bought drinks for city whiz kids, rich bankers and portly brokers in the hotel bar. They told him all about their great city, its lights and music, and especially about their jobs and their wonderful bonus payments. They even told him about the great and majestic bank at the heart of the city, about its chairman and about the chairman's very pretty daughter.

"Where can I find this lovely girl?" asked the soldier.

"Oh, you can't see her", they replied. "Her Daddy keeps her working on mergers and acquisitions all day and every day. No one but the chairman sees her because it's prophesied that one day she'll marry a common soldier. Her father thinks that's so last year."

"Even so", said the soldier, "I'd very much like to see her".

But, all things considered, and after the third bottle of shampoo, he supposed that it simply wasn't meant to be.

The soldier lived well in the city, going out for expensive dinners at the finest restaurants, attending the theatre regularly, spending pleasant evenings in the brightest of celebrity haunts and even doing a little work for charity when time permitted. He was particularly proud of his charity work, which was a good thing, for he well remembered being a poor squaddie. Now, though, he was rich, handsome, had fine clothes and he had a new set of friends, who were all eager to join with him in his good fortune. His great pile of cash dwindled slowly at first, but as the weeks progressed the pile seemed to shrink more and more quickly. For every penny that he spent he got nothing back at all until, at last, there was nothing left but two fifty-pound notes, and after the incident with the old lady he dare not return to the cash machines under the oak tree.

The soldier had to leave the Ritz that night and move into a tiny little room in a traveller's motel out by Heathrow airport. He saved every penny he could by washing his own clothes, eating in burger bars and buying cheap plonk from the local off-licence. He pawned his fine clothes, sold his gold wristwatch and hocked his patent leather shoes, until he had nothing left but his old army clothes. None of his new friends seemed to have the time to come and see him anymore, saying that business commitments were just too demanding. For a while he believed them when they said they would do lunch very soon, but the phone never rang.

A few weeks after his flight from the swanky city hotel, the soldier found himself in a dire situation, unable to afford a bottle of Chateau Maggot even. He was about to fall into the deepest, blackest depression, when he suddenly remembered the old woman and her mobile phone. He checked his army jacket and sure enough there it still was.

There was a pawnshop around the corner and he might get a few pounds for it, he thought, so he took the phone out of his jacket and gave it a cursory inspection. It was a very old model, more monolith than mobile, and the battery was as dead as a doorknob. More out of frustration than hope, the soldier started to press the buttons randomly, and as he did so the door to his meagre little motel room crashed open and in sprang the dog with eyes the size of sparkling Catherine Wheels. It lurched to a halt in front of him, panting and dribbling on the carpet.

"What", ...pant, "doth", ...wheeze, "my mathter want?" it lisped.

"Poke me sideways with a fish fork", said the soldier, "what a funny old world. Did the phone bring you here, dog?"

"Yeth, mathter"

"Right, well, can I really have anything I want?"

"Yeth", said the dog, "I am yourth to command".

"Right", said the soldier, "fill this tartan shopping trolley with fifty-pound notes. Oh, and pop in a lamb Madras, Pilau rice, a mushroom bhaji, and a couple of bottles of Spanish brandy while you're at it".

The dog careered back out of the hotel doorway, pushing the trolley in front of him with his big, slobbery mouth. No more than a few moments ticked by before the dog and the shopping trolley crashed back into the door frame, spinning the dog into the room bottom first. The shopping trolley was full to overflowing with fifty-pound notes, some of them covered in curry sauce, and two bottles of cheap hooch.

The soldier began to understand what a marvellous mobile phone this was, and he thoroughly understood why the old woman had wanted it back so urgently. If he pressed one, then the dog with eyes as big as compact disks would come. If he pressed two, the dog with eyes as big as saucepan lids would come. If he pressed three, then the dog with eyes as wide as sparkling Catherine Wheels would come.

The soldier played with the phone all night long, until he was as rich as Croesus. He moved straight back into the Ritz, bought new clothes, bought a brand new sports car and almost immediately found that his fair weather friends, now that the rain had ceased to fall in the soldier's life, all suddenly had sunny windows in their diaries.

With the magical phone and his team of wonder dogs at his command, the soldier rapidly became one of the richest young blades in the city. He spent every moment that he could collecting shopping trolleys full of ready cash and, when he finally had enough money to hand, he opened an account with the great and majestic bank that pulsed at the heart of London's financial community.

This, of course, was all part of his plan and the soldier mused on this later that night; "Now, it's really too bad that no one is allowed to see the chairman's daughter. Everyone says she's a stonker, even if they do say she's also a bit of a ball-breaker. But there's no use in her being lovely if no one can ever see her. So..."

He pressed one on his mobile phone and with a whoosh, up popped the dog with eyes as wide as compact disks.

"I know it's late", said the soldier, "but I'd like to see the bank chairman's daughter ".

The dog, by now on more familiar terms with its new master, raised a paw, licked its lips and waited. As soon as the soldier gave him a marrow bone biscuit, the dog rushed back out into the night. After about half an hour the dog crashed back into the soldier's hotel room, panting and wheezing, with the chairman's daughter lying upon his back. She was fast asleep and she was, indeed very lovely to look at. Even her pyjamas smelled of silver spoons and the soldier simply couldn't resist temptation. He kissed her on the lips as she slept, proving, despite his newfound wealth and status, that he was a romantic old thing at heart.

When he eventually finished gazing at this vision in flannelette, the dog returned her to the penthouse apartment that she shared with her parents. In the morning, when she joined her father and mother at their seven A,M. power breakfast, she told them about her strange dream in which she had been whisked away by a large brown dog with weird eyes and that a soldier had kissed her. Her father smiled serenely without looking up from the business pages of his newspaper, while the lovely young woman's mother made a mental note to check her daughter's bathroom for signs of illegal drugs. The Filipino maid, however, believing in ghosts and witches, made a mental note to keep watch the very next night. Where she came from such things were not at all unknown, especially when they concerned beautiful young maidens.

The soldier really did want to see the young lady again, and so the dog was despatched the very next night to fetch her while she slept. The dog brought her as fast as he could, but the maid was waiting for him and she followed the dog and his package at a discreet distance in the back of her cousin's minicab. The maid followed the dog right up to the door of the soldier's suite at the hotel, where, so that she would remember things properly in the morning, the maid chalked a white cross onto the door. Then she went home to wait and see when the dog would bring her mistress back again.

When the dog left his master's room to take the girl home, he noticed the chalk mark on the door. Having eyes as wide as compact disks has its advantages. As soon as he delivered his package home, the dog returned to the hotel, made another piece of chalk appear by magic, and proceeded to mark a white cross on every door in the hotel.

Early the next morning a fleet of black limousines sped into the hotel car park and with much slamming of car doors and with the heavy echo of rushing footsteps reverberating off the marble walls, the chairman, his wife and various members of his personal security team crashed through reception. Moving like a well-oiled machine the security unit covered each other, took up positions, made sure that all was safe and beckoned the chairman and his wife forward.

"There it is", shouted the chairman, pointing at a door with a white chalk cross on it.

"No, there it is", shouted his wife, pointing at another door.

Having kicked open three doors with white crosses on them they had to admit defeat. With the best will in the world, they couldn't see how their daughter had been spirited into a broom cupboard, a conference room and an octogenarian couple's golden wedding anniversary suite. They soon realised that every door in the hotel had a white chalk cross on it and that their search had ended in failure.

The great bank's chairman was ready to fire the maid for causing so much confusion and embarrassment, but his wife had extensive experience in the realm of hotels and subterfuge, and she persuaded him to go to work and that she would sort things out with the domestic staff. She had, after all, met her husband at a banking conference in Switzerland many years before and the sight of so many white crosses immediately made her smell a rat. Instead of firing the poor girl, the chairman's wife asked the maid to sew a little bag of the finest silk and fill it with ground up Puy lentils. When her daughter, tired as usual after a long day at the coal face of international mergers and acquisitions, went to bed, her mother tied the bag to the back of her pyjamas. Then she cut a tiny whole in the bag so that the ground up lentils would leave a trail if she were abducted once again.

True to form, the dog came that night and took the sleeping young woman to the soldier, who by now was madly in love with her. He wished for nothing more than to be an international banker too, so that he could make her his wife.

Even with eyes as big as compact disks, the wonder dog did not notice the fine trail of lentils leading all the way from the girl's bed to the soldier's suite at the Ritz. The very next morning, and much to the chagrin of the concierge and the paying guests, the chairman, his wife and their security team came crashing through the hotel once again. They followed the trail of ground lentils right up to the soldier's door, smashed their way into his room and had him arrested immediately. He was indicted for stalking, for abduction and for a host of other charges, which lead, with a nod and a wink and some party donations, to the minister responsible for such matters making stalking a capital offence. The soldier was tried, convicted and sentenced to hang by the neck the very next day.

*

The poor soldier sat on the bunk in his cell, alone and without shoelaces in his shoes or a belt to secure his modesty. He had been force-marched out of his hotel room in only his bathrobe, and now he wore the condemned man's prison blue overalls. His army jacket, where he always kept the magic mobile phone, was still hanging in his hotel suite wardrobe, which meant that he was feeling very sorry for himself.

"If only I had my phone", he thought to himself sadly.

The very next morning the soldier watched through the bars of his cell as a huge crowd started to assemble in a public square outside the prison's front gates. There was a brand new gallows standing there and the steadily growing crowd seemed very excited because there had not been a hanging in the City for years and years and years. Gantries, platforms and temporary grandstands surrounded the gallows where television crews were setting up and radio presenters were practicing their lines. The soldier sighed, resigned to his fate. Then he spotted a boy working his way down a line of parked cars, who was taking advantage of the crowds to steal the radiator badges from the more expensive sporting models.

"Psst", hissed the soldier. "You there, yes you. Do you want to earn five hundred notes?"

Although startled at first, the boy came over to the cell window when he heard mention of easy money.

"There's still an hour to go before they stretch my neck. If you can get to the Ritz and bring me my mobile phone, I'll give you the cash as soon as you get back".

Now the boy, while not an A grade student, was quick and cunning and he'd heard that the soldier was absolutely loaded. He spotted an opportunity to do himself a favour, wrote down the number of the suite and sped off in pursuit of serious wedge. He broke into the suite with little trouble, changed out of his Baggies into an Italian designer suit and a pair of handmade brogues, picked up some loose cash for good measure and pocketed the mobile phone.

With just five minutes to go before the soldier was due to be led out to the gallows, he heard a shrill whistle, and when he looked through his cell window a remarkably well-dressed young man threw an old and battered mobile phone into the cell.

The soldier pressed one, two and then three. There was a whooshing sound and a second or two later a bundle of fifty-pound notes was passed through the cell bars to the young boy. The soldier then composed himself and waited for his escort to come and lead him out to his place of execution.

Despite the chill air, the early hour and his impending death, the soldier cut a fine, bold figure as he accompanied his guards to the gallows, where he stood to attention on the raised platform and looked at the crowd. The best seats were on a dais to his left and in these seats sat the bank's chairman and his wife, their daughter, government ministers, the chief judge and the Superintendent of the Metropolitan Police. To great applause, the hangman placed the noose around the soldier's neck and made ready to pull the lever that would send the soldier to his death.

All went quiet. The director of the live television special whispered into his microphone and the cameras panned in on the hangman, on the judge and on the soldier. Through the latest audio communications wizardry, the director asked the hangman to wait. He then asked the judge to stand and ask the soldier if he might have any last requests. The director wanted to build both the atmosphere and his chance of a gong at the annual television awards ceremony.

The soldier responded to the judge by asking if he would grant a sinner one last favour. He wanted to phone his dear old mother to say goodbye and to say that he was sorry. The hangman reached into the soldier's overall pockets, took out the mobile phone and pressed the numbers one, two and then three as instructed. In a blinding flash of light, accompanied by a deep roll of thunder, all three dogs appeared at once.

"Help me now so I won't be hanged", yelled the soldier.

The dogs flew to the right and to the left, up and down the aisles and rows, savaging all of the dignitaries with their massive fangs until there was nothing left of the government ministers, the judiciary and upper echelons of the police service but rags and bones. The hangman, fearing for his own life, immediately cut the soldier down and untied the ropes that bound his hands and legs. All of the policemen on crowd duty turned and fled the carnage, but the ordinary people in the crowd started to cheer and whoop with delight, carrying the soldier around on their shoulders and yelling and shouting that they'd never liked bankers at all.

Later that year, being the largest account holder at the great and majestic bank, and because of his newfound fame as a television celebrity, the soldier was unanimously elected as its new chairman. After a short but intense period of mourning, the soldier married the old chairman's daughter, which she liked very much because he made her Chief Executive Officer and together they cornered the world's markets in gold and oil, before retiring in their late thirties to live in Antibes and raise a gaggle of spoilt but happy children.

As for the dogs? Well, it took them a little while to get used to the sunshine in the South of France, but these days they can usually be found lounging by their master's pool, getting fat on the finest sirloin steak and freshly made marrow bone chews.

For The Love Of Comets

THERE ARE TWO MULTI-FACETED and massively asymmetrical lumps snuggled quite distinctly and quite separately, under a thick, winter duvet. These lumps are hills major and minor with a deep valley running lengthways down the bed between them as if cut by the fast flowing waters of a glacial melt stream. Under the duvet two people lay with back facing back, she curled and foetal, he on his side over towards the far edge of the bed, one arm continually searching out comfort underneath his pillow. He turns onto his back and stares up at the Artex. Hills Major now resemble a single central volcanic peak.

Courtesy of a streetlamp three doors up along the Cheltenham Road there is just enough light coming into the room to make out the broad swirls pulled out of the plaster by some ancient, twentieth century craftsman. He, Hills Major, has been meaning to fit a blackout blind these last three or four years. He corrects himself. It is seven years since she and he moved to this picaresque South Gloucestershire market town to be closer to the grandchildren, grandchildren who now live thousands of miles away in a place called Mountain View in California. They have been gone these last three years and still neither he nor she nor they have visited one another. That is something else that he must get around to fixing. He loses himself momentarily in the ceiling swirls within swirls. In the half-life of his waking he remembers a song from the nineteen-sixties but can't quite grasp the tune. Circles and minds. Something or someone French. Bloody windmills…

He is drawn outwards as if by the gravity of some compelling foreign body. He needs to pee. He resists the compulsion to move for as long as he can under the duvet, drifting through those Canute like minutes when he firmly believes that a simple act of will can change his physiognomy and mentally dredge his bladder so that it is deep enough to cope with this currently pressing volume of urine. He knows that he is doomed to failure yet again, but still he tries. The house is silent. Heating pipes and cooling floorboards have long since ticked and cracked away to a point of equilibrium with the March chills outside.

Still staring upwards he tries to blend in with the spinning circles and the revolutions in the ceiling above his head. He imagines the atoms and the molecules that make up his latterly substantial physical form splitting and flowing down like that glacial melt water through the fractal layers of plaster. He imagines himself like the character in a nineteen-fifties 'B' movie, shrinking inexorably through Dante's circles of the universe. He will battle a spider with a pin. He will swim with sharp finned quarks and bosons. He will discover the ultimate components that shape creation, but no one will ever hear him shout 'Eureka!' They never do.

*

He is not alone in the waking. She is his wife, the mother of their children, beloved grandmother to a boy and a girl learning to speak with East Coast affectations. She stirs too, disturbed by his abdominal fretting. She is a light sleeper. He is an annoying lump of a man. She breathes more deeply in the waking and shifts her topside leg to a more comfortable position. Laying on her side she can see through her lashes the bright green numbers on her bedside alarm clock. Four thirty-four. A witching hour if ever there was one. She wonders what a Valley Girl is and whether her granddaughter will ever become one?

She switches back to the here and now. It is time for him to visit the bathroom. His bladder seems to work to a tight but choreographed schedule. He always seems to wake roughly one and a half hours before the alarm, whatever the setting. Sometimes she thinks that he does it deliberately. At other times she thinks that he should see a doctor. He is of an age, a paid up member of the Prostrate Club, a man at risk in that mid-fifties bracket when so many of them start to fail. She wonders why she worries. Is it that, after all of these years together, she fears solitude? She wonders on this in the drift towards wakefulness. Is that all that binds them? Surely a little peace and quiet in her twilight years would not be such a bad thing? God knows, she thinks, she has wished for it often enough. Is that fair, though?

He will wait. She knows his routines and she thinks that he probably does know hers too, though he never seems to care enough to show it. As annoying as he is, her man is not totally stupid and they have reached a certain state of symbiosis because somewhere in the dim and distant past they reached a comfortable intellectual accommodation. It is his more recent inactivity that grates upon her sensibilities. If only... but she sees no point in going down that route at this time in the morning. That subject is better voiced in the company of the gin soaked ladies in lavender who frequent the wine bar in town after an afternoon stint on the counter at the charity shop.

She too can make out signposts in the half-light cast by the Cheltenham Road streetlamp. He will, when he gets up the gumption, walk around the end of the bed and pass through the door to their en-suite, the door that she is watching. He will throw his green fleece dressing gown around his shoulders but he will not do it up. He will be naked underneath and his middle-aged belly will wobble limpidly as he waddles towards the bathroom door. She thinks that his insistence on sleeping in the buff is probably his one last throwback to a more rebellious age, and it is, she muses, utterly nonsensical. She feels the chill these days and much prefers the sanity and the chastity of cotton pyjamas. He will, she knows, sit rather than stand when it comes time to do his business. He will take his mobile phone and play a hand of solitaire while he ponders whatever it is that men ponder while sat on a toilet confronted by their quietly, deadly, artery choking obesity.

She cannot quite let the inactivity thing go. As she waits and watches the white wooden panel door in the wall opposite her bed, she thinks back to their last conversation before they retired for the evening. She feels that he is marking time. He turns up for work simply because he must. He has three more years to grind out in order to qualify for his local government pension. He goes through the motions. He is now so long in the tooth that they, the local government bean counters, will not dare to make him redundant. There is, she thinks, catching a bar or two of an old anthem echoing against the walls of her skull, power in a union after all.

That is, of course, a good thing, and she is mostly thankful for his steadfastness now that they are growing older, but none of it excites her. And, she thinks, given that he is hardly breaking sweat in any aspect or endeavour in these final decaying orbits it would be a little more encouraging for them both if he made more of an effort at home. She has her charity shop work. She has her classes. She is always busy. He sits and tries to watch television while she reminds him of his wider obligations. He drinks coffee or wine or both and makes marmite toast. He bloody well has the nerve to complain when she asks, simply asks again, that he do… something.

She sighs gently and closes her eyes. There is no telling how long he will take to stir, although stir he must. She too feels a need. His selfish act of waking has shifted her bodily functions along the waking curve as well. Time and ritual. She will wait for him to finish and then, when he is back in his side of their marital pit and turned away towards the window, she will visit the bathroom herself. She snuggles a little deeper under the duvet. The warmth is luxurious. She could smother herself away forever, and in that moment she wonders whether she is really being too harsh on him. Whatever else the man might be he is surely hers until death or sheer, bloody and murderous frustrations do them part.

It is now or never. The force is strong with this one. Pee he must… His love of science fiction colours his thinking. In his throwing off of the duvet, in his donning of his green fleece dressing gown, he imagines that he is Obi-Wan throwing off the malign weight of some obvious Sith Lord nemesis. At his side dangles an imaginary light sabre. He is confident that should he ever feel the need, really feel the need, then he could lay the beast, could slice and dice that slow revolving maelstrom that broods beside him in the marital bed, with one humming blow. But then, as he sits on the edge of the bed and realises that he cannot see his toes, in either night darks or day lights, he considers himself more Jabba The Hut than Obi-Wan. It is his turn to sigh.

*

She shifts under the duvet, making a sleep muffled whimper while pulling the cover up closer to her chin.

He knows that she is awake. Film themes abound. He looks over at her and mentally makes a note to remind his number two that this mission requires absolute radio silence. The metaphors drift in the early morning twilight. He is bound now to fly across black moonlit waters, engines roaring and winds rushing through the flimsy cockpit, to drop a bouncing bomb against a dam wall.

He fishes for his dressing gown at the end of the bed. It is impossible to tell which way up it is, and as he stands to drape the thing around his shoulders he realises that he has it hanging sideways. He feels around the hemmed edge of the garment for the little loop at the collar. He overbalances in the darkness and steps heavily to his right. He pretends to be sorry, muttering something indistinct as he steadies himself and draws the folds of his dressing gown about his rotund stomach and belly.

He pauses. The next steps require a moment of orientation. He must plot the course of his turn to avoid mentally mapped obstacles, namely the dog bed at the foot of their marital sack and the dog within, a Jack Russell named Chewy. The dog does not stir. The pilot knows that Chewy is watching him avidly, just as he senses that the maelstrom is aware of his corpulent procession across the bedroom. Needs must. He reaches the en-suite door and presses down gently on the brass lever handle.

He does not turn on the light, preferring not to disturb his imaginary aircraft's delicate thermal balance nor to diminish his acute eyesight with the harshness of electric light. He leaves the bathroom door slightly ajar so that just enough of the street light illumination creeps into the enclosed toilet to allow him to safely reverse back towards the toilet bowl. When he feels something cold press against his upper calf muscles he reaches down behind his buttocks, makes sure that the lid is up and the seat down, and then gently lowers himself to a sitting position so that he can relax into the job. He has power management set to low on his mobile phone so that the glow from the screen does not disturb the night darks too much while he plays a hand of Vegas scored three card draw Solitaire.

*

She is wide awake now and contemplating a cup of tea. There is a counterpoint here, a tipping point. The thought of tannins and caffeine and heat in her gullet are immensely appealing, but these thoughts weigh heavily on her own bladder. She has watched her leviathan break upon the shores of night and haul its vast and menacing bulk into its black-mouthed lair. The creature is all milky-white of breast and midriff and would be vaguely disgusting if she could be bothered enough to let her imagination run full riot. Her mind is set, however, upon the wandering stars as an antidote to these earthly horrors. She must move. She must stand. She must become marginally active to relieve the tensions that brew while she waits for her time in the bathroom.

As she rises and pads over to the bedroom window she wonders how the states of things are arrived at. Surely there must have been signs and wonders somewhere along their shared, star-spangled road? She parts the curtains and gazes up through the white halo cast by the streetlight at a clear sky too town bright to reveal the galaxy of stars that she knows is out there. When did they become so insular? When did they stop sharing? She remembers nights sat out in the garden, nights buoyed by chilled rosé, when he used some app on his mobile phone to identify the constellations and show her where the International Space Station was tracking across the heavens. They used to sit out and watch the Perseids until the wee small hours when the summers allowed. Before that she remembers stars cast by glitter balls, stars that waltzed across red brick walls, and dancing and bands and laughter. Now she watches toast crumbs orbit the stretched neckline of his jumpers.

The double-glazing is blown. Condensation is forming a triangle of water droplets in the bottom left hand corner as she looks at the window. It seems to form a graph. The curve descends and flattens as time progresses revealing trends of youthful expectation descending by the year to a mean firmly rooted in middle-aged disappointment and boredom. That is the moment when she looks up and sees at the far, upper right corner of the window a single bright star breaking through the clouds and through the up-lit glow. Polaris, perhaps, she muses, although she has her doubts. He would know, of course. Bloody science fiction. Bloody science fact. She watches the star twinkle through the clearing night sky.

She can hear him tinkle as the star twinkles. Saving graces, she thinks. At least when he sits there are no seat dribbles to wipe away, although the warmth of the seat can be a little disturbing at times. She listens as he turns on the cold tap just enough to rinse his hands. She wonders why he pretends to be quiet and considerate. He knows that she knows. They are time served veterans, barely speaking at times like this, but instinctively one creature. As he pads gingerly across the foot of the bed, careful to avoid stepping on Chewy, she turns from the window, grimaces at him, and marches to the toilet, firmly and loudly shutting the door behind her and locking it.

*

He wonders what she has been looking at in the night sky. He knows that you cannot see anything much beyond the streetlamp glow. You need some place like a Welsh hillside or a desert wilderness for such wonders, for watching the spiral arms of the Milky Way spin above your head as each spiral catches and whisks away all of those youthful dreams. He could almost cry at times like this. Instead, though, he hears the toilet flush and the sputtering of the hot water tap. She will smell of bottled lavender when she slides back underneath the duvet. Her hands will be pink and scrubbed. In place of the star in the upper right hand corner of the window he can see her delicately pale hands waving down to him.

He breaks away from his night gazing and looks down at his own hands. He has fat fingers. He sports a similarly matched and over-ripe torso. How, he wonders, can anyone love a thing like this? He is a gross creature in his own eyes and cannot understand how any other eye could rest upon him and feel desire. He is both a raging monster and a lost boy. He dare not show his teeth. He cannot ever seem to summon the strength to change, to make that effort of will that would see him step into a training shoe with some definite purpose in mind.

Better, he thinks, to listen to her slide back into their marital bed and tuck herself up safely for the night, wrapped and buttressed against his inevitable, boulder-rolling invasion of their sleeping space. He continues to look out and up. The hour is drifting on towards five o'clock in the morning and the darkness will soon recede with the coming of spring. It is too late for Obi-Wan to take heart in the force, too late for comets tailing a diving moon, but still he lives in hope. He spots the flashing lights of an early flight heading towards London, out beyond his earthly orbit. He imagines a star-drive, a warp engine, hears that signature hum as crystals and fusion reactors fire up and haul a human cargo across the edges of the galaxy. He wishes that he were weightless. He turns, closes the curtains and feels gravity acting empirically upon his layers of fat.

As he too folds the duvet under his chin, laying on his back and looking up at the ceiling swirls one last time before he slips down into that unrewarding hour of deep morning sleep, he breathes out heavily. He is, he thinks, surrounded by emphatic slumber and the endless orbit of the draining board. He drifts towards the apologetically poetic. He is, within these folds, a small rag-arsed boy who dreams of surfing solar winds on dragon wings.

His beloved maelstrom shifts onto her side and eases her body towards the middle of the bed, sliding slightly downhill into the dip caused by his heavy frame. Bedsprings creak. He closes his eyes and turns gently and slowly to face her back. In his imagination they are once again the burlesque delights of youth, he thin, top-hatted and dapper, she bright, sequinned and sparkling. His feet touch solid earth. Dragon tails flick once and disappear behind the moon.

He knows that his arm is heavy. He places a hand on her shoulder. He feels the warmth of her in his fingers. The waters of their glacial melt have warmed under these twenty-first century night-time skies. He inches a little closer to feel her back against his chest and stomach. The mattress sags a little more pulling her closer still. He remains silent for a moment. He knows that she too is still awake.

*

She smiles to herself as she feels the weight of his hand upon her shoulder. She too remembers those dancing days as she drifts down under his familiar touch. They could not have been that long ago, surely? And then all becomes clear to her. Time is the bloody reason. Time is why they are here now. They cannot move fast enough to warp reality. Despite the years of gazing upwards at the stars in their varying degrees and stages of hope…

*

He strokes her head and her neck before resting his hand once more upon her shoulder. "Love you", he says softly just the once as he closes his eyes for the final time.

*

He is incredibly gentle. He always has been. "Love you too", she whispers and snuggles a little deeper into his warmth. She too closes her eyes.

*

Unseen by anyone at this early morning hour but burning gloriously through the upper atmosphere, a shooting star glides across Hills Major's local patch of heaven before it fades as it dips down towards the horizon. A man shifts onto his back and after a moment begins to snore. A drowsy woman digs him in the ribs with her elbow.

The Tender Kiss

THEY TALKED ABOUT HER. She knew of their wide ranging speculations and their over-active imaginations. It has always been thus and would remain so throughout the generations that must, inevitably come. She, the Countess, heir of an imperial blood-line, stirred on her bed, uncrossing her arms, breathing in deeply the scent of basil and jasmine that rose like sweet perfume on warm, glowing skin in the viscous air of this hanging Cretan night. September. A small studio room in a cheap block of identical rooms just a little way off the coast to the east of Rethymno. Simple pleasures. Great risks. The joy of the chase.

The Countess stood up from the low bed and walked slowly around the small room. From the tiny bare metal kitchenette she took a bottle of the local, thin, dry red wine, unscrewed the cap, and poured herself a small glass. Thirst was a strange companion and one that she understood only too well. For her it was a ravening beast as well as a simple, pleasurable act that might slake a dry throat. The wine was too warm, but it would do well enough for now. It would bring a little colour to her pallid cheeks, although she would only permit herself one glass for now. She prided herself on the almost mineral paleness of her skin.

How odd, she thought, as she picked up a brush from the bedside table and started to pull it gently through her sleek, long, black hair, how odd that they still gossip so. If only they knew the truth, poor lambs. Always they gossiped. Never did they ask. It had been the same for her and her mother back in their ancestral home. People talked, people feared, and slowly the fat faced peasants dwindled away leaving only the meek and mildewed behind.

Her hair fell in thick, straight waves across her pale shoulders, her skin being almost translucently white, like a moon veiled by the lightest gauze of a high, grey cloud. The only light in the room came from a lantern strung up on a pole outside to help guide tourists along a winding path from these studios to the taverna that occupied the frontage of the building. With the curtains drawn across the large glass door to her balcony, the Countess could drift through her evening rituals in that sweet and comforting half-light that makes the world enticing. She lived for the dusky anticipation of each evening.

The Countess ran her free hand along the contours of her body, tracing the curve of her firm, full and neatly upturned breasts. Entranced, lost in the revelation of change in her body, she ran her fingertips over her taught stomach and down to her groin. It was time. She could feel the need, could sense the exquisite pain of that once in a lifetime craving, a passion that inflamed her entire being beyond anything that she had known in all these years of absolute and necessary thirst.

All these years. How many years more, she wondered. Not many. She would hand on the challenge of her line soon enough if she could but find the right one, the right boy, strong and beautiful, but preferably not too bright, who might join with her. She would kill two birds with one stone.

The Countess rose and walked over to the rustic, blue painted wardrobe and pulled from its hanger one of a number of simple cotton summer dresses, long and plain, cream in colour, with just a hint of flow and swirl towards the hem. Unlike her mother, a poor and feeble creature tied to the old days, a woman who shimmered like a pallid ghost among the ruins of their estates in the mountains, a woman who wore the same, disgustingly stained gown throughout her long and decrepit life, this Countess had broken with those dusty traditions. Her dresses were simple, worn only the once, and never stained when she put them on.

She liked to think about change while she dressed for the evening. The breaking of the taboos that had dogged her line down the centuries gave her a strength and a purpose. She was the first to see that the old ways need not be the only way. Ever since the great patriarch had sworn a pact with the dark stars, ever since he had fought the Turk and the Christian, drinking their blood in his fury after battle, they, his progeny, had never let off the work. He changed the world in making them what they were, so why, she thought, couldn't she do the same. She was of his line. She embraced the same arts and wielded the same powers. This heritage was too precious a thing to betray. So far they had been lucky, perhaps, or fated. She would not be the one to let it all end.

Her great and fell ancestor made the world anew and in so doing left them to live with a curse, the price to be paid for greatness. Each generation could breed only once, and in so doing, in the raising of the child, the parent was doomed. Each child, when they reached puberty, took their first drink of life from the parent, a fatal drink, laced with power and death for ever more. So had it been when the great one's son was born of a strong peasant girl chosen for the task and then discarded, a dry husk blown away on the winds of maternal fate. The boy child had, when the time came, embraced his father, told him he loved him, and then sunk his mouth to the old man's neck to taste the acrid, metallic taste of heaven for the first time. The second Count of long years had been her grandfather. Her mother had performed the same ritual when coming of age, although for her it seemed the bitter pleasure of awakening touched her mind. And finally she, the Countess, had rejoiced that she could end her mother's suffering and then fulfil her own destiny.

Her destiny, however, was not that of the cold mountains and the lonely snow bejewelled passes that brought fitful life to their lands. You could only feed for so long on fresh meat in one place. The peasants feared you at first. Some fought back, but eventually they grew weary and resigned. Villages became haunted places, fit only for wraiths and fools. The pickings became sour and few, you hungered endlessly and the glories and splendours of your surroundings grew shabby and mean. You relied on stealth and cruelty to maintain your position and your way. That was her mother's choice, the path that lead to feeding on carrion, of chasing down the rabbit and the rat and vole just to fill your belly and your veins. It was not the modus operandi of this Countess.

After the joy and exaltation of awakening, the Countess stayed true to her upbringing for some years, making the best that she could out of the debilitation and decay around her. Unlike her mother, though, she sought out images and tales of the wider world. Things had changed there too. Machines did the work of a hundred peasants. They waged war across continents. Oh, she had thought, if only great-grandpapa could have seen that. Money flowed around the world in great rivers of wealth. Why then, was she shut up in the wasted mountains, where winter was the only season and fresh meat such a dream?

When the blood-lust was done with, when the corpse was nothing more than a dried out shell, then she studied until dawn, ordering books from cities far and wide. She learned to control her lusts so that she could meet with the mortals, taking advice at strange hours of the night from men who knew of the great metropolitan stratagems. She rarely succumbed to temptation.

After time and knowledge had broadened her view of things she made a decision. The estates in the mountains, the never visited, decrepit palazzos, everything that she could lay claim to was sold. The money realised from this fire sale of the broken and the decayed was sufficient to invest and to bank. She worked out that if she were frugal for a few years, and given the likely length of her life, then the glories of compound interest and stock markets might make her fabulously wealthy. And so it came to be. The Countess through her financial foundations and partnerships moved in quiet splendour wherever and whenever she wished. Today she wished to holiday in Crete and live like they did, these people who provided succour, and tonight, she was sure, would provide the next heir to her line. With the night sky calling forth the hunter in her soul, she opened the curtains, stepped out onto the balcony and gazed down the dusty little lane that ran towards the local coastal strip, with its bright lights, its noise and its scurrying human possibilities.

*

Another night on the town, as delightful as it might be, just didn't seem right to Stu. Rethymno itself was fine, although a little too bookish for his taste, possessing insufficient an air of debauchery despite Crete's bloody history. Stu was more a Malia type of guy. Tonight, though, he fancied quiet and peaceful, which he had to admit was a bit of a departure from the norm. The rugby boys could stuff their less than subtle gibes and always rowdy insults where the sun rarely ever shined (you could never quite tell with one or two of them). He really didn't care, and being from one of those hail-fellow-well-met backgrounds, it was all water off a duck's back. He was, anyway, the fittest and fastest of the assembled pre-season breakers, playing at centre with all of the modern power and grace required of a rugger boy. His main claim to fame in these still relatively tender years had been a youth appearance for Scotland, although sadly a combination of injury and a tendency towards dilettantism meant that such early promise remained as yet unfulfilled. As the bus squeezed and wheezed its way through streets full of bars and girls Stu hoped that his chosen destination might have something at least a little different to offer tonight.

Stu stepped off the coast road bus at Adelianos, having left the boys to their beer and their eager-eyed and insatiable game of spot the girlie. This was going to be a quiet, thoughtful night, which would suit the locale. Adelianos looked sleepy and quiet and, frankly, pretty boring, providing a thin string of tavernas and bars set back a little from the beach. Everything looked the same; Souvlaki, Kleftiko, Stifado, grilled fish, Mythos beer, waiters standing on doorsteps trying to persuade you to eat at their establishment. He wanted something different tonight, a place of quiet solitude, where, despite being built like a row small northern industrial terraced houses, he might not stand out, where he might just sit and eat and while away some time without having to enjoy himself quite so much as he had during the first three days and nights on the island. Stu wanted to watch other people tonight.

He looked around the main square of Adelianos. Nothing caught his eye as being suitable, but there was a sign, faded and hanging at an angle because one of the cable ties holding it to a chain link fence had snapped. A taverna. Demetriou's. One kilometre as the arrow points inland. Stu smiled. Perfect. Inland meant up hill and that meant a little bit of exercise before scoff. Stu hoped that the place would be full of locals, bewhiskered old men rattling their rosaries and maybe playing backgammon, with their wives, those little old bewhiskered crones huddled in a corner chattering away noisily.

Even on a September evening it was still warm enough to raise a little moisture on Stu's forehead and top lip as he made the gentle climb inland. During the walk the night sky shifted from the hazy blues, reds and oranges of sunset, through the leavening purples of dusk and then into the jet black of the quiet cicada hum that calls forth the first star. With the closing in of the day the air filled with the gentle aromas of basil and wild garlic. The sounds of the night began to break free as Stu left the coastal strip and climbed slowly across the ancient Cretan soils; a cat mewling with excitement at the chases to come, something ferreting in the undergrowth, the whine of a moped in the distance. He felt strangely at home, like a ripe and powerful Palikare of old.

Stu represented the epitome health and vitality, walking with all of the swagger that a broad shouldered and confident young man at ease amid a timeless landscape should possess. Not that such thoughts occurred to Stu as he sauntered through those final dusty yards towards the taverna. He was getting slightly concerned by the apartment complex that he could see set back against the fields and olive groves. Bloody tourists.

No, such lofty and poetic thoughts were not his, but they did fill the mind of one shadow-souled creature who watched the world below from her balcony.

*

As the boy sat at table and ordered half a litre of the house red while he perused the by now predictable menu his heart sank in converse proportion to the rising pulse in the veins of the aforementioned lady. While he foresaw an evening of single mediocrity, she could feel the ravening joy of her twin cravings rising in her gorge. There would be a little moment of thrill when she stretched her legs out on the threads of her invisible web, a subtly delicious hour of play as she watched him eat, and then there would be the ultimate liaison dangereux. She was the spider, this place and time her hunting ground, and with the primeval urge satisfied she would then indulge herself within the joyous pain of bestial desire. It would be an evening of anticipation, frolics and, for the Countess at least, a late dinner. Such fun.

Before leaving her room the Countess took one precaution. Not for her the mosquito plug-ins, nor the net or the salve. She lifted the mirror from the wall and stowed it under her bed. Then, wearing simple thongs and clad in her delicate cream cotton dress, she drifted out of her apartment, cascaded down the steps to the taverna and voila! She made her entrance.

The locals, Demetriou and his sons waiting on customers, as one made the sign of the cross as she entered. Such superstition, she thought, in these modern days. They prattle on because they think that I only come out at night. Do they not see my alabaster skin? How could I risk the sun?

She spotted the boy at a table looking out onto the road, the only new customer so far tonight. Trade had been slow for Demetriou these last few days. The shepherds further up the mountain were talking about a white skinned ghost, a raven mistress, who called to them under the stars. Local people were staying at home. Only the tourists came, and now that the season was nearing an end there were only two apartments occupied.

The Countess appeared to hesitate, looking around the taverna as though unsure where to sit. Demtriou waved his hand and tried not to look into her eyes, all the time flicking his rosary beads against his thigh. The Countess smiled at the balding crown of the man's lowered head, and then walked boldly up to the boy's table.

"Would you mind if I joined you?" she asked in her clear but still accented voice.

She dipped sweetly into his eye line. It was a Ding-Dong moment, a Bloody Hell epiphany. The boy looked up. He could almost taste the promise held in the way that her dress clung to her taught, pale body. He saw how her hair fell straight and lustrously across her shoulders and down her back. Then he gazed into her eyes. She had the most amazing, the most beautiful and captivating eyes. They seemed to shimmer with a moonlight of their own making, set deep into black hearts, and there too he saw the flame of the candle on the table reflected back at him as if she hungered eternally.

He smiled weakly and mumbled his agreement. As she pulled out the blue wooden chair opposite him and sat down he couldn't believe his luck. He feasted on her, taking in the rise of her breasts and measuring the beauty of her long and supple limbs as if he were admiring a fabulous Pieta. Her skin shone in the candlelight. She seemed almost translucent, but deep and ancient in her marble perfection. Stu felt as if he were falling into a well. She wore a strange perfume that filled his nostrils with sweet unguents, with jasmine and rose and lavenders and with something else. It made him think of time, of ages passed under moon light. Bloody hell!

They struck up conversation easily. She declined his offer of dinner, saying that she would eat later, that she had not long finished a late lunch, but she would stay and keep him company while he ate. There was something fascinating about watching these creatures eat, something sordidly gratifying about the way that little dribbles of sauce might run down their chins. The boy was a fine specimen, vigorous and young, and engaging in his own sweet and innocent way.

While he ate and drank his wine, of which she accepted one small glass to be sociable, she talked of her home in the mountains, of how it had all been sold and how she roamed the world now, stateless but always with a casket of earth from her own land by her side as a reminder of home and her beloved family. She spun webs of silver thread through the evening air, always making direct eye contact, always drawing him in towards her desperate need for love on this particular night.

Once the food was done with they stayed sitting at the table to finish the wine, and the lady even found the patience to wait and talk idly about his life while he drank a coffee and a brandy, even though her own heat and lust for the gift of life was raging like a furnace beneath the demur cream cotton shift.

And then the talking was done with. She asked him to walk with her a little as she needed some air. She told Demetriou to add the food and drink to her bill and she would settle all with him the following evening when she was due to leave for her next as yet undecided port of call. She took Stu's hand in hers and walked out into the dark night, heading up into the hills, slowly but surely away from the fetid breath of everyday life. As the pair left his taverna, Demetriou crossed himself once more and said a silent prayer for the young Englishman's soul.

*

"Here", she said, "we rest here for a while"

Whilst not always the sharpest knife in the box, Stu's libidinous sense of what was possible confirmed the Countess's assessment of the situation. The olive grove was secluded, the grass thick and soft, the trees full and weeping heavily with fruit, and the air was still and calm. With his hand held firmly in her soft, white and cool embrace he let himself be lead to the far corner of the olive grove. She sat with her back against the tree, revealing a shapely if thin alabaster leg, and pulled him towards her. She met no resistance. Stu knelt before her and brushed her hair away from her shoulder. He leaned forward and kissed the limpid skin of her neck gently, afraid that he would break her into a thousand pieces if he exerted any force upon her frail form.

He need not have worried. There followed a storm of soundless lovemaking during which she engulfed him, forcing his penetration ever deeper until they ultimately found their symphonic tempo, and always, even in climax, their eyes remained locked together. Now satiated, dripping sweat and smeared with Cretan soil, they lay side by side staring at the rising field of stars that glistened above the olive trees. Her snow white body lay naked and revealed to the world of men for the first and only time, and she found, for a moment or two, that the urgency of her other bottomless hunger abated. She wanted to talk, to hear his voice one last time so that she would be able to tell her new-born of a father.

She rolled onto her side and propped her head up on her hand, her black hair falling dishevelled across shoulders and curving round her breasts. "Tell me about your family" she said softly. "Tell me about your brothers and sisters and your father. A memory of a good father is always something that I missed growing up."

"Not much to tell, really." Stu paused. Maybe if they talked for a while, maybe if they got their breath back they could try it all again, he thought. There couldn't be any harm in a little potted history.

"One brother, a twin. Funny thing that. My Dad was a twin and so was Grandpa. In the genes, I suppose, but Mum always said it was one hell of a job looking after us as babies. I thought it missed out generations but apparently not. Dad was an archi…"

She stayed his lips with a slender white finger. "Rest now", she said. "Close your eyes and rest."

Stu looked up into her eyes and there he saw reflected twin boys, curled up, arm in arm, growing by the moment into fine young men, dark and pale like their mother but blessed with a good, manly physique. He smiled. She smiled too, for in that moment she knew that she would change the world. There would be two little ones to bring up, and although it might take centuries, two would become four, then four become eight, until the line of her great ancestor filled the world in numbers sufficient to make extinction an impossibility.

At that moment she made the one truly human choice in her life. She placed her hands on Stu's eyelids and gently closed them while whispering sweet incantations. He would sleep and wake refreshed with the rising sun of a new day. It was a small gift from a grateful mother to this fine father of the race of Nosferatu. She would drink elsewhere of Crete tonight.

Only The Names Change

(Loosely based on Andersen's The Evil Prince)

HISTORY BOOKS ARE FULL of names and dates. They are full of stories about great lords and ladies and about the things that men do in the world, and some of these stories may even be true to a degree. Much the same can be said for little stories such as this one, except little stories like this are usually much more accurate than any history book. This is a tale with roots that run deep into the folds and the valleys of the country, a story from a time before enlightenment brought its own challenges to the people of this dark land.

The world is a very big place, with room enough for everyone and room besides for all of their differences. Unfortunately some people prefer a world that bends to one particular will rather than a world that reflects the views of the many. There was once just such a person. He was, at the outset, an ordinary man, whose only thought was to make a world more comfortable for him and his own kind. We shall call him a prince, for every story should have a prince.

Our prince began life in a humble way, growing into and learning some of the methods of the world common to his people. He sought their approval, promising them much and delivering on some of his promises. In short, he was no better, but no worse, than any other prince. He strived for the public good, especially when it coincided with his own interests, and took thanks in as many ways as such thanks became available to him. He tried to face the dangers and the troubles of his people as well as he might, until, faced one day by a strange and threatening combination of events from the far side of the then known world, he decided that this confluence of opportunity and challenge was his moment of destiny.

Our prince was skilled in many ways, not least in his powers of persuasion. Faced by something that he did not really understand, he listened to advice and sought out experts, and he found himself having to make a choice. Should he open his heart to the world or should he seek protection from it? He made his choice.

He convinced his people, his courtiers and his councils that the only way to secure peace was by striking fear into the hearts of his enemies. One by one he sent his armies out to the far corners of the wide, wide world bearing fire and sharp edged blades. His soldiers trampled down the grains in the fields and set mills and workshops and cities ablaze with red fire. He looked on as the fruits of one civilisation after another charred and burned on the branch. Everywhere mothers hid with their babes behind smoke drenched walls, but the soldiers marched on, rooting these potential assassins out for their pleasure.

Wherever his soldiers ranged, the prince's name became fear and dread, and his power grew and grew. He sucked wealth and might from every conquered land and city. His treasuries overflowed and his warehouses filled with every luxury and every loaf. At no time and in no other place had anyone amassed so many of the riches of the world.

Mindful of his place in the history books, our prince used his vast wealth to build huge palaces, monuments and castles. He commissioned epic poems and stirring stories about his ferocious deeds and he employed the cleverest scholars to write true accounts of his great crusades. All who saw the wonders in stone that he erected and all who read the towering texts that carried his name beyond the clouds were moved to say, "What a truly magnificent prince".

Nowhere was the suffering of others ever mentioned. The prince's own people did not, could not, would not, hear the sighs and the laments rising from the scorched fields and the ash filled streets in foreign lands.

After many years the prince surveyed his realm. He looked at his piles of gold, at his huge and glorious palaces and at his subject peoples, and he thought, "This is good. This is as it should be. I am, indeed, a great prince".

But even after such unprecedented success he still felt the emptiness of the great world around him. He decided there and then that he must bring order to the chaos surrounding his perfect world; he must ensure that there were no powers equal to his own, much less any power greater.

The prince marshalled his forces, made plans and waged wars against every neighbour and every enemy and, one way or another, he conquered them all. Each one of these vanquished kings, queens and princes were bound and gagged and shown at trials, where their unworthy souls were metaphorically flogged.

They were chained like dogs, made to lie down at the prince's feet and made to beg for scraps of food from his table.

With the world at his command, with his own men running the cities and the fields and the seas of the world, the prince had reason to be well satisfied. He raised new statues in every square, he made proclamations in every place of congregation and he sent orders to his priests and to the holy souls of the realm that his likeness should stand shoulder to shoulder with the highest of their many Gods.

As one the priests and the holy souls said, "You are a mighty prince, but our Gods are surely mightier. We cannot do what you ask".

The prince considered this. He asked himself if such a thing could, indeed, be true.

"Of course not", said a voice. "You are one of us. We have chosen you to command the earth and to rule the sky. Hear our voice, for we are legion, and know that what we say is true".

The prince was dumbfounded when he first heard the voices of the Gods speaking with him personally, but he quickly came to realise that this was as it should be. He was a most powerful prince and it was only to be expected that the Gods would side with him. And so, with the voices of the Gods in his left ear, it took but a little time to extend his dominion to every soul and across every inch of the earth.

And this too was good for a while. With new palaces raised and with statues and books exalting the prince and his friends, the world and the heavens were joined as one. But, even in such a time of plenty, the prince was not satisfied. He filled the earth with his name, but still he felt the emptiness of the skies.

"Why", he asked himself, "should I share this. What have these Gods done but talk. It is I who has struggled and fought for truth and glory all of my life".

The prince called his peoples together. He called his lords, his ladies and his priests to him and announced, "I am your Lord. I am the greatest prince ever known. Now I will conquer the Gods".

The riches and the resources, the minerals and the great minds of the earth were assembled and the prince built a great fleet of ships to carry him far into the heavens to meet these Gods face to face. Each ship was as black as a heart and bristled with a thousand blades, but each blade was a missile that the prince could fire into the soul of the universe. Great, steaming engines spewed out fire and heat as the ships rose from the ground, climbing higher and higher until all of the prince's dominions lay beneath his feet like a map. Every art and every science was employed to fashion this vast fleet. His soldiers and his sailors searched the heavens, scoured the stars, bombarded every comet and fired cannonades into every asteroid in their path.

But the Gods did not wish to be found.

And so it was, with a vengeful wrath building in his heart that the prince returned to his own world. He was determined to expunge the Gods completely. He wanted to obliterate their names and their memory.

The Gods watched as the days unfurled. They decided that enough was enough. They sent forth a single virus, complex in its own way, but no match, on paper at least, for the science and for the technology employed by the prince. The virus had no firepower with which it could outgun the armies of the world of men. The virus was nothing but a carrier of the common cold, no more, no less.

The virus twisted and turned, flew somersaults in the air and made men cough and sneeze. It changed and modified itself, becoming more virulent, more invasive, and with every infection its strength grew until it became a killer of flesh. The virus waxed and multiplied, infecting the young and the old, the rich and the poor, and the strong and the weak without mercy or allowance for wealth and status.

At last the chains that bound our prince to the world were yanked tight. Standing at the head of his armies, surrounded by his vast wealth and his walls of science, he came face to face with the Gods. There were no bullets capable of shooting the virus, no speech could influence it, no rhetoric could inflame the mob to protect him from it and no history book could provide a vaccine against the virus.

He was vanquished. Our prince, who commanded the riches of the earth, sneezed once, retired to his bed in terror, and there he died, snivelling and delirious just a day or two later. He was extinguished and, if not forgotten, he was certainly relegated over time to the pages of fairy stories like this one, which is where, as I said at the very beginning of this story, the truth is often found.

Jamul's Happy Day

CHOKING DUST FROM CRUMBLED plaster filled the hot, still air whenever a four-wheel drive careered past the leeched wooden frame of the window. Glass lay on hard baked earth, a thousand pieces shimmering together to form dirty, jagged pools under a blistering summer sun. The thin burn-white stems of long dead grasses stood dry and brittle on the stagnant breath of a world becalmed. Hanging on the outside of the wall below the window an air conditioning unit, held up by two straining bolts, dropped thin flakes of rust onto the dirt. The fan was fused on its spindle, the bearings having seized up over too many long hot summers and too many freezing winters, becoming a fusion of age and decay, just like the people and the towns and the spinning whirl of calloused hand on hand amid a sea of sad eyes above gap-toothed smiles.

Within the buildings a derelict office lay bare save for a few marks where Sellotape had once stuck posters to the walls. Wide cracks, fissures in the fabric of the place, revealed the brown mud of handmade bricks underneath layers of dull, dust-coated paint that was scratched and faded, a reminder of better times. The telephones worked then. Lights burned at night and footsteps in the corridor were light and soft.

In one corner of the room, as far from the gaping window as it was possible to position it, a desk stood shrouded in the drift of slow days under a clear blue sky. A bleached and shell shocked telephone, with a dial that wheezed round on accumulated grit, trailed a fraying chord across the desk's surface. The wall socket into which it was still plugged lay on the floor, where it had been ripped from the wall years ago. The broken heads of the screws that had once held the telephone socket to the wall now mouldered in plaster caked Rawlplugs. The surface of the desk was clear of any sign or implement of work, showing only the slow, osmotic colour change of dust in wood grain. Leaning with his back against the rough surface of a brick wall, fused into the patina of the room, a shabby middle aged man sat on a raffia-backed chair tapping his fingers on the edge of the desk. His eyes were closed.

Underneath a heavy fringe of thick grey hair the lines and ridges of age and care cracked white as the man smiled quietly. He whispered a few words to the blown out seed heads beyond the window and continued to tap out the rhythm of his memories on the desk. In his head he watched the grain and flicker of celluloid images and heard the sibilance of tin sounds. A young woman with long dark hair was walking towards a camera under the same bright sun that shone down outside his office window. She cast no shadow on the world, shining through the liver spots and chemical blemishes of his mind's reel. Music faded out as she spoke. Cymbals, drums and flutes fell silent before her simple but absolute beauty. Her voice was deep and soft, a cool liquid melt. Television. In his head he could replay programs from the days when he worked, when there was electricity and the comforting hum and flicker of spooled tape. Right now he was reliving pictures of a goddess. Her eyes were a soft glow, were deep black wells reflected in moonlight, and she smiled as she described giant statuary that formed a backdrop to the camera shot, revealing curves and subtleties of expression that held him in total thrall. She walked on the water that spilled from the corners of his eyes.

His reverie was broken by a sudden shudder of noise. Car horns braying on compressed air shattered the stained glass of his dream and scattered his tears into a wilderness of confusion, shattering the lens in his mind and spilling reams of spinning videotape into the dust at his feet. Toppling forward, he ducked instinctively down into his chair and tried to work out how far away the monstrous vehicles were. He could hear the growl of an engine, the discord of metal and the rumble of rubber on loose stones. He could feel them coming from the far end of the street, where, in the days before the current flavour of truth had been tasted, a market had once blossomed with coloured awnings and a chorus of voices at dawn. The lunatics were on the loose. He tried to twist into himself. His stomach fluttered and a diamond hard stone of fear rose in his throat. He heard repeated bursts of automatic rifle fire in the air and the clink of spent casings hitting shattered concrete. A beastly whine of hot metal roared down between lines of low, bunkered buildings, spraying loose rocks out from under tyres and throwing clouds of hot summer dust into the sky. He wrapped a worn out handkerchief over the lower part of his face and waited. A staccato rattle of stones pummelled the little patches of plaster that still clung onto the outside walls of his redundant office and then, drawn away to parade before the rough mortared blocks of some other Jericho, the men in the four wheel drive were gone, leaving fresh clouds of fine dust hanging in the air.

There had been a time when they stopped right outside the door. He coughed and spat dry phlegm onto the new layer of dust that was already settling onto the desk. He found it difficult to remember dates. He seemed to have spent so long sitting in this room, waiting. Six years? Seven? He remembered faces, though, and their sullen eyes and their rifle butts, remembered all too clearly their acrylic colours and the needle taste of his own blood. He tried to blot the faces and the voices out of his scarred memory, but these new images played just as brightly as the footage of his angel. The lunatics hurt him. The only reason that he survived was because films of his seraph played on a constant loop in his head.

*

The camera shot in his head changed. The world turned and everything was different. At first, when the small men came, he had just got on with his job. In those early days he had thought that it was nothing to worry about, that the faces of the men who hung around the offices had changed, that was all. Then warlords came with their freebooter comrades in arms, with their extorted wealth, and their greed for more, throwing down into the streets other, older men whose time and money was spent. There was killing and random brutality, but no more or less than the centuries had brought to his ancestors. He had been allowed to get on with his job. The new men, the ones who towered above you but left no impression in the mirrors of your mind except for the smudge of their fingerprints, still wanted pictures and sounds. In a funny way it was a good time. He kept the archives, just as he had always done, and helped to prepare new programs for them.

They wanted revolutionary tales and heroic descriptions of struggle, never minding that the revolution was really just another tribal gathering and a settling of blood feuds. The quality of his work then was poor but these new lords knew what they wanted, and what they wanted were farmers with big smiles on their faces scratching at parched earth. They wanted girls in school rooms looking serious and concerned over their books. Larger than life portraits appeared on the shelled out ruins of buildings, portraits in primary colours to remind the people of a new order personified by the Great Leader. What they wanted were pictures that earned foreign money, bribes for their good behaviour with palms greased all round, dollar bills for services rendered. They wanted the smallness of the world laid at their feet and he had helped them because he wanted to make sure that his name was not on the lists of those who might disappear.

That was when she had gone. She stuck it for a few months at the beginning, making documentaries and news programs with all of those happy farmers and working sisters, but then, one day, in late November, three months after the revolution, when the snows lay thick on the hills, she slipped quietly across a border with her film crew while making a piece about land reform. The apparatchiks and the newly devoted men of faction were furious. That was when the cars had come, just like today, except that they had not roared past the doors of the television studios. He expected to be on the list, but these men with guns came and simply pushed him out of their way. They spirited greater men than he off to the dark corners of their frenzied imagination. Of course, it was all caught on camera and delivered in sombre tones by fidgeting newsreaders. Rumours became apocryphal stories. Tales were told with a shrug of the shoulders, the common currency of the streets, but he kept his silence, working on with the catalogues and the endless filing of videotapes. Nothing much changed. His daily routine, sipping thick black coffee at roadside stalls and busying himself with paperwork went on largely as usual, except that people, friends even, avoided him and his notebooks and pens, wary of the list. He simply lingered on, untouched in his quiet little storeroom, surrounded by circular tins of celluloid, videotapes and tape cassettes. When the fractures in the Homeland eventually healed over and everything settled back into the basic routines of revolutionary life and death he found that the newfound wealth of party members and tribal elders included video recorders and he made a little extra income from copying western films.

*

It was said, or so he believed, that the far away streets of London were paved with gold and that buses drove down crowded streets without the aid of men in armoured Toyota pick-ups. London must have many buses, maybe a hundred or more. At his favourite coffee stall he often made a joke. It was the same with revolutions. You could wait a lifetime at the bus stop of the barricade and then, all at once, driven with abandon by disciples of Tito and Vladimir Ilyich, many, many buses, some as red as London's finest double-deckers, would all hove into view at the same time. The differences, he thought, were twofold. The conductors on local buses carried an AK47; and no one told the passengers waiting patiently for the ninety-seven that the driver was a Prophet and that their final destination was Heaven on earth. Crowded onto the back of trucks and Japanese four by fours, shooting from the hip, the warlords and the fanatics from the provinces had finally put paid to the glorious experiment of fraternal corruption. Collective farms and incompetence were replaced by the truth, by words of faith and the rocket propelled grenade.

In with the old…the newly shod foot wearing a worn out boot. The sound of raised hallelujah voices and heavy souls was a sound that he could recall from his own personal archives just as vividly as if he was watching old news footage from his storeroom. In the rampage that followed the fanatic, when all the stones were kicked over and the dust rose to obscure his people's desperation from a pre-occupied world, the lunatics had come for him and his kind. Boot heels kicked in doors. Rifle butts broke open heads and video machines. They lit fires in the television studios and ripped wires from walls. A time of broken glass and broken bones, for the lucky ones at least.

When they came in their cars, bristling with automatic weapons, shouting and screaming at the infidel world, he, like everyone else, stood in a corner and looked on in bewilderment. Like everyone else, he was beaten and bent double. Men tore at the walls and smashed his machines, spilling wires, circuit boards and half full cups of coffee onto floors that were already stained by years of abuse. These new fanatics, these men of religion, made electricians, janitors, secretaries and engineers stand in line while they quoted scripture at the solid state circuits that lay abandoned and broken around them. The younger men were herded into trucks and ferried away to one of the front lines. Those who remained were made to clear away the devil's hardware and write their own names in the traces of dust beneath their feet. In the midst of the maelstrom, with bruises and cuts and trembling hands, he had done the one thing that he could.

At the beginning of each day he went to his place of work as usual. Each day they came and screamed at him. Each day they pulled and pushed him, making faces and calling him simple and stupid. Each day they beat him and burned him with cigarettes. Each day he squatted on the floor of his storeroom, degraded and dirty. Each day he collected videotapes and cassettes, cans of film and soundtracks and filled their boxes and bags. Each day he watched them pour petrol on his life and send towers of smoke up into the blue sky to mingle and merge with the dust and smoke that they raised across the city skyline. He persevered, putting one foot in front of the other and kept going, kept walking, until they got bored with him turning up for work in this derelict shell of a building. They should have killed him but, with the blessing of the Prophet, they did not and with the passing of their interest in him, he quietly gathered up the tapes and reels that he had hidden from them, folded them into his robes and stumbled out into the night with their half-hearted insults drifting around his ears. He knew that if they found the tapes he would join the pilgrimage of the damned but he continued his work of salvation. It took nearly a year of sifting through the wreckage to move the remaining tapes and cassettes from their hiding places. At times he felt as if his veins were full of nothing but madness, but once he realized that it his apparent imbecility was a mask that allowed him to stumble onwards, he used it to save what he could and hide what was left of his life's work under the floorboards at his home. It was a home without doors but a home clothed in hope. So much was lost, so many tapes could not be carried, so many were burnt and trodden under boot heels, but those that he could save were saved.

He gently swung his chair back to the perpendicular and leaned forward over the desk, taking his handkerchief from his face and putting it back into a pocket. He let his fingers make geometric shapes in the ever present dust. He drew a quaint caricature of a nineteen-thirties camera, all Mickey Mouse ears and tripod legs. He ran his fingertip along a thick scar on his forehead, a memento of unhappier times, and smiled, leaving a trail of white particles on his cheek. He looked up through the punched out window and saw a kite flying above low, corrugated iron rooftops and squat, tin chimneystacks. The fanatics had withdrawn from the world of DNA and computer chips for five years, banning music and television, pigeon breeding and long hair. They looted museums and destroyed the relics and customs of a culture centuries old.

For what?

They had left, just like all the others. Forcing young men to hold a rifle and stand firm against a world that had finally turned from gazing at some distant horizon and was looking straight at them did not help the soldiers of religion. Massacring thousands in the north did not save them. Seizing foreign aid did not succour them. Banning women from work, schools and healthcare did not make them stronger. The privations and chastisements visited upon the sinful by the Ministry of Virtue brought forth no miracles. They should have watched him more closely. Destroying his life and beating him senseless did not stop Jamul. Calling him names and laughing at his madness only served to save his sanity.

The world spun through another cycle and then another. Men with money and bombs had come and now, as the spokesman of the new government had said on an impromptu broadcast only last night, the world was going to be different. Just how different things would be Jamul could not tell. There was nothing material that he could point to, no machines, no cameras, nothing that he could touch that suggested some true orbit. Japanese four by fours, white, blue or fanatically dirty, still rattled the doorframes of the buildings that they lived in, but he could see with his own eyes that the faces of these men were different. It was not their faces, however, that worried Jamul, no, not their faces.

He stood up, pushing his chair along the floor behind him with the backs of his legs. In the shadows of his bare office, with its trailing telephone flex and exposed brickwork, he smoothed down his clothes and breathed in deeply, tasting the heat of the afternoon and faint traces of cooking on his tongue. Taking long, firm steps he walked over to the open door and stood there, framed by its cracked architrave. Jamul squinted as the full force of the summer sun blazed down upon his face. He had an appointment to keep.

When the bombs came and the lunatics ran away, men in strange skins had come and found him at his work. He took them to his home and lifted the floorboards. Amazed by the lights and the pictures in miniature that they showed him, beaming a toothless grin to a phantasm of global networks and satellite magic, he was feted as a hero of the free world and a true sign of the indomitable spirit of his people. They promised him a roof and shoes and food. They said he could continue his work and so now he waited in his bare office for the machines to come back. He had given them the videotapes and cassettes and soundtracks and they had cheered. He cheered too, not daring to tell them that the pictures were all of her, of his angel.

Today she was coming home. After the beatings, after the disappearances, after the nadir of hope and expectation from which she had fled long years ago, she was finally coming home. Jamul stepped out into the full glare of the sun. He walked along streets tumbling down with decay and along the dirt road that would take him past bomb craters and bullet holes, past wrecked shells of houses and shops that had long ago given up the pretence of selling non-existent goods to ghosts. He would find a car or truck and hitch a ride out to the airport and be there for her. She might have put on weight. She might be grey and tired. Jamul could not care less.

The lunatics had called him insane but he had endured it all for her. Today Jamul knew himself to be alive. All of the hardships, all of the despair, all of the hazards to come in this brave new world, were as nothing to the lightness in his heart. Jamul was on his way to bathe in the deep black wells of her moonlight eyes. He was going to dance to the soft timbre of her smooth and reassuring voice. That was how the world turned. He caught sight of the flashing tail of a kite dipping and soaring in cavernous deeps of red and brilliant nylon yellows above the rooftops. The lunatics had banned the flying of kites in favour of their own monstrous magic carpet. He breathed deeply, filling his lungs with hot, arid air and began to sing as he walked.

Jack and Jill Went Up the Hill

ALTHOUGH THE GREAT AND the good of this feted land have, in recent times at least, attempted to develop a responsible and ethical relationship with their own population, with their neighbours, with foreign potentates and with the leaders of other races, factions and interest groups, nonetheless the pressures placed on any free society by the complexities of modern statehood have taken their toll on the patience of our law makers. Nowhere has this been more apparent than in London's shimmering streets of gold, where the right of the individual to express his or her free will has not always been appreciated or encouraged, despite the avowed intent of worthy politicians from all shades of the political spectrum to protect the very basic tenets of free liberal democracy.

A few years ago the policy makers in the country's parliament were faced with making one of any truly democratic nation's most unpalatable decisions; namely whether to take the country to war or to reject violence in favour of an attempt at a diplomatic solution to their problem. Now, the purpose of this story is most definitely not to debate the merits of the choice made by the politicians of that day, for this has already been the subject of considerable vitriol and public argument. However, if you cast your minds back to the newspapers of the time, there is every possibility that you will remember hearing something about Jack and Jill, and their unfortunate walk along the paths of our political uplands.

That the nation's politicians had chosen the option of war in a foreign land rather than the continuation of diplomatic and economic methods of problem resolution had irked Jack and Jill considerably, so much so, in fact, that they willingly joined a protest march that snaked and chanted its way along their local suburban high street. The march was held on a bright and crisp spring day, and the assembled crowd was a refreshing mixture of young and old, of blue and red, and of creed and colour. Rather than being a riot of the usual suspects, at least as portrayed in the media, Jack and Jill really felt that this time the commoners of the land, the everyday jobbing folk, were standing up for what they believed in. The numbers varied according to the witness, but the country as a whole saw millions of Jacks and Jills walking under a clear blue sky peppered with banners and filled with the harmony vocal slogans. In every borough and every ward, under familiar high street signs and shop displays, the streets echoed to the sound of tooting car horns and good natured but serious protest.

Jack joined in with the chorus line on every marshalled step, "Not in my name…No War…Freedom, not oppression…".

Jill, feeling herself to be at one with the ebb and flow of the crowd all around her, found her voice breaking with emotion as she too called out, "What do we want? Peace and understanding! When do we want it? Now!"

Neither of them had ever actually participated in any form of public protest prior to this, preferring to comment quietly from the relative safety of the front room in their semi-detached home. Jack had supported the government's taming of the wilder elements of the socialist movement some years earlier, had despaired of the more recent sleaze bound affairs of state and had even questioned the merits of voting on one or two occasions, but on this matter both he and his wife were of one opinion. It mattered desperately. It mattered that they stand up and be counted in a way that would really make the politicians think.

Ever since the debacle of "Honest John" Skuttle's forced resignation following the blank speech scandal, Jack and Jill had grown both disillusioned and militant in their own particular, socially responsible manner, picking issues on which they could hold definite opinions amid the general torpor that they felt in relation to the general body politic. The war helped to galvanise them into belated action, giving them common cause with thousands upon thousands of similarly confused and worried men and women who lived everyday lives and dealt with everyday problems just like their own.

Things had changed in the country's parliament and now that fresh faced and youthful Mike "Mickey" Gambol had assumed the reins of power, it was most decidedly time for Jack, Jill and the rest of the little people to remind the establishment of who it was that really stalked the corridors of power in England's green and pleasant land.

*

In the Houses of Parliament, "Mickey" Gambol, having accepted the poisoned chalice of a foreign war, tried desperately to persuade his fellow parliamentarians and the wider constituency of voters that they were all fighting for the same ideals.

"Despite our differences, despite our deeply held convictions", he asked, "are we not really brothers? This great country has seen a thousand years of history, during which we have developed as a nation to value beyond measure the freedoms and securities that only a true and open society can yield. That this government has embarked upon a policy that some of you disagree with is, understandably, a bone of contention among many of us, but this government's actions and policies are designed to protect exactly the right that you are exercising, the right to dissent in a proportionate and measured way.

We will debate these issues. We will reach a consensus and we will remain, now and forever, arbiters of freedom, democracy and inclusion amid the chaos of a fractured and hostile world.

It is precisely because we can air our views without fear of reprisal, that millions of our citizens can conduct peaceful and considered protest and that we, as a government, will listen to your protests.

It is precisely because of these ancient traditions of fair play and accountability that we can stand tall in the world and defend the rights of the oppressed against the dark forces of persecution and oppression".

The debate in the media raged on, as it did around dinner tables and in taverns throughout the land. Points of view differed immensely, but in general people understood that, although opinions differed and that arguments could become quite lively and heated, they lived in a reasonably balanced land where the state, despite the occasional bout of nannying, preferred to leave the individual some scope for making choices and for taking responsibility for their actions.

Away from the public eye the debate raged within government circles too, although it assumed a slightly more hushed and cautious tone. Away from the hurly burly of the parliamentary debating chamber, "Mickey" Gambol and his advisers from the governing party and from the civil service took the whole debate about the protection of democracy very seriously. Over a plate of chocolate hobnobs and plastic cups of a vaguely tanned tea-like substance, they met in secret conclave to discuss the issue and to decide upon the best way forward.

"Of course", said the leader's chief policy adviser, "we cannot endanger the rights and freedoms of individuals, but we should remember that such freedoms have been, and will continue to be, our Achilles heel in times of crisis like this. It's all very well saying that we have to respect considered debate and responsible protest, but the laws, as they stand, protect any sort of protest, no matter how wild and inflammatory it may be. We have to distinguish between legitimate protest and incitement".

And so, after a tough but productive session, the assembled ministers of state, private secretaries and political consigliore agreed that a combination of closed circuit television, internal surveillance and intelligence gathering, improved police responsiveness, and a few new clauses tacked onto the forthcoming Freedom of Speech legislation ought to be sufficient to keep a lid on the more extreme members of society.

*

Jack and Jill retired from the world of public protest as soon as the first wave of popular enthusiasm for the anti-war march had broken on the breakwater of political indifference to their cause. They muttered and mused on how a government that claimed to listen so intently to the voices of the common people could so completely ignore those voices when raised outside of the normal focus group channels.

Over one too many glasses of reasonably priced red plonk, Jack suggested and Jill discounted the options of shoe bombing, egg throwing, naked building scaling and petitioning. Anthrax was discussed, as was direct action of the Red Army Faction variety, but neither over the dinner table nor over the long wooden bar at their local pub, could they decide on how best to wake the buggers up and get them to smell the roses.

Every form of anarchy and every form of peaceful protest withered in their minds as the days and weeks passed into the obscurity of history, until, wrapped up in the mundane chores and stresses of normal life, Jack and Jill's brief flirtation with political protest and activism dissipated and dwindled, becoming nothing more than the sound of a dog gnawing at a bone in a neighbouring garden. With the sound of birdsong in the branches, of lawnmowers droning on a Sunday morning and the inevitable chatter of the daily grind, they could hardly make out the sound of chewing canine teeth at all, but during the quiet hours of the night, when most of the usual suburban noise polluters had given up the ghost and finally fallen asleep, Jack and Jill were sometimes able to hear the gentle crack of a splintering bovine hock.

With time and the continued commitment of forces in overseas lands, buried bones came fresh to the surface and the dogs of war chewed enthusiastically. Jack and Jill found that the daily casualty lists weighed more and more heavily upon them. A continual diet of sanitised news reports, of ineffective debates and the inevitable slump into response fatigue by a general population whose attention wavered and drifted in the summer heat haze, tickled their own consciences lightly but persistently. With the war's general death toll rising inexorably and with the losses experienced by Britain's own forces of liberation approaching a significantly rounded number, Jack and Jill finally heard the dogs leave off from their chewing to bark and howl from the shadows.

"It's really not good enough", said Jack one evening over a light supper of smoked mackerel salad. "I mean, everyone's saying how bad the war is but no one's doing anything. Bloody Gambol is ignoring everyone. If only we could do something".

"I know, love, I know", replied Jill, "but what can we do? There doesn't seem to be much in the way of organised opposition to the war. None of the political parties are doing anything and no one else seems bothered anymore".

Evenings drifted by like this, interspersed with the usual distractions on the television and in the pub, without any real progress being made on the issue of how to make their voices heard. The dogs, however, continued to gnaw away and Jill's private thoughts kept company with the hounds, whittling the bone down to the marrow of the problem as it nagged and badgered at the seams of her considered sense of justice. The words that really stuck in her mind were 'no one' and 'organised'. It seemed to Jill that perhaps she and her husband were looking in the wrong place for inspiration.

"Perhaps we should think about this in a different way", she said a few days later as she and Jack finished off a lovely late night snack of cheese slices on slimming rye bread wafers. "Perhaps we should think about doing something ourselves, you know, just making a small statement on our own. It's a start and maybe, when a few people see us they'll think the same and maybe it'll grow, maybe it'll be like a chain letter or something".

"You've got a point, you know", said her husband "I mean, even if there was a group to join or whatever, all they'd really want was our money and a signature. Even if we did buy a rubber bracelet, they probably wouldn't actually want to listen to us, to you and me personally. Of course, they'd say they were listening to 'Us', but we'd never really have any say in anything. Look at that march, I mean, it was a lovely day out, but it didn't actually achieve anything lasting, did it".

Jill topped up her husband's glass of Merlot. "I was thinking maybe if we did something simple, something nice, maybe if we just made a small point it might help. I've got an idea. I'd like to read out the names of the dead soldiers at Trafalgar Square. No one could object to that, could they? I mean, it would be peaceful and quiet and over in a jiffy".

"And I could wear a t-shirt and hold a banner or something, you know like those protest t-shirts that were all the fashion twenty years ago. And if the banner said something like 'quiet please' or 'just listen', then who could object?"

There followed a week of planning and painting on torn up bed sheets. From a local screen-printing shop Jack ordered two bright pink t-shirts with their chosen slogan emblazoned across the chest. On the Friday afternoon, having travelled to the heart of the political district in Westminster, Jack and Jill started their ascent up the shallow rise from Whitehall, passed the Foreign Office, Downing Street and the old Admiralty buildings and eventually emerged onto Trafalgar Square carrying two sheets of A4 paper, a rolled up banner made out of an old bed sheet, an empty bucket and a bag containing one hundred small pebbles. Directly underneath Nelson's column, they walked over to the white marble steps of one of the country's most famous and recognisable martial memorials, and set about their quiet, peaceful and considered protest in the hope that someone, that anyone, would listen.

Jill stood on the bottom step of the memorial and prepared to read out the names that were printed on the A4 sheets of paper. Jack filled his bucket with water from a couple of bottles of Tesco stripy, stood on the second step and placed the bucket between his feet. As Jill started to read out the names in a normal, everyday tone of voice he unfurled the banner above his head, tied the posts to the pedestal of one of the lions and proceeded to drop one pebble into the bucket for each name that was read out aloud. In a simple, dignified and personally significant gesture, Jill waited for each gentle pulse of ripples to subside before reading out the next name.

Above them the sky was filled with scudding grey clouds and a light breeze made their banner flap and snap on its broom handle poles. Together, reading and dropping pebbles into a bucket, they worked through their protest, name by name, wearing bright pink t-shirts bearing the slogan, 'Maybe if we're all quiet' on the front, and 'Gambol might get the bloody message' on the back. The banner simply asked anyone who could read it to please respect 'The Silence of the Dead' as they passed the strange couple dressed in pink t-shirts.

Government workers on their way to and from meetings, rubber necking tourists and the occasional meandering, unworldly vagabond strolled through the square, catching sight of the protest and registering the usual mix of momentary confusion, annoyance, interest and amusement. Jack and Jill plodded on, one name at a time, one pebble at a time, in the simple hope that one of these passers-by would see and think and take up the challenge. The possibility that television cameras would relay their activities to a much wider audience had simply not entered their heads.

*

Of course, the television cameras in question were those that had been installed as part of the government's response to the perceived threat of wild and inflammatory protest. As Jill read out name number thirty-seven and as Jack dropped pebble number thirty-seven into the bucket, the high pitched snarl of a revving engine pierced the quiet dignity of their polite little memorial ceremony. Even in the afternoon hustle and bustle of the tourist throng, the whine of gears and the rumble of tyres on tarmac seemed to them to be a gross intrusion on the solemnity of their act and they watched, rubber necking just like the ambling tourists, as a white van rushed up Whitehall to where they were protesting.

They assumed, as did everyone else who had stopped to look at the van, that there must be an emergency, that there must be some dastardly act of terror or vandalism taking place somewhere in the government district, against which a fully armed response squad had been despatched to ensure that all who obeyed the law and worked hard would be protected.

The men in the van were, indeed, armed, armed with the weapons of state that allowed them to protect the great and the good, the high and the low, the strong and the frail, from rogue elements in a society threatened by extreme views and an unfettered willingness to create chaos.

They were armed with legislation that gave them wide discretionary powers, powers that allowed them to determine just what constituted wild and inflammatory protest, and so it was that the van screeched to a halt by the memorial, that seven uniformed officers bundled out of the van and these same officers managed, with a great expense of arm twisting and wrestling, to manhandle Jack and Jill into the secure environs of the vehicle's transportation cell. The van containing the police officers and their securely bound charges careered back down the road.

Sporting bruises and cuts to their heads and hands, and with the bucket tumbled down the memorial steps, Jack and Jill nursed their aching limbs and broken crowns, and prepared, finally, to speak to the one member of the state apparatus who seemed inclined to listen to their story; namely the presiding judge in their forthcoming trial for crimes against public order and incitement to terrorism.

Where the Grass Is Greenest

(Loosely based on Andersen's The Butterfly)

AS A YOUNG MAN, Tom Bowler was naturally keen to find himself a girlfriend. Progressing through his teenage years he committed all of the usual fumbling faux pas and awkward lunges that boys the world over are obliged to do before they become men. His chat up lines developed from monosyllabic grunting into the crudely embarrassing hope of youth before finally passing into the hopelessly threatening swagger of the seventeen year old. By the time that he was twenty, however, his urgent desire for a shag, for any shag, was growing and maturing into a desire to find a partner. Of course, if a willing young lady fluttered her come-to-bed eyes at him he was still game, but on the whole his thoughts were crystallising into shapes that combined the simplicity of out and out lust with the complexities of mutual respect and life-long friendship.

Tom had a system. He spent most Friday and Saturday nights in the pub and then went to his local nightclub. Whether stood at the bar or on the balcony overlooking the dance floor, he believed that he could classify girls into a number of different types.

Depending on the state of their dress, their general fashion sense, their hairstyle and the amount of cleavage on show, Tom could calculate their "Naughty" ratio.

He was, as is only natural at his age, most attracted to those girls that he deemed to be pretty, and would watch girls huddle together in groups, gazing at them as they lost themselves in the rhythm of the dance, and he fell in love at least once every half an hour. Tom's trouble was that there were just too many lovely young girls for him to choose from. As soon as he spied his next great love and started to work out how he would introduce himself to her his attention would wander and be caught by another girl's smiling eyes. Girls seemed to like him and Tom was as convinced of his own beauty as he was certain that every pretty girl in the room really wanted to be on his arm.

After another engaging but ultimately unsuccessful foray into the beating heart of Saturday night, Tom spent a quiet Sunday afternoon lazing in the summer sun in a local park. He lay on his back under the drowsy influence of the heat haze and pondered his future, concluding that he really must think about settling down. He rolled over onto his left side and looked into the gentle eye of a simple little daisy. Tom vaguely remembered that the French called daisies by a woman's name, and he ran his finger along the plant's stem while he tried to recall what that name might be. He settled on Deirdre and asked her very quietly if she could really tell the future. She did not deign to reply. Rather than picking her petals off one by one in the time honoured fashion of lovers everywhere, Tom elected, being in a romantic mood and disinclined to do harm to such a simple little bloom, to kiss each petal in turn.

With each kiss he asked, "Loves me? Loves me not. Loves me

loads? Just a teeny bit? Not at all? Oh, sweet little Deirdre, oh wise little flower, tell me your secret, who am I to marry? If you let me in on the secret I'll go over to her right now and propose".

But Deirdre had no answer for the boy, knowing in her sap that boys were made up of many things but rarely of a constant heart. Tom grew impatient with her dallying and, placing his soft lips upon her petals, he bit off her head and spat it out onto the grass.

Over the next few months Tom worked overtime on his project. He met and dated young women of all shapes, sizes and temperaments. Some were still at school or college, some were working and some even had a child or two of their own, but Tom had an open heart and an open mind and he always tried to see the good in the person rather than the difficulty in the circumstance of their lives. His conquests ranged through prim and proper young misses all the way up, or down, to the most brazen of womankind. He tried girls who said yes and girls who said no and girls who answered his inevitable question in every shade of grey imaginable, but none of these relationships lasted. Like the daisy, they were too young and too green.

Tom's next revelation came one Thursday night at a music bar in town. He didn't usually go out on a Thursday, preferring instead to drop by the gym to work on his muscular definition, but he fancied a change that night. When he saw the "Grab-A-Granny" sign posted on the door of the bar he felt a gobbet of quiet revulsion rising from the pit of his stomach and was about to turn on his heel and head for home when the command centre in his brain kicked in and flashed the words, "Older Woman" before his eyes.

Like many young men Tom felt the excitement inherent in the

imminent promise of resting his head in the arms and on the bosom of an older and more experienced woman. There was no shortage of interest in the bar and Tom found himself at the centre of a veritable storm of hormonal posturing and pouting. It was great. He'd never had so much fun in public before and by the time that dawn's hopeful head rose above the far horizon of the duvet he was thoroughly and utterly shagged out.

Throughout his twenties and into his early thirties Tom played the part of a very willing Casanova, flitting from one bed to another, living for the moment and for the beauty of every freshly explored country. He tried on for size the role of lover, of the other man, of concubine and of predator, all of which thrilled and excited. He looked for many things in his partners, varying their age, their hair colour, their breast size and the length of their legs as if he were a dictator's wife in a shoe shop. There was, however, one significant drawback with the whole process. The girls and ladies who he really liked were invariably unwilling or unavailable to him for long. On the other hand he found that the women who wanted something more permanent from him were just too tart and cloying for his palette. Nonetheless, Tom swept into his mid-thirties with the absolute confidence of someone who knows that the chosen one is waiting for him just around the corner.

On his thirty-ninth birthday the stars crossed and the finger of fate wagged in Tom's general direction. He met a lovely woman called Rose, who was, in every sense, a true and natural beauty. Her smile was crisp and bright, her eyes shone with a wicked sparkle, and she knew her way around the bedroom, the living room and the kitchen. Much to Tom's delight, Rose even had a pretty good idea where the garage was. Tom dated Rose on an exclusive basis for nearly two months and was seriously considering the ring thing when disaster struck. Rose asked Tom to meet her parents and her older sister one Sunday afternoon and he willingly agreed to go along. After all, if he was going to pop the question he really ought to buy into the whole family kit and caboodle.

As soon as he walked through the door of her parent's modest semi-detached, Tom knew that it had all gone terribly wrong, there being something about paisley carpet that he just couldn't stand. Worse still was the fact that Rose's mother was four foot two inches high and at least six feet wide. The final nail in the coffin lid was the sight of Rose's older sister. She was clearly of the same breeding stock as her sister, although she was, being in her early forties, some seven years older, and those years had not been kind to her. Tom saw in her faded looks and in her dimming eyes a future that he was not inclined to embrace. Shortly after this visit the relationship with Rose foundered on a sea of unreturned telephone calls and ignored emails.

After his experience with Rose, Tom drifted through a series of ever more desperate relationships. He found that his disappointment in the collapse of his hopes and dreams for Rose carried through into each new liaison. He came to see the women that he met in pastel shades, as if the strong and vibrant colours that had once filled their lives had been bleached by the time they'd spent being weathered and beaten down by life. He tried to recapture some of the spirit and verve of his younger days by dating women in their twenties, but the effort of it all was rarely rewarded. More often than not he just got annoyed with these younger conquests because after sex, and even before it on some occasions, there was nothing that he wanted to say to them.

By the time that he reached his mid-forties, Tom's good looks and the firmness of his buttocks were on that inevitable, gravitational slide southwards. In his mind's eye, of course, he was still the young buck about town, but the invitations to cuddle and schmooze on a Thursday night at the music bar were becoming increasingly rare and when they did arrive, it wasn't uncommon for the lady in question to resemble Tom's own mother. Of course, he knew that wasn't really the case, but once the thought had thrown its grappling hook and caught on the battlements of Tom's mental castle, there was nothing he could do about the waves of nausea that battered at the door of his mental redoubt.

In the autumn of his years Tom still watched the girls in pubs and at clubs. He watched them in the town's marble halled shopping mall of a Saturday afternoon and at work during the week. He still found the beauty of fresh skin and bright, expectant eyes utterly compelling, but his flesh was weak and he was tired. That fresh, fragrant lightness of being that had once filled his heart was somehow lacking. Fragrance is what the heart needs to remain young and the sundry, intermittent associations that Tom engaged in were based on the satisfying of dull need rather than on the delicate perfume of hope and future expectations.

Not long after Tom had chalked up half a century of summers in the flower garden, he did meet a woman who he thought it might be possible to establish contact with. She was a divorcee with two grown up sons and while she might not be in raging bloom, she was, nonetheless, strong of stem and full of the subtle aromas of experience and a life lived well. Unfortunately for Tom, her history was the undoing of his hopes. She recognised in him a man of shallow roots falling into decline as the breath of winter touched his leaves, and she had no time and no inclination, now that she was free of encumbrance, to add Tom to her list of permanent worries.

She offered him friendship and an occasional night in by the fire, but nothing more. The simple truth was that Tom had searched for too long. The blooms of spring and summer were long gone from his garden and faced with the late flowering of honeysuckle women, Tom found that he was too set in his ways to flap his wings and fly up into the Indian Summer skies to greet them. He was a died-in-the-wool bachelor.

Winter set in as it always does. Tom settled for the comfort of a roaring fire in the snug of his local pub rather than the bright lights and the thump of whatever music the kids listened to these days. A pint of beer and a whisky chaser represented a little slice of heaven. Life was just about perfect if he could manage the price of a small cigar to accompany his drink.

Women still featured in his life, but only via the electronic highway of his one true indulgence. He found the plasticised, superficiality of staged Internet sex far more satisfying than having to deal with the real thing. Not that he actually did anything like that anymore. As he dwindled though his sixties and settled into his final decade, it was enough now to look. To be honest, he preferred to watch the big match on the television on a Saturday night if he could stay awake long enough.

Towards the end of Tom's days on this earth he became a little forgetful. He was wrapped in blankets and given a new place to live in a municipal home, where forgetful people of all kinds and classes waited for the snows to fall and cover their heads. Sitting in a high-backed chair in front of daytime television soap operas, Tom would stare out at the world through glass eyes as a reel of film ticked rapidly as it spooled through the projector in his head.

Tom flitted and flew across the silver screen of his mind's eye like a butterfly flapping its wings against a window pain.

His beautiful, his lovely, thorny, darling Rose stood there in her faded winter finery in the middle of the flower bed with her head lifted up to a pale noon sun. Around her the images of his summer garden were there for him to see in all of their wonderful glory but old Tom couldn't break through the glass. He raised a sallow skinned hand to his eye to wipe away a solitary tear because he understood now that he would never reach out to kiss the daisies again.

Hesperus Wrecked

THIS IS A WORLD viewed through half closed eyes, a world drawn by degrees of cross-hatching through blurred eyelash blacks and blue-hued shadows from shuttered windows. This is a world of sepia stains and the pastel blue washes that flow through the disintegration of an eastern Mediterranean sun briefly waxing a thick but brilliant orange in the midst of its inevitable late afternoon wane, mimicking the final throws of its future solar death with a yellow-orange-red-purple phase shift. In the distance, across the curling peaks and troughs of a Meltemi agitated sea, a range of distant Pariki Attic-Cycladic Crystalline hills lose contour and detail in the lowering light. Shadows lengthen and the peaks and serrations of ridge and cliff are blunted.

Erich Jackard plots more local Koufonissi contours, feeling rather than seeing the elevations and the depressions of calf and thigh and hip and stomach and breast. His remote classification of the nearby profile of tear-drop Paros marks him simply and obviously for what he once was; a delver in and chipper out of rocks. His more intimate classification of pore and follicle and sun-drenched skin marks him out as a man with more than just time on his hands. This afternoon he prefers this local domestic geography. He is, anyway, a jobbing silversmith these days, working the Scandinavian tourist seams in the long summer melt that engulfs this small Greek island. Geology comes in strips to be hand beaten into bangles.

Erich is happy. He is sated. He feels that universal sense of sublimation that comes in the drift down to the mundane parcelling of life and love and boredom. He is laying on his back, one arm stretched out under the pillow upon which his partner lays, a blonde haired head nestled into his shoulder. They touch in the shadows, rib upon rib, hip upon hip, toes resting against toes. This is the after burn. This is the sinking time, when lust and need and that primeval, brutal scream subsides to leave a moment of unspoiled quiet. To speak now would be to ruin the world, and Erich has, he thinks, more than enough experience of such ruin. He deserves this moment of lonely companionship, this moment when the world stops, when breathing is faint, and the sound of a glassy teardrop sliding down a cheek is as rough and as seductive as any Shakespearean sonnet.

Erich smiles and stifles a chuckle. He has just remembered their homecoming after a long, slow and hot walk along a dusty path by the boatyard and down to the ruins of a Second World War German gun emplacement on the far side of the main town bay. Erich should have been hammering away at those silver bangles ordered by the weekly brigades of backpackers and tented families, plying a trade that keeps him in simple accommodation and copious bottles of thin, red vino, but today he had shut his little workshop at lunch time and was now enjoying the fruits of a long and intimate siesta. He is still of the opinion that he will open up with the dusk and pluck Euros from the hands of tipsy travellers. Erich sighs contentedly.

When he and his partner returned from their earlier ramblings they had come home to find one huge beefsteak tomato and six inches of bent and twisted cucumber on the white plastic table on the veranda outside of his paramour's apartment. "Cucumberi…" That is what the impossibly wrinkled and tar crusted Giannis had called that odd green carbuncle when they queried his horticultural arrangement with smiles and laughter and pidgin English. "For you… From this gardenia…" Much nodding. A peek from behind her grandfather's knees by little Anastasia, the granddaughter, all olive tans and thick black curls and a heart breaker at just five years old.

Erich wonders whether one is allowed to think such things anymore but decides that the politically correct bandwagon that his conscience seems to have jumped on can go and fuck itself. Little Anastasia will wreck the lives of countless teenage island boys. It is a delicious thought.

The conversation with Giannis ended with a wave of a hand and the expletives that spew forth with rolled tobacco fits and starts. The cucumberi sits now on the top shelf of an otherwise food free fridge. A half-drunk bottle of Prosecco is all that occupies that unnaturally cold space, standing with a teaspoon in its neck in the door rack. Erich remembers again his polite smiles and waves as the thick, studded apartment door closed, and this time he does chuckle softly. How long has he known Giannis? Half a lifetime, it seems, and the old leopard has never once changed his spots. Heaven forbid, thinks Erich. If ever one of those heartbroken teenage boys so much as swears in Anastasia's presence Erich is convinced that they will soon feel the sharp claws of leopard

Giannis in their wiry young necks.

Erich's smile broadens. The cucumberi reminds him of something. He smirks quietly, relishing the still puerile element in his forty-seven-year-old persona. He moves his free hand and brushes the back of his fingers against his partner's belly. A soft intake of breath in the shadows by his head. He traces a love handle with a fingertip before resting the flat of his hand on that soft, warm abdomen once again in the fading blue-purple descent. A moment passes. Erich feels that slicing of time that severs the now and passes it back into foggy memory. He imagines that he is that gentle tear drop sliding across his partner's cheek.

Erich breathes in deeply, feeling his partner's head rise upon his chest with this strong inhalation, and he turns slightly towards this other prone body on the bed. A fingertip runs gently across a cheek. He wipes that fingertip upon his own cheek. It is undeniably wet. Erich stares through the darkening afternoon and sees the black caress of matted eyelashes against a pale, naturally blonde forehead. He curls into the shape beside him and cradles his partner's head tightly to his chest. He feels the shudder and hears the sigh. This is the moment. This should be… this will be that leaving moment, that grasping moment, when two threaten to become one but like oil and vinegar they can never truly merge. They are foreign substances in a bowl, thrown together briefly for culinary effect, waiting to be discarded at the end of the meal. This is the place and the time when all hope is lost. There is no going back. The otherwise well-ordered ship that bears Erich's life across the ocean swell is once again breached and broken upon the rocks. The crew of the Hesperus lie twisted and shattered on bloody sands under a dog-day heat haze.

But perhaps, just perhaps, Erich is not yet ready to abandon all hope of survivors. Another shift. Tangled sheets around feet. The sweat of the afterglow sticking hair to forehead and skin to cotton. It is still too warm to get up but sweat pools rather than evaporates. Erich feels suddenly uncomfortable. He arches his back to relieve a minor cramp and his partner starts awake. A soothing brush of a forehead. Confusion. A hushing. They resume their former positions, one head nuzzled into the crook of a shoulder, but this time their bodies are barely touching because of the heat.

*

The grind of an old diesel and the dusty rumble of thickly treaded tyres on white, disintegrating bedrock. Giannis is back from the tiny island port with back-packers game enough to pick a room advertised on a laminated page by a smoke shrouded Greek grandfather. As ever the spelling of words like "rom" and "cumfe" seem only ever to charm the boys and girls streaming off of the boats, although streaming might be an exaggeration where Koufonissia is concerned. Erich sighs with delight. His favourite mistranslation has always been, "Lamp in the Oven".

The world beyond the room's window shutters is black now and the room hums to the tune of a cicada treble beat. They have both slept. Erich is the first to awake. Outside children's voices drift on the wind and the bleat of one solitary, bell-necked goat tethers the world to a harsh white moon. Erich's right arm, the arm still under his partner's pillow, is numb. He flexes fingers and feels that delicious stab and prickle of flowing blood. His partner has rolled over and now lays with back exposed and knees tucked up. Spoons. Erich obliges, all the while thinking about that half bottle of Prosecco or, even more fancifully because of its absence, a hob brewed mug of Nescafe… or both… with a cigarette. Erich has not smoked for more than three years. He is fit. He does not hack in the mornings. A bitching God is the only creature who truly understands how much Erich wants a cigarette right now.

Beside him a body stirs and yawns. The ripping heat of the afternoon has drifted down to the low ebb of early evening and dried sweat chills cause Erich to feel the stippling of goose-bumps. A body turns around amid the night shades and the veranda lights that have snapped on with the passing of some iridescent moth or sharp fanged hornet. Erich can just make out a smile and iris wide hazel-blue eyes. Hazel-blue is the colour of love today. A moment when foreheads touch. A tender brush of lip on lip. The sudden, bed-sprung leap of faith that bounds towards a shower. Erich laughs out loud.

"The last of the wine, Stefan?" he calls out as the sound of a sun-warmed shower patters out fecundly from the bathroom. He stands up and wonders if he will ever walk straight again.

"Of course, you old goat…" The sound of shampoo suds hitting a tiled floor. That Scandinavian lilt. "… and where do you want to eat tonight? The beach or the old town?"

Erich does not care. Stefan is still three days away from the ferry back to the northern pines. They will eat Smelts and Red Snapper and drink thin pink wines before retiring to the Internet Bar to drink Espressos and Metaxas while playing backgammon to the tune of ten-year-old euro-pop records, the highlight of the evening always being The Race…

Erich will not open his workshop as originally planned. He will eat with Stefan tonight. Sod the tourists and their freshly minted Euros, he thinks. Hesperus is indeed totally, utterly and magnificently wrecked…

Picking the Wings off Crane Flies

(Loosely based on Andersen's The Girl Who Trod On A Loaf)

YOU'VE PROBABLY HEARD about the boy who trod on an Indian take away meal so as not to spoil his brand new training shoes, and of how badly he fared. It was in all of the red top newspapers at the time. The boy in question was well known locally for his fastidious way of dressing, and although his choice of clothes wasn't everyone's cup of tea, he had already become something of a legend in his neighbourhood for his sharp temper and his vain and overbearing nature. In short, he was the sort of boy who, when five years old, delighted in picking the legs off crane flies to see if they could still fly, and if they could still fly he plucked off their wings as well.

As he grew older the boy's manners and his sulky disposition became steadily worse, but he was blessed with a strapping physique and sultry looks that turned girls' heads. He knew he was handsome and as his school days wound down and he matured into a young man, his looks and his personality were the very undoing of him. His physique and his winning smile were all that stood between him and many more beatings than he ever received.

His father often said to him, "It'll take something desperate to cure you of your mean little ways. You'll be the ruin of us all if you don't grow up and accept some responsibility".

But try as they might, his family couldn't cure him of his pride and his temper. His friends, such as they were, had neither the wit nor the inclination to take him to task. He preferred it that way and chose his friends accordingly.

Having left school without many qualifications, trusting his fortune to his smile and the forcefulness of his personality, the young man started work at a factory run by one of his father's friends. Because of the esteem in which his father was held, his new employer treated him very well and Billy almost became part of his employer's family. He was trained and paid a good wage for his age, all of which allowed him to indulge his passion for designer label clothes, shoes and jewellery. He looked good, he felt good, and his arrogance increased with the purchase of every new shirt and every new pair of tight fitting trousers.

He spent so much time with his new employer, both at work and on a social basis, that it soon became clear that he preferred money to blood. After a year had passed his kind and considerate employer said, "Really, Billy, you should spend more time with your parents. They're not getting any younger and your Dad could do with some help around the place. Why don't you make a bit more of an effort?"

Billy could think of nothing worse than having to spend an entire weekend with his folks, much preferring the company of his employer's spoilt and wealthy sons, but he had also learned that it was good to listen to his surrogate father, that it was good for his image and for his prospects, and so, one fine summer weekend, he stayed at home as a means of garnering brownie points. He managed to grunt his way through breakfast and even managed some meagre civility when his father asked him to help in the garden, but as the morning dragged on and as his father prattled away about trivial rubbish and the incomprehensible doings of maiden aunts, Billy started to scream inside his head. He had to get out of there. As soon as his father's back was turned he slipped out of the garden by the side gate, gunned his small but heavily customised hatchback car down the drive and fled towards the nearest decent shopping mall.

Billy was ashamed of his parents. He was ashamed of their petty little lifestyle and of their inane and constant chatter. His father, who was a book-keeper for a local firm and had worked there all of his adult life, was a grave disappointment to Billy. His mother, who worked as a cleaner at the local primary school, was beneath him. He felt humiliated by the fact that he was making an effort, making a real splash in the world, and his parents were so boring and tedious. Billy had no regrets about spending the rest of the day drinking Cappuccinos and hanging out in designer clothes shops, being, by now, quite experienced in the use of retail therapy as a way to mitigate the irritations caused by the thought of his home and of his family.

As soon as he was able to, Billy rented a small studio flat and left home for good with his stereo, his compact disks, his wardrobe and his collection of soft porn magazines. For six months he carried on working, going to the shops, drinking luridly coloured alco-pops and dating girls for a week at most. Not once did he visit his parents or pick up the telephone. He even set his email account to automatically delete any communications from them.

Then, at work one day his employer called him over and said, "I was having a chat with your father in the pub the other night. He was telling me that since you moved out they've seen neither hide nor hair of you. I know you're young and eager to make your own way in the world, but you really should try to get on with them a little better. Blood is thicker than water, after all".

"Right", replied Billy from under his fringe, shifting his weight from foot to foot, "suppose you're right, it's been a while".

"Good boy. Now, I've got an idea. Mrs Spencer and I are having a takeaway curry with your mum and dad on Friday night and I think it would be a lovely surprise if you turned up with the takeaway and joined us for the meal. What do you think? They'll be delighted to see you".

*

On Friday night Billy put on his tightest jeans, his most flamboyant French shirt and his latest purchase; a pair of red and gold trainers made by the coolest sportswear manufacturer this side of last month. Despite the fact that it was raining, Billy parked his souped up roller skate of a car a couple of streets away from his parents' house and walked round to the local Indian take away. After all, he might manage a visit but he didn't want to advertise the fact that he was spending a Friday night at home with his mum and dad.

The streets were full of puddles and dirty brown mud where people had been walking on the grass verges and Billy trod as carefully and as delicately as he could through all of the muck and grime, desperate not to spoil his pristine shoes. He'd borrowed from the rent fund to afford them and he was not going to see them ruined on account of a stupid family obligation.

After Billy picked up the curry, the popadoms and the pot of minty yoghurt, he set off at a brisk pace for his parents' house, but at the bottom of the road where they lived Billy came face to face with his worst nightmare. Somewhere, somehow, one of the drains had backed up and was spilling a cold and dirty mixture of rainwater and sewage right across the pavement and into the gardens on both sides of the street. The stream of murky brown liquid was just too wide to jump across. Billy was stuck. There was no way on this earth that he was going to put his shiny new training shoes in that mess. Billy had an idea. The curry was in a plastic bag. If he put the bag into the middle of the stream and used it as a stepping-stone, then his trainers would be saved. "After all", he thought, "I can say I'm broke and they'll just have to get their own bloody curry".

Billy pushed the plastic bag full of cartons into the stream of dirty brown sewer water and, attempting something akin to levitation, he tried to step as lightly as he could on the bag so as to avoid both the water and the possibility of curry sauce splashing his designer trainers. But as Billy's right foot landed on the carrier bag and his left foot started on its arc towards dry land on the far side of the stream, the takeaway meal started to sink. Everything seemed to happen in slow motion, but try as he might Billy couldn't reach dry land. The bag of curry sank deeper and deeper, taking Billy with it, until he disappeared completely and there was only a thick, gurgling stream of water to be seen in the cold and empty street.

Billy continued to fall and fall until he thought that he was going to end up on the other side of the world, but then, with a sudden bump in the darkness, he came to rest with his cheek against a cold and clammy brick wall. Billy was in the great hall of the King of the Sewer Rats and the King of the Sewer Rats loves rain and dirt and all things foul. He brews his potions out of the world's stinking detritus and Billy knew from the smells all around him that he couldn't stay here for long. The stink that rose up from King Rat's cauldrons made Billy's head spin. He searched desperately for a chink of light, for any sign of a doorway, but there was no way out because all of the exits and entrances to the hall were full of squirming, wriggling, horn tailed rat soldiers. Billy sank to his knees in the middle of this loathsome, writhing mat of warm, twitching flesh and he started to shiver and shake and moan.

On this foul weather day the hall was full of commotion because King Rat was playing host to a much-esteemed visitor for whom he was conjuring potions. He was entertaining the Devil's grandmother, who is a virulent old woman at the best of times, spending her days sewing unrest into people's shoes so that they can never settle down. She is keen on needlework of many varieties, embroidering unfulfilled wants and needs in people's pockets and crocheting lies and thoughtless remarks in busy people's underwear. In short she does anything based on the sewing crafts that will cause harm and corruption in the daylight world of men.

The old woman looked at Billy as he knelt in the mire and said, "Now, there's a man-child with attitude! Give him to me as a token of my visit here and I'll set him up for eternity as a Toby Jug in my grandson's living room".

Of course, King Rat was only too pleased to be able to make a gift of this foul creature of the sun, and that is how Billy ended up spending the rest of his days in the Devil's living room as part of his prize collection of amusing caricature pottery. The Devil's living room is really quite small, unlike his eternal and unending halls of pain, and he likes to relax in a well-worn armchair that stands beside a cosy fire. In fact, the room looks like the parlour of a small Victorian terraced house, except for the fact that the walls are lined with shelf upon shelf filled to the gunwales with grotesque faced Toby Jugs.

Perched high up on one of the shelves, Billy felt as cold and as stiff as an earthenware flowerpot, for cold glazed pottery was what his body had become. Like the rest of the damned souls immortalised in pottery, Billy could still move his eyes and as he did so his head filled with shapes and dreams of absolute horror. Huge bulbous bodied spiders were spinning thick strands of silk over the jugs, building webs that lasted for a thousand years or more and Billy could sense the torment in the souls around him. The contorted faces of loan sharks and estate agents, of fat corporate cats and smug warmongers, filled his view of the room. It was a truly dreadful thing for Billy to find himself stacked on these shelves.

"This is what you get for wanting to keep your shoes clean", he whimpered to himself in a terracotta voice. "It's awful, dreadful, quite the ugliest thing to see them all glowering back at me like that".

It was true. Every one of the Toby jugs flashed an evil grin at him, shooting stars of menace across the room. Billy could hear their demonic mumblings even though none of them could move their mouths, set as they were for eternity beneath paint and glaze.

Billy looked down at the bulbous shape of his own jug and saw that it was painted to look like just like the clothes and shoes that he had been wearing when he set the Indian take away in the stream of water. "Well, at least I still have a sense of style", he mumbled to himself, "which means they're all jealous. What a terrible pleasure it must be for them to see me in all my glory".

Billy continued to stare at his own painted body. The general effect was pretty cool, but now that he looked closely he felt that something, somewhere was wrong. As he stared and stared he realised that he must have been covered in grime and filth after his fall into the hall of the King Rat, and someone had painted all of that grime onto his pot bound body. It was awful to see how his trainers were covered in thick globules of mud. At least he hoped it was mud.

"Still", he muttered, "none of the other ugly pot-bellied bastards are looking too hot to trot either".

It was then that Billy noticed the smell of burnt chicken Madras. He felt pangs of hunger rising from the pit of his earthenware stomach all the way up to his painted eyebrows and he felt a lump of something settle in the bottom of his hollowed out body. Billy screamed silently inside his own head as he realised that he was full of cold chicken curry. His hunger pangs drove him into a frenzy but there was simply no way that he could satisfy his ravenous appetite despite the ample source of food that he held within his own portly shell.

And then the flies came, attracted by the smell of coagulating Madras. They came in their thousands, swarming all over his eyes and his mouth and his ears. He couldn't even blink. Billy was stiff and cold. He shuddered and started to cry non-existent tears when he realised that the flies were wingless, legless crane flies, but worst of all was the endless hunger. It seemed to Billy that his entrails were eating themselves and he felt nothing but emptiness inside, nothing but hollowness and loneliness.

"I can't stand it", he yelled at the top of his voice, but stand it he did, for he had no choice.

It was then that Billy felt a tear fall upon his glazed face. The tear trickled down his cheek, down his chin and all the way down to his china training shoes. More tears fell upon him, each hotter than the last, because up above him, through the darkness and the cold, his mother was crying over her lost son. She was crying tears of grief and a mother's tears always reach her child, although in this case they were of no comfort for they burned as they fell, adding to Billy's torment. He was consumed by hunger and by the knowledge that he was full of chicken curry and couldn't eat a drop of it. He was convinced he was devouring himself from the inside out. He was like a black hole sucking everything into his black heart, which was how he came to hear the words of his parents up there on earth.

What he heard was harsh and painful. Although his mother wept deep tears of sorrow, her words were full of anguish and anger.

"Pride goes before a fall", she moaned. "That was your undoing, boy. That's why we suffer so".

Billy was mortified.

"If only I'd never been born", he thought, "then we'd all be so much better off. Now my mother is snivelling and crying like a banshee but she's no help to me. They should've cured me of my attitude, should've made me into a better person, should've cured me of my temper... not that they're bloody saints, the miserable bastards".

Billy's attitude was cast in hard, eternal relief, just like his face and his hands, and he fumed quietly on the shelf as he heard every word that was said about him up on earth. None of it was complimentary. He consoled himself by thinking, "Well, if I'm as bad as they say it's their fault and they should be punished for their sins as well. Oh yes, then these shelves would be full to overflowing. Can't they see how tormented I am?"

Billy's soul grew progressively harder and colder, his heart filling with icy fury and spite. He ranted and raved over many, many years, until he realised that his story, that the words that he could hear from the world above were fading almost to silence. Billy realised that his parents, that his employer and his friends were all dying, one by one, and that his story was passing into folk-lore.

Now all that he heard were other children's parents telling them not to be like the boy who loved his shoes so much that he sank down into the pits of Hell. Children everywhere were told Billy's story to stop them being hateful and full of pride. Most of these children just stood there silently or cried in fear, but one day, as he listened and ranted back at these disembodied sounds, Billy heard a little boy cry not in fear but in despair.

"Mummy, please, won't Billy ever rise up again, won't he ever be saved?" pleaded the little boy. "He can't be punished forever just because he liked his shoes so much, can he?"

The little boy's heart was breaking for Billy. He showered tears of compassion down upon Billy's hard coated face, but unlike the tears of Billy's mother, these tears were soft and gentle. One of the little boy's tears ran in through a crack in the glaze and reached all the way to Billy's soul, filling him with warmth and hope.

As the years have drifted by, and as Billy has continued to shout back at the human voices that he can hear, that one tear has worked its slow magic. Billy's anger has gradually waned and his voice turned to a gentler tone. Billy knows that he can never expect anything more than this darkness. Billy knows that the flies will still come to gorge themselves on the never emptying slops in his pottery body. Billy knows that flames will lick and crack his glaze, turning his once bright colours to shades of grey and black, and that his hunger will never abate, but he also knows the love of a small innocent child. He just wishes, when the flies stop buzzing and the flames stop crackling, that he'd put the plastic bag down a few yards to the left all those years ago.

Lord of the North Wind

A COLD CHILL TO the skin. A fine, faint spray hung in the air, cocooning the sodium light of a market town evening as if the world were lit by giant bumbling glow worms. Lucy was tired and ever so slightly tipsy. The Mad Hatter in fresher's week. Girls and boys from the Royal Agricultural College wearing spiders webs for clothes and daring September's spiny little teeth to bite if they could. Youth and optimism and the first rush of freedom combined with Bacardi mixers to make Lucy feel just a little giddy. The boy in the red polo shirt, the boy with defiantly tousled hair and yard boots, he would be the one. Virginity sucks, she thought, and spun round once on the pavement outside W H Smiths.

The low greyness of the sky blotted out the stars, but as Lucy headed up the road towards Waitrose and the uphill walk towards Chesterton, past the old hospital and the mouldering bones of the old Roman amphitheatre, she felt sure that some astral guardian would bring the boy to her arms and to her digs soon enough. She felt a tingle of excitement at the thought of her own nakedness before him, warming her from within as she walked.

September's clarion call to looming winter began to gnaw at the flesh on her exposed legs. The skirt that she was wearing was a last throw of a summer wardrobe designed for hot, sultry Greek nights, and barely covered her modesty. Great in the bar, so long as you remembered to bend the knees when sitting, but of little use in preventing the onrush of hyperthermia amid winter's close called icy tendrils. The light fleece top that she had ultimately decided to bring along sat snugly over her shoulders, not worn, as that would be too much admission of sensibility, but comforting nonetheless.

Her boots, brown and calf length, heeled but slim and forgiving, were the only part of Lucy's attire suited to the time of year. Lucy was particularly attached to the boots, reminding her as they did of her mother and father's glinting lasciviousness. The example set for Lucy by her parental role models was neatly summed up in her father's succinct way of describing her mother's love of long, tall boots…"Chase me, shag me, boots".

Despite having reached the age of eighteen intact and undefiled, Lucy had definite views about Fresher's week. The right time and place. She was grown up, away from home, an independent woman dealing with a bright and shining world on her terms. The boy in the red polo shirt. Lucy grinned inanely as she reached the main Tetbury road and started to walk up hill towards the underpass that opened out onto Chesterton Lane and her new home.

There seemed a deepening of the chill in the air as she climbed up and out of the town, as though the imminence of winter was more profoundly announced away from the lights and the chirpy clatter of bars and restaurants. Lucy shivered and felt the reverie slip away from her grasp. She was alone. Why? Her new friends, the girls sharing her digs had elected to go on to a small club a few yards down the street, but not she. In the bar, wrapped in the warm embrace of alcohol and the fantastic promise of the boy with the tousled hair and that cheeky smile, she had suddenly felt compelled to decline the offer of more fun. She wanted to go home. It was an imperative, an unquenchable thirst, almost a universal longing for an end to this particular night. So here she was, about to walk down the ramp and into the underpass, with the first dread impulse to run back to the lights and bars rising from the pit of her stomach.

As she took her first step down towards the underpass she noticed a slight change in the atmosphere. The sound of rumbling rubber from the cars on the dual carriageway seemed to drift above her and hold its metaphorical breath. The sky weighed upon her shoulders as if she was walking into the maw of a deeply black and ebonised catafalque. The spindle limbed bushes that edged the footpath seemed to tangle and spin around her, casting her into the middle of a trawling net. Her heart raced, thumping against her ribs fit to split them asunder. Another step. She wanted to turn and run back towards the light, anywhere other than here. The usual horrors of the Waitrose car park seemed ambrosially soft compared to this hard, cold, terminal descent. Instead of turning, however, Lucy placed one unwilling foot in front of another, feeling amid the were-growl at the base of the world as if she must and without delay enter the realm of the beast. The tingle engendered by thoughts of the boy in the bar remained with her, stronger now, so much so that the strange compulsion to return home positively engulfed her.

The sound of cars faded completely as Lucy took a tentative step off the ramp and into the underpass proper. There was no other place in the world than this dank, graffiti covered passageway between the streets of her new place of abode. Lucy's nostrils filled with the inevitable familiarity of the damp earth musk of the subterranean, of watered down piss pools, and the reek of old, decaying tobacco. On the wall, halfway along and to her right a security light shone weakly from behind its cage, singing a song of light as plaintive as the lark held captive beneath a towering sky. Motifs and signals. Colours splashed across the walls.

She walked slowly on. Shadow. Lucy thought that she could make out one patch of other darkness at the far end of the underpass. She hesitated, catching her breath on the barb of her fear, her heart pounding on and on. Her eyes watered and she tried to wipe away the blindness, but merely managed to shift the focus of dread to the dead pool of black something blocking her way. She had no choice. On she must go.

The shape shifted. An irregular mass elongated and stretched itself, revealing the rough shape of torso, limbs and head, all of them covered in what seemed to be a coating of thick, black, flowing cloth. The head was hooded. On the ground the shape seemed almost frail, as though it could not carry the burden of terror that forever dogged its tracks, but as Lucy moved closer, as the figure gathered its limbs together and began to unbend, began to straighten and stand, she saw with horror that he, for it must be masculine, was tall and thick set and lithe, as if he were a wolf or a hunting cat.

Lucy swallowed, desperate to bring succour to her parched throat. She could not see any feature on the man except for darkness. She could sense no personality save for that one weird sense of longing that seemed to flow from his soul. Lucy was afraid of the moment but somehow she was not terrified. She felt the fear that comes with expectation still wrapped in tinsel and bright paper. Strange, she thought, as if a logical examination of the moment might reveal the joke. She sensed something other here but not evil, not in its own right, describing it to herself as rather a feral air, as though the man were wild and untamed as yet. The tingle. The compulsion. Lucy could not help herself. She stopped beneath the squalid light.

"I just want to go home", she said, trying to breathe softly while mustering the militia of authority to protect her exposed flanks.

The creature growled rather than spoke, a belly-growl, a bark almost, but the words were plain enough to Lucy. "That is all anybody wants".

"Will you move out of my way, please", she continued, struggling to form the words and sounds as a coherent whole. "Will you?"

The creature reached his full height and girth, his hands stuffed into deep jacket pockets, the hood low over his forehead. Lucy thought for a moment that she saw what she could only describe as a whisker twitch at the edge of that black hood. Was that fur she could spy tufting out of his trouser leg bottoms?

"If that is what you really want, then I will move", the creature replied in his low, guttural purr. "But first I want to ask something of you."

Hell, thought Lucy, this is it. This is the stuff my mother always warned me about, the perv in the park, the bogeyman offering venomous sweeties, the wolf in sheep's clothing. In a childish attempt to make the creature disappear she closed her eyes tightly and tried to breathe slowly.

"Think", she muttered to herself. Could she outrun him? Where was there to go? It seemed to Lucy as if the whole world existed within this short, dank passageway. She opened her eyes slowly, as if that might make the world around her change. She looked up expecting to see rough, serrated concrete but saw instead and to her utter amazement stars in their millions. Where the feeble lamp had spewed out sluggish particles of light there now hung a low, full moon. The painted walls were swaying tufts of long eared grass. Lucy gasped. Her heart rate quickened once again. The creature withdrew his right hand from his jacket pocket to reveal a slender, grey-brown paw, talons gleaming like black diamonds in the moonlight. He beckoned her towards him and spoke with that soft, serrated, killing voice.

"A kiss is all I ask, just a simple kiss from your soft, ruby girlish lips. One kiss for the beast, for the Lord of the North Wind, and you will be utterly free."

Lucy took a step forward, knowing that with movement that she would reveal herself to him, but the musky smell of this noble carnivore seeped into Lucy's soul. She should cut and run. She should think about the boy in the red polo shirt, think about marriage and babies and college and so, so many things, but not one of them meant anything at all to her in this moment. She felt the tingle, felt the longing in her groin spread throughout her body, warming and teasing her, making her skin sensitive to the touch of hem and weave and seam. She couldn't help but let out a long, low sigh.

Lucy took another step forward towards the outstretched paw. She caught a brief reflection from within the hood, a pale white howling light cast back at her from his eyes, a reflection of the moon and his ice cold soul. Lucy longed to nuzzle into his fur, to bury her face in the texture of death. She knew that one touch would be enough. Lucy saw with absolute clarity under this calm but deep moonlight, that accepting the request would bring freedom of a kind that, at her tender and exciting age, she had never yet considered. It tasted delicious. Those eyes. How she longed to look into those eyes just once before the fang and the crack of her neck.

The wolf spoke again, smothering the moment with his reek and the furnace heat of his breath. "You think you know what freedom means. I see it in your eyes. But you are mistaken. My kiss is not death. It is the one truth of a life immortal in the time of man."

This was not what Lucy expected. She felt the magic in the air begin to waver around her head, revealing glimpses of stone cold wall and hard, puddled tarmacadamed floor amongst the grasses and the starry sky. This was the instant of doubt, the point where the prey loses its fear of those mesmerising eyes and runs for dear sanctuary, but in that instant when Lucy felt that she might regain control of her legs and speed back towards the light of town, the wolf slid the hood from his head.

What big eyes, full of fire and wind. What big teeth, slavering and razor sharp. The light changed once again. The sweet smelling air of a cold, crisp open plain standing before the wooded foothills of some primeval mountain range filled the world, an air that brings with it the promise of silence on snowfall, of the wandering track of paws discovered on a bright, blue freeze of a morning.

Lucy watched as the beast flung off the black cloak. She gaped and swooned as the wolf prince, this Lord of the North Winds, revealed himself to her. Time stood still around her, the grasses hushing their endless tidal sweep, and now, without any further movement of her feet, she felt herself glide towards his beckoning paw. With every inch covered her senses reeled with ever deeper revelation. The smell of him; taught and unfettered, canine and warm, dripping with libido. The look of him; rippling and strong, lithe and leggy, powerfully quick to the prey. The sound of him; deep and endless, a calling wind from the birth of time itself, assured and confident. The taste of him; oh the taste to come, the wetness of his muzzle, the razor edge of his teeth, the fetid and yielding lust on his hot breath as the bite went home.

"I…I don't…understand", she whimpered as she placed her delicate pink hand onto his rough skinned canine pads.

If a wolf and a man combined can truly ever smile, then he did so now, revealing the full width and depth of the terror of the world in that one reflexive response to emotion and the kill.

"All this and more is mine. Every field, every mountain range, every wood. I roam free, beyond the gun and skinning knife. I wait in dark places, in alleyways and passages, amid dereliction and decay, and once in a white killing moon I listen for the call, and take a willing kiss from an innocent. Not from the unknowing but from one whose potential is as boundless as my realm, from one who feels my strength but knows not yet how they will be set free. I can set you free."

"But…who are you?" Lucy asked quietly, laying herself down beneath the wolf, feeling soft grass prick her bare legs.

The wolf sank onto all fours, straddling the girl, nuzzling at her breasts and her cheek softly. His eyes burned red with the fire of his kind now. He looked directly at Lucy and spoke his last words softly, like a lover spent after the first new tenderness of the night.

"These places are my trails between worlds. You came calling my name. I am simply he who answers your call. Soon the wolves of your world will be no more. My mortal folk are lost. But as with all things the time of man will end. Until then I answer the call of those like you who know in their hearts what it is to be free. When the time comes you will tread this path again into a cleansed and virgin world and you will howl at mother moon and set my folk free. Know, girl, that I am the Lord of the North Wind and that I love you with all my heart."

Lucy could swim in his eyes forever, she felt, as she gazed at her own reflection in the deep ruby fire of his timeless stare. She saw there not the girl, but the she-wolf, the alpha female, in her prime, maned and dripping blood from the kill, suckling at pups, standing at the edge of the world baying for the return of her great lunar matriarch. She saw a time to come when the world would be at peace and left without the mark of human death, a time when lone wolves would appear as out of the air to reclaim their eternal place in the heart. She heard the welcoming in the hills and forests as each of these immortal beasts sang with joy in the bright light of full moons.

As Lucy felt the waters of the wolf rising above her head, entombing her in his flesh, as she watched, fascinated by the bending of his neck and felt the first exquisite piercing of his canines within her flesh, she whispered one last question.

"Am I really like her, the wolf-woman in your eyes?"

The Assistant Shop Manager

IN A SMALL TOWN set upon the flat plains of England's far flung eastern lowlands there once lived a very pleasant young man. He came from a very pleasant family with a father who worked hard and diligently and with a mother who stayed at home and brought up her children until they were old enough to attend the local senior school. The young man had a pretty older sister, who married well enough and settled down to raise her own family. He also had two sets of doting grandparents together with a host of happy aunts, contented uncles and aspirational cousins.

On leaving school with good, but not necessarily spectacular qualifications, the young man found a job in the retail sector. He progressed through a variety of jobs in a variety of shops until, at the age of twenty-one, he decided that he had made sufficient progress in life to get married. He had a reasonable salary, some nice perks and had just been promoted to the responsible role of Assistant Shop Manager with a very caring company selling mobile telephones.

Late one Thursday afternoon in the run up to Christmas the shop was full to bursting with young teenagers on the way home from school or college. One of the young man's employees called him over to authorise a sale to a young lady and as soon as the young man saw her he knew that she was the one that he would marry. He saw her standing there in her black puffer jacket, with her long black hair and her belly button piercing, and his heart started to pound. She was perfect. She was cute beyond belief, especially in the way her nose twitched as she chewed gum.

Now it was, of course, very presumptuous of him to dare to say to her: "Fancy a drink on Friday?", but he dared, for he had a good job, was full of the confidence of youth and he knew deep in his bones that there was many a young lady who would be glad to join him for a drink.

The young girl gave him the look. He loved women with attitude. She signed the contract for her phone, said nothing at all to him, and walked out of the shop. It was all a code, thought the young man, and having noted down her address, her home telephone number and her date of birth, he started to plan for his future. She was called Tiffany, according to the form, lived just a few streets away from his own home, and she was seventeen years of age; a perfect match.

The next morning the young man rang a local florist and arranged for a bouquet of the finest mixed winter blooms to be sent round to her house, hoping that she would be shocked, surprised and then intrigued by this wonderful gift. He dictated a cryptic message to the florist, signed himself as The Telephone Man, and even remembered to put his own mobile number on the bottom of the card. He had, of course, already stored the young woman's new number in his own mobile phone's memory.

When Tiffany arrived home from another hard day at the

grindstone of academia, her father called her into the living room. On the coffee table there was a huge bouquet of flowers and an opened message card. Tiffany's first reaction was one of sheer joy.

"At last", she thought, "my prince has come".

She clapped her hands together, dreaming of DJ Reckless, the wizard mixer of trance and acid bass at the student union, with whom she was madly in love.

"Who the hell is The Telephone Man?" growled her father. He was, of course, unprepared for this only too visible sign that his little princess was growing up. "What have you been up to?"

It dawned on Tiffany that her father had opened the card that had come with the flowers, which was an outrageous breach of privacy. She deserved more respect than that.

"Ugh!" she mumbled before giving her father a look that she hoped would convey the message that he was a complete embarrassment to her. Then she ran up the stairs, slammed her bedroom door and turned the volume button on her compact disc player up to maximum.

Over tea there was an almighty row that ended with Tiffany crying, her mother shouting at her father and the bunch of flowers being thrust headfirst into a wheeled dustbin standing out on the pavement ready for emptying the next morning.

The young man stood in the shadows on the opposite side of the street and watched as Tiffany's father thrust the blooms into the dustbin and slammed down the lid. He was disappointed, of course, that the flowers had not been allowed to brighten up his darling fiancé's home for longer, but he thought that he understood.

"Well, her father is just being protective", he said to himself as he rescued a single red rose from the rubbish, "but no matter, she will be mine".

He walked down the street towards his home plucking the petals from the flower as he repeated that lover's mantra of old: "She loves me, she loves me not". He was overjoyed when he plucked the last petal from the now bald flower head and found that she loved him.

For a whole week Tiffany wracked her brains trying to work out who The Telephone Man might be. She looked long and hard at a telephone engineer who was working in the street, which resulted in her hurrying home in tears, her ears ringing with the sound of wolf whistles. She checked with her college friends to see if anyone went by the nickname, but she couldn't find anyone who she could identify as the sender of her flowers. She did see a young man, who seemed oddly familiar, watching her at the Friday night rave in the student union, but then boys always watched her and she was hopeless with names and faces.

The young man bided his time and was rewarded for his patience the very next Saturday afternoon. A gaggle of young girls came into the shop to look at the latest mobile telephony wonder in pink and there, in the middle of the group, was his princess. He knew exactly what to do. He rang the number of the display model that they were looking at. Instead of the usual ring tone, the phone burst into life playing Tiffany's favourite dance tune. She was delighted and grabbed the phone out of her friend's hand, flipped open the clamshell display and pressed the connect button.

"Hello", said a voice, "this is The Telephone Man. I'd really like to take you out for a drink. I'll even give you that beautiful pink phone…in exchange for a kiss".

Tiffany stood there in a state of shock. The Telephone Man! She turned around very slowly and looked at the young man who had served her when she bought her current mobile phone just a few days ago. It all came flooding back. She shut the pink phone and thrust it back into the hand of her bemused friend. Tiffany's cheeks matched the colour of the pink phone's case perfectly.

She stormed out of the shop closely followed by her coterie of giggling young ladies and once they were all outside in the mall they held a heated debate about The Telephone Man. There were differences of opinion, ranging from weird through cute to typical boy. After a couple of minutes one of Tiffany's friends was nudged and prodded back into the shop. She walked up to the young man and said, "She says if you kiss me, can she have the phone?"

"No thanks", said the young man. "No disrespect, love, but either I get a kiss from her, or I keep the phone".

"Shit!" said Tiffany, on hearing her friend's report. "Oh well, in for a penny, but you've all got to come in with me", and so, surrounded by a multitude of sniggering young girls, the young man got his kiss and Tiffany got a really good deal on a mobile phone that would be the envy of everyone at college.

For the whole of the next week Tiffany was a rock and roll goddess. Whenever she received a call or a text message her phone made her the centre of attention. It was so much fun showing everyone how bright and pink her mobile phone was. The other kids and quite a few of the lecturers thought her ring tone was really funky and they all agreed it was definitely a cool bit of kit.

The following Saturday Tiffany received a message on her wonder phone from the young man. It read: "Wht abt tht drnk? Free calls 4 life = 10 X".

Tiffany understood the text message only too well. For 10 kisses she could get the young man to fix her account so that she never had to pay for another top up ever again. Perhaps he wasn't quite so bad after all. He clearly liked her and even if he was a little geeky, a kiss or two couldn't really hurt.

Later that day, and as before, the girls assembled outside the shop and one of Tiffany's friends was sent inside to ask, "She says you can have two kisses and she'll think about a drink".

"Sorry, no deal", said the young man, "ten kisses and the drink or she pays forever like the rest of you".

"If I kiss you can I have free calls?" asked the girl.

The young man smiled sweetly and told her that he couldn't possibly be unfaithful to Tiffany. Once again, surrounded by her giggling friends, Tiffany went into the shop, kissed the young man ten times, and said that she would definitely think about a drink but could he wait until next week as she already had plans for Saturday night. The young man agreed to wait another week, gave the young girl a new sim card that was already prepared, and sneaked an eleventh kiss just for good measure.

Another week went by, during which Tiffany called everyone that she knew over and over again. She sent text messages by the score and took pictures of everything and anything that moved, but, and much to her delight, every time that she checked the credit on her phone it was full. She was over the moon with her new pink phone and her limitless line of mobile telephony funding. In fact, Tiffany started to see the young man in quite a different light.

"He's not that bad, I suppose", she said to one of her friends on the following Friday night as they walked into the pub. "I mean, it's all a bit freaky, but he's got a job and a car and seems keen enough. I think I will meet him for a drink…as long as you and Robbie come along too".

The following morning Tiffany woke up and checked her messages. She tried to send a text to her friend to arrange to meet up outside the phone shop, but her phone wouldn't work. She checked her credit and checked the battery but she couldn't find anything wrong. "Typical", she thought, "that nerd's making sure I turn up at his shop today so he can ask me out for a drink".

Later that same morning Tiffany and her friends were in no mood to compromise as they approached the place where the young man worked. Demanding kisses for free telephony services was one thing, but being mean and spiteful just to get your own way was something else. As one of her friends had said, it was disrespectful; it was definitely not the way to win a young woman's heart.

They all marched into the shop expecting to see the young man lurking in the shadows, but he was nowhere to be found. Instead, there was a new man, older and stern looking, standing behind the counter. Tiffany was momentarily confused by this new situation, but then she remembered that she had stored the young man's mobile number in her phone. Even if she didn't have any credit she could display his number and call him on one of her friends' telephones.

As soon as she pulled the bright pink mobile from her pocket the older shop manager spotted it and walked up to her.

"Would you be Miss Tiffany Lemon?" he asked.

"Might be…" mumbled Tiffany.

"I'm afraid I'm going to have to ask you to return your phone. It appears there's been a problem, as it were. The young man who sold you the phone was acting outside of his sphere of authority. Oh, and these gentlemen want a word too".

Tiffany looked over her shoulder and, to her horror, she saw two uniformed policemen rocking backwards and forwards on the heels of their big black boots. She nearly fainted as they explained that, while she was not under arrest, they felt that it would be in her best interests to accompany them to the local police station. Tiffany was escorted out of the shopping centre by the two big and burly police officers, put into the back of their patrol car and whisked off into the busy Saturday morning streets.

The next few hours were, indeed, some of the worst in Tiffany's short but eventful teenage life. Her father went berserk when he was informed that Tiffany was helping the police with their enquiries and was quite ready to give her a good thrashing and to call her all sorts of nasty names. Then, when he heard all of the details concerning the young man, who was, as it was now becoming clear, quite widely known as The Telephone Man, he realised that it had, in fact, been a very close shave for his daughter. After all of the questions were done with and the lady from social services was satisfied that all was well, he was simply relieved to have his little princess back at home, safe and sound.

It transpired that The Telephone Man had stolen many, many kisses from young girls in exchange for free pink mobile telephones. He had stolen even more kisses in return for doctoring telephone sim cards. He had even persuaded some of his many and varied young, female customers to join him for a drink. In fact, he was now on remand waiting for a court date to answer charges relating to a number of accusations of very persistent stalking.

Within a day or two the local press got hold of the story and the whole situation became public knowledge. It was a dreadful shock for the young man's family. His father refused to talk about his son, preferring to bury himself in his diligent duties at work. His mother felt unable to attend any more coffee mornings, preferring a gin and tonic with her mid-morning biscuits. His sister, while feeling very sad for her brother, found herself looking at her own baby son in a strange new way.

But, as Tiffany's father said as he downed another large brandy late one evening, "Now it's that young perv's turn to be pretty and vulnerable".

And as fate would have it, at exactly the same time that Tiffany's father said this, the young man was lying on his bunk bed crying his eyes out. Of all the dreadful shocks experienced that day, nothing compared to the sudden and degrading catastrophe that he had just suffered as he'd bent down to pick up the soap in the prison shower.

Pigs and Dogs

CRISP CLEAN SHEETS. BECCA loved that late night slide under a fresh, wind-dried, duvet. The bed sheet was taut and uncrumpled, the elastic corners still holding their own against the frayed mattress cover underneath. She slept in a pair of shorts and a vest these days, all greys and pinks and girlie with small cat motifs, knowing that her three years and three months old son, Ollie, might call her out of her slumbers at any point during the night.

To be fair, she thought, as she sipped the evening's last full glass of Riesling, he was pretty good these days. The night wets were already a thing of the past and as yet his dreams seemed to be as sweet and as natural as they should be. He was a good boy. Tiring, yes, but intrinsically a very good little man. To Becca, Ollie was simply perfect, sweetly curled and blonde like her and his dad, but without any of that man's side and snide. There were just the two of them now and Becca much preferred her life to be organised that way.

Becca settled back against her recently plumped pillows, rested her head against the matt-blacked metal frame of her Ikea bedstead, and took another sip of her nightly sleep tonic. Sometimes she thought about the Riesling and wondered whether she should ease up a little, but the truth these days was that she relied on it. The once-upon-a-time glass that helped her to relax was now usually a bottle to knock her out for a solid hour or two in the dead hours when the boy was sound asleep himself. She felt the effects less and less as the days passed, but she remained steadfast in limiting her intake. Becca hid her drinking well. She could function. She could be the mother that Ollie deserved for most of the day, but she did need a little help when it came time to settle down in the wee small hours.

Even now, in her mid-thirties, right at the point when she thought that life and things generally should be getting clearer, Becca felt the unsettling churn of contradictory thoughts jumbling in her head. She knew that she should not drink so much but no matter how bad her guilt trip she also loved that twilight moment when the world became hazy and the sounds of the house settling for the night reassured her that bricks and mortar and tiles and trusses kept her and Ollie safe from harm.

She should not fear the dark and its dreamscapes anymore. Becca was thirty-four, a grown up in so many ways, and yet her inner child, her personal demon, seemed to need that numbness brought about by the Riesling. The annoying thing was that Becca's soundless stupors only ever lasted for an hour or three before her body reacted to the poisons and she became sleeplessly restless, but again there was a clear juxtaposition. Becca craved that hour or two of peace, and yet she was equally grateful that she could rouse herself quickly should Ollie ever need her.

Right now, in these final moments before another bout of fitful sleep briefly smothered her, Becca allowed herself to luxuriate in a newly made bed, letting the tick-tick-tick of cooling heating pipes beat out the rhythm that accompanied her final mouthful of warming white wine as she slowly lowered her eyelids. Her little house was, for just this moment, a haven, a bastion against the night, a two-up two-down fortress of red brick and double-glazed windows. She felt warm and cosy and fuzzy and so she rolled onto her side, put her now empty wine glass on her bedside table and switched off her bedside lamp, safe in the knowledge that all was well and that she would be making her first cup of tea on a bright new day in just about four hours from whenever now might be.

Four thirty-four. The blackout blinds were drawn. The bedside light remained switched off. Becca's bedroom was illuminated slightly by light seeping in through the crack at the base of her bedroom door. There was no carpet on the landing yet, just bare floorboards. She tasted bitters and grit. Becca lay awake again now, sifting through the detritus of recently disturbed sleep. She never remembered dreams. Rather she focussed on the simple things that combined to keep her and Ollie safely tucked away here in their little house. She had no plans, no strategies. Keep it simple stupid seemed to be her vital modus operandi.

Becca contemplated the night just passed. It had been as peaceful as they come. She had slept for nearly four hours straight, and apart from the bitters and grit she felt clear headed and no more fatigued than ever she did. She stretched out underneath her toastie warm duvet. The digital numbers on her radio alarm clicked over to thirty-five, a promissory note for the safety of daylight to come. Becca pulled the duvet up underneath her chin. She would take five more minutes before the hushed pad down to a cold kitchen. The central heating was not timed to come on until six o'clock, and then only for long enough to take the chill off the early morning and to ensure that there was enough hot water for both her to shower in and for Ollie to bathe in later in the day.

There were moments when Becca looked vicariously at the many worlds around and about her, the worlds that she helped to clean, and she wondered whether her life was all that it could be. Those moments of envy, of dissatisfaction, remained few and when they did occur Becca could dismiss them easily enough. Cleaning for other people, taking in ironing, the anything and everything of tax credits, universal benefits and cash in hand meant one simple thing. She survived. She and Ollie survived. They survived together, never apart, one and the same and indivisible. Today she would watch over him. One day, many years from now, he would watch over her like a guardian angel. It was a simple thing. An absolute truth.

Becca shivered despite the warmth of her bed. She felt a footstep fall heavily upon her grave. Becca mentally corrected herself. Another footstep upon her grave. This continual pacing across her dead soil was the reason why she had never quite settled here in the land of the living. These heavy treads were the reason why she was on constant watch. The old man who Becca imagined to be walking on her corpse wore thick-soled boots.

Becca tried to reason away the jitters. She and Ollie lived in a small space, an enclosure, a fortress, four walled and square. She could protect the boy. She could make this world her own, insular and protected. Cash-in-hand and benefits kept Ollie safely by her side and away from the bleeding edges of her own childhood dreams.

Ollie. Becca smiled broadly in the darkness. Her little soldier. She was saving up for him. A few pounds sometimes, just pence at others. It all depended on the time of the month and the cash to hand. It all depended on her habitual craving for juice of the grape. She was nearly ready to buy a present for him, something for him to cherish, to look at or play with and think of his loving mother, even at three years and three months. Becca had asked him what he wanted most in the world just a few days previously. She had just over twenty pounds stashed away in a jar on top of one of her kitchen cupboards and she was starting to see toys and clothes and gifts take shape in her mind's eye.

Her darkling smile twisted as she remembered his words. Ollie had thought long and hard before he answered her. He wanted, he said, a pet. Becca had tried to change the subject but Ollie had remained firm in his three year old wanting. Becca offered him an option - maybe, one day, a hamster.

"No hamster", he had said. "Want cat. Black cat." His cheeks had puffed red and his tiny blonde brows had inched downwards with absolute, uncompromising determination.

"Oh, Ollie. Don't be silly. We can't keep a cat. Do you know how much they cost? Food and animal doctors and they run out in the road and get killed by cars. You don't want a cat, my darling…"

"Want cat… dog… rabbit…" and so the list began. Ollie answered everything for the next thirty minutes of their child-centred conversation with one of or a combination of cat, dog or rabbit. The episode ended in a full floor bitten tantrum, a maternal walk away to peer from behind a door, a messily shared chocolate milkshake, and a wrap up warm because we're going off to Mrs Hopcroft's to clean her bathrooms. Despite the obvious frustrations of coping with a three year old and the certain knowledge that she would have to disappoint her suddenly pet mad son, Becca remained confident in their unselfish love for one another. She quietly dreaded the day when school would rear its ugly head.

*

Later the next morning Ollie sat out on the landing at, as fate would have it, that same Mrs Hopcroft's village cottage. The good lady was out at work, doing something executive in Oxford, which was, Becca supposed, why she could afford such a house and such a cleaner.

"Hey ho, hey ho, it's off to work we go…" Becca whistled as she set to work cleaning dried faeces off the rear of the toilet bowl with a good dose of strong bleach and a stiff brush. Such was life for such a cleaner in just such a village house. The whistling helped to pass the time and Ollie seemed to like it too. He tried to join in with Becca's whistling but usually ended up blowing raspberries in weird child-time synchronicity. Neither he nor Becca ever finished a song, always collapsing into a fit of giggles by the end of any second verse.

The raspberry blowing was short lived this morning, however, and was replaced by the sound of something heavy being bumped into a wooden skirting board. Oh God, thought Becca, he's bored… She poured one final dose of bleach around the toilet bowl and under the rim, carefully screwed the bottle top back on and then pulled off her bright yellow Marigold gloves. Becca stepped back out onto the landing and sure enough, Ollie was flying one of his Transformer toys around his head, making whooshing noises, before crashing the toy down onto the carpet and into the skirting board. There were already a series of dents and scratches in the wood that seemed to form a distressed sort of face that, to Becca's eyes, screamed; 'a small, annoying child was here…'

"Ollie, Ollie, stop doing that. Bad. Mustn't do that…" Becca pointed to the marks on the skirting board as she grabbed Ollie's flying wrist. Immediately she did so she saw the boy's eyes well with tears. His lower lip trembled for a moment before shifting to form the base of an oval through which a long, keening moan morphed into a full-blown wail.

In a moment the boy was wrapped in Becca's arms, his head against her shoulder as she stroked the back of his head. "It's all right, my lovely, it's all right. No harm done, not really. Mummy's not cross, darling. Mrs Hopcroft, remember, darling. Mrs Hopcroft."

Plan D. The television. Mrs Hopcroft had a good selection of assorted children's DVDs in a rack downstairs for when her niece and two nephews came to stay, now that her own daughter was an undergraduate at university in Exeter. Ollie loved Wallace and Gromit. Half an hour of The Wrong Trousers was all that Becca needed to finish the upstairs bathroom and that would be her morning done. The afternoon would be easier. They would once again be safely tucked up at home. Becca had Mrs Mobb's ironing to do for pick up at six that same evening.

Outwardly soothed but inwardly still seething with three-year-old effervescence, Ollie threw his Transformer toy at the bathroom door with all his might before convulsing in one final, almighty sob.

"Come on, my love, that's not how we behave, is it?" suggested Becca, knowing full well that the child would be asleep in her arms in moments. She had to keep him talking for a few minutes longer while she got ready to stand up and carry him down to his stroller for his television interlude before the walk home. "What's wrong with Transformer?" she asked.

Ollie didn't look up, burying his face firmly into her shoulder. "Want a farm", he said softly into Becca's jumper. "Want farm and tractor and sheep and cows and pigs and dogs…"

Becca shuddered inwardly, holding onto Ollie as tightly as she could. Pigs and dogs. Whatever other animals he might have on his toy farm she would never stand to see pigs and dogs. Never again.

*

Becca and Ollie reached the end of another day, with Mrs Mobb's ironing done for the week and a little more cash tucked away. Becca had the usual bills to pay, an electricity meter to feed, and a toy farm set to save up for. She had given in. Again. She told herself that she would do a little Internet research and find out how much a really nice farm set might cost before she finally committed to buy the toy for the boy, but Becca already knew that this particular game was lost. Ollie's poker face was already so much better than her own. She settled back against her pillow, resting her head on the usual spot on the bedframe and thought about the day to come. No cleaning tomorrow. No ironing. No visits to the social. Wednesdays were a park day, weather permitting, and it comforted Becca that Ollie would like that.

She continued to muse on the day just closing as she drifted slowly down towards sleep. The only other downside to Becca's day, and far more worrying than the damage done to Mrs Hopcroft's skirting board, was the barren state of her kitchen cupboards come teatime. Mrs Mobbs had collected and paid for her ironing too late in the day for Becca to make it to the village shop, so she and Ollie had shared two rounds of toast with half a slice of ham on each and with the last half of an already opened tin of baked beans shared out on top. They had played the usual game of trains, with Becca cutting up and forking Ollie's choo-choo tea for him while her own plate congealed as it chilled. No matter, she thought, time for a bath and then bed.

While Ollie splashed joyously in six inches of lukewarm water, converting a set squidgy, sponge letters into zooming submarines and flying terra-dinosaurs, Becca knelt by the side of the bath, resting her left forearm on the olive green plastic edge. She had long ago given up any pretence of staying dry. A bombing run by a Pleistocene letter F momentarily sunk a bobbing letter M in an explosion of soapy bubbles. Ollie laughed out loud as Becca sat up and wiped froth off of her nose. Ollie lost himself again in the dive-bombing game and Becca drifted off with her own, tired thoughts.

As Becca half watched her son play in the bath she sensed in him questions. Why just we two? Like you watch over me, who watches over you? Who watches over us? Where do the dreams come from, mummy?

A clever boy, thought Becca, but then she realised that these were her questions and not the wise-beyond-his-years thoughts of her infant son. Ollie was just three years and three months old. He had no cares to bear down upon his dreams and turn them sour. He knew nothing of such strains and disappointments. Becca breathed in sharply. She had startled herself out of her day-tired daydream.

"Right, little man", she said softly, "time to dry…"

A howl of protest and flat palms slamming into the waters.

Becca stood quickly, bent down, placed her hands underneath Ollie's armpits, and lifted her little soldier out of the bath, while his legs kicked the last suds from his toes into his mother's damp stomach.

"Ollie, no. Bad" Becca whispered as she lowered her son to the floor and immediately wrapped him in a large white bath sheet. The smothering instantly stopped his struggles. A drying and a tickling. Happy bunnies in a soft, warm burrow.

And so Becca moved through rituals and lists and cuddles before she could finally struggle down the stairs, and enter into her own time, into that small moment of solitude that allowed her to sort and fix the day. To get to her happy place Becca dressed Ollie in blue robot pyjamas and tucked him into his bed. She twice read out loud The Hungry Caterpillar and Little Red Riding Hood just the once. She made sure that there was a bottle of water on Ollie's bedside table, that the duvet was safely tucked under his chin, and that his night light glowed a gentle shade of green. With everything sorted Becca kissed her son on his forehead and finally stole away, shutting his bedroom door ever so gently behind her.

With Walford's finest doing their damnedest to be miserable on a low volume on the television, Becca waited out the half hour during which Ollie was most likely to stir and call out before she opened a chilled bottle and took her first sip of liquid relief. She felt the wine, as chill as it was, warm her gullet and spin her down into a state of exhausted bliss. It was eight o'clock when Becca took that first sip. She drifted through a series of television programmes, idly flicking across the channels, and only stirred again as she poured the last glass from the bottle. It was now eleven-thirty and time to take her last glass with her to her own bed.

In her happily dazed state she too soon found herself safely washed and tucked up. Becca tried to sink into that final languor that brought forth that sense of total relaxation that came just before sleep, but the usually soporific effects of work, childcare and Riesling did not seem to be combining in happy slumber. Becca felt very awake. Her neck felt strangely stiff and she ached in her joints, as if coming down with a fever or an influenza, Around her the midnight ticks and clicks of a house shutting down for the night seemed somehow wrong, seemed to shift out of time, as though the walls and the pipework and glass in the windows were being drawn by the unsteady hand of her sleeping child.

Becca fought an urge to check in on Ollie one last time. It was late and she feared that in her present state of nervousness she would be clumsy and wake him. Steeling herself for a frustrating, sleepless struggle wrapped in a hot and sticky duvet, Becca lay on her side so that she could reach the bedside lamp switch, paused for just a moment, sighed, and turned out the light. Around her she sensed the darkness fall.

The shift from lamplight to night darks was not instantaneous. Becca was sure that the shadows slid rather than plunged across her vision. Her breathing quickened. She felt the muscles in her neck tighten by another notch. Across her chest she felt a band of pressure bear down on her lungs and adrenalin pumped through her veins. The darkness, now fully formed, drifted through walls and doors and floors like thick, dense cloud seen through an airplane window. Becca fought an urge to succumb to the terrors in sheer childish panic.

Through the shifting clouds Becca sensed once more an old and familiar gaze coming to rest upon her face. She was being watched. Time shifted and she was a small child again. She knew not who the watcher might be. Becca never had known the answer to that question. She knew only that nights here in this dislocated space were long and dark. She was paralysed. The eyes that watched were never seen. These piercing blues were always at the edge of her vision, beyond the frames of solid reality, a flickering in the margins through which she passed her days.

Becca sensed again breathy warmth upon her skin. A pane of glass broke somewhere in the house. Winds rushed across her face. There was a distant peel of laughter. Something tugged at the corner of her duvet. Becca could not breathe. She remained wide-eyed but rigidly paralysed. The warm breath on her arm was feral and borne of the wilderness. She felt as though she was being pulled, this way and that. A decision was called for. She must make a choice…

Becca stared up at the ceiling. To each side of the bed she could hear things, snorts and whimpers and scratchings. She was sure that at the foot of the bed stood that same old man with the heavy boots, the one who walked across her dead earth with such alarming regularity. His were the eyes that stared in the darkness. These creatures beside her bed were his as well.

A sudden convulsion. A full body spasm. Becca was suddenly wide awake, and she understood completely. These were the clouds that came with the dreaming. These were the mists and the blights brought down upon her head by the ghosts that walked upon her grave. She pulled the covers up over her head and closed her eyes tight. Her heart raced. She thought she must surely burst but slowly, slowly she relaxed her grip and started to breathe again. As the shadows and the sparkling star bursts behind her eyelids shifted and drifted and merged and spun, she began an incantation.

"There are no animals in this house… there are no animals in this house… there are no animals in this house… not in this house… this is my house… this is my…"

And once again Becca could feel the sour warmth of the creatures that had dogged her childhood dreams. She could feel the soft panting of some fauna, of some dumb beast crouched next to her bed. Under the thin protection of her duvet the hairs on her bare arms lifted. Her tongue felt hugely swollen in her mouth and Becca was sure that she would choke. She must cast these creatures out. She must exorcise these old friends and enemies. She tried to swallow, tried to moisten her tongue. Her voice sounded thick and vague in her head.

"There are no animals in this house…", she whispered, her voice slowly rising with the repeated cadence of the recitation. "There are no animals in this house… there are no animals in this house… there are no animals in this house… there are no…"

Becca ceased her spell making abruptly when she realised that she was almost shouting. For the first time since waking amid the memories and the irrational fears of her youth she remembered her son in the room next door. She remembered the way the darkness seemed to drift through the wall. She remembered Ollie's daytime mantra, "…cows and sheep and pigs and dogs".

Becca pulled the duvet away from her face, sat up and glanced into all four corners of her bedroom. There was a faint lightening of space and time. The clouds were gone. Becca saw that the landing light still shone through the gap at the base of her bedroom door. Out of the corner of her eye she saw… no… she felt the last wisp of something deep and sombre pour itself through a skirting board.

This time she did shout. "There are no animals in this house… there are no animals in this house…" Becca threw back the duvet and launched herself out of bed and towards the lighted landing.

"There are no animals in this house… there are no…" She threw open her bedroom door and stood for a moment in the light before moving her hand to the switch on the wall. Her voice returned to a faint whisper as she decided not to turn off the landing light. She and Ollie needed the safety of electricity. Becca slowly and quietly completed the last line of her mantra, "…animals in this house."

Becca padded over to Ollie's door and listened intently, her ear pressed against one of the door's upper wooden panels. Becca's mind raced. Could she hear something? What was that? "Ollie…" she whispered and gingerly Becca started to press down on her son's door handle.

On opening Ollie's bedroom door Becca instantly felt the drag on her skin caused by time shifting backwards again. Ollie's night-light was off now. The illumination thrown into the space beyond the doorway by the bare upstairs landing bulb seemed to break and splinter at the threshold to the boy's bedroom, throwing weird misshapes into the inner darkness. As Becca took her first faltering steps towards her son's bed, and as her eyes grew accustomed to the diffused half-light, she saw that he was still sleeping, thumb in mouth, on his side. He faced out towards the door. He looked utterly serene.

Becca could feel the drifting darks falling across her face like the faintly fluttering wings of a candle burned moth. She gasped as she sank to her knees by Ollie's toy box. She reached out to steady herself and as she did so she touched a sponge letter still damp from the bath. The air around her was thick and clogging as she tried to draw it down into her lungs. She started to pant, and with her laboured breathing there came a companion sound, a stereo image, a doppelganger effect. She tried to orientate herself, but the blood pounding in her temples created an uneven landscape in a space that she could usually navigate through without thinking.

No more than a couple of metres from where she knelt, Becca thought that she could see shapes forming amid the smoky shades of these night darks. She could make out heads, one to the left of the bed, on the far side, and one to the right, nearer to where she now sat. Both heads, as yet disembodied by the night shades, simultaneously turned to look directly at Becca, as if on some unspoken command. Becca saw the iridescence of dull light reflected back at her. She thought that she saw browns and yellows and dirty pinks. She imagined for a moment that she heard again those sympathetic snorts and whimpers and wheezes accompanying her own laboured breathing. Something feral, something instinctively impatient rooted through the core fibres of her soul. She sensed surprise and anger. She sensed a question. She sensed words forming… "Now… Now… Now…"

 A choosing was asked for by a shadow drifting more blackly than any other in the room, back beyond the edge of her vision. She could hardly break away from the staring creatures by her boy's bed, but slowly, by painful degree upon degree, she shifted her gaze to the floor, where she saw the outline of one huge, shaggy paw and a thickly cast metal chain. In her looking away the shadows lightened and she could describe definite outlines at the periphery. A dog. A pig. Both wearing wide black collars, from which hung chains that fell and snaked back into the vast well of darkness settling by the wall opposite the foot of Ollie's bed.

Underneath the driving beat of the blood still pumping at her temples Becca heard a voice. Voices. A tandem craving. And then a third voice, weathered and cracked and faded. "Time to make a choice… we've waited… we've waited… pig and dog… dog and pig… chained all these years… pig and dog… dog and pig… you and him… him or you… we've waited…"

Becca let a flood of tears fall onto her cheeks. She bit back on her sobs. Ollie stirred slightly and rolled over to face the far wall, but he remained in gentle peace under the watchful gaze of his mother and her companion creatures. As her tears filled her eyes and her normal vision blurred, so she started to see the world in which she now existed far more clearly than she had since her earliest recollections had taken form and shape. Her childhood friends were back. She saw them clearly again after such a long absence. She must choose. Pig or Dog. Girl or boy. Becca or Ollie.

Becca steeled herself. She gulped in air. Through her tears she could now see the old man in heavy boots quite clearly. She shivered. He trod gently up and down upon black earth. She felt an impulse to say a name, but before she spoke out loud one last thought flashed across her retreating mind. Please let it be my name, she thought, please let it be mine.

Adrenalin. The world slowed. Becca felt every twitch of muscle and cartilage and tendon as she picked up her son's discarded Transformer toy and stood up. Becca felt her mouth shape sounds Becca felt her vocal chords tighten. She thought of the letter B.

Her mouth shaped to form a vowel.

Bastille Day

COLD STONE WALLS. TO touch them was to recoil. The prisoner opened his eyes and felt as if he was some strange, wide-eyed, lidless creature lost in a sea of thick black oil. The darkness was viscous, dripping slowly onto flakes of straw that lay rotting on the puddled floor. This complete absence of light was the hardest thing to bear. The stench of wet decay was almost a comfort. The scurrying of sharp little claws on flagstones was a reminder of life and the slightest feather touch of frayed rags on his bare legs was a breath of civilisation, a small memento of his humanity. All of these things, all of these slight, needle tip sensations, were a lullaby for the child afraid of the dark.

In his head he pieced together the letters of a name over and over again, trying to fit them together in any one of a thousand combinations, only one of which would form the shape of a man. By repeating his name, by bouncing the echo of his voice off the cold stone walls that surrounded him, he somehow found the strength to hold at bay the constriction, the weight of fear that otherwise would have crushed him. The sheer mass of stone and brick surrounding him compressed his sight. His awareness of being was a single point of focus. Curled up in the middle of a bleak and hooded cell he waited for grains of shadow to float between the bars of a small arrow-slit window high above him. Deep within the darkest hours the purple shades of a newly rising day would come and with them the rattle-bag voice that ground out the hours of his incarceration.

"I, the voice of the people am being smothered, strangled…assassinated!"

And so another day began, timed by the insane mutterings of Citizen Marat, the one-time darling of the revolution now made mechanical and ever vigilant while enemies of the state lay in foetal balls on freezing flagstones. He drifted on waves of nausea. Heart-pounding tension washed through the man in the cell, who sat huddled and buried deep beneath the crumbling vaults of stone that formed the roof of the world. The pitch of Marat's voice was sharp and angular, cutting through the thick prison air like a knife, and when the mechanised grind of his jaws finally ceased, an echo hung in the still morning air like a noose biting ever deeper into the prisoner's bare neck. Wide-eyed, rocking back and forth, curled up into the smallest space that he could physically make for himself, MacKenzie waited for dawn's faint lustre to break on high.

As Citizen Marat settled into another all too brief period of silence MacKenzie watched the bleeding edges of dawn fall from the sky. Wisps of cloud drifted across the narrow opening in the arrow-slit high above him, its outline drawn in pitch against the faintest murmur of a grey-purple softening in the counter glow outside. A rat, brown and sleek, scratched at scraps and bare bones in the shadows. Beyond the window MacKenzie heard faint, skeletal bird calls, which caught on the square-cut edges of the thick cell walls and dissolved the shifting shapes of the man that he had been trying to form. Bird song called MacKenzie back to the hungry frailty that made flesh of his present reality. He watched the light break above his head and stopped whispering the letters of his name.

*

Beyond sleep, Danton, grizzly Danton, the bear, the motive power behind the revolution, prowled the corridors of La Force Nouveau. He should have come before this. MacKenzie had been a friend in a world where true-bloods and the likes of Danton rarely got close. In Danton's wake a red capped guard hurried on, head bowed, taking two pigeon steps for everyone that the committee chairman slammed down onto the unyielding flagstones as they swept past heavy browed doors set in frames of rough cut, foot square timbers. On every door a faceplate rusted on wrought iron runners, closed against the light of real wax candles guttering on stone ledges set into the walls. The sharp retort of metalled boot heels struck out at the early morning stillness, announcing the arrival of Danton and his scowling, out of breath companion to every inmate as they bore down on the door at the end of the corridor like cannon balls, casting their grotesquely elongated shadows across the floor and up the walls. When they reached the end of the corridor a small man in a leather jerkin jumped out of the shadows and Danton's voice boomed out, smothering the chill of morning in burning impatience.

"Gaoler… If there's no sleep for me, I'll be damned if there's any for you. Look sharp, man."

The gaoler, wrapped in high collars and thick furs beneath his jerkin, muttered a series of barely audible imprecations and stumbled forward into the flickering light cast by one of the candles. He continued to curse the dog that dared to stalk his halls this early in the day, but thought better of raising his voice in anger when he saw the shaggy shape of the bear that marked Citizen Danton out from the usual visitors.

"Take me to MacKenzie..."

"Sir, yes... this way."

The gaoler fiddled with his keys and unlocked the door at the end of the passage, pushing it back to reveal a short flight of steps carved out of natural rock. The ceiling was low and narrow, forcing Danton to move forward with his knees bent, crouched down beneath the mountain. God alone knew who dreamt up this vision of Hell, he thought, as he ascended a flight of narrow, pinched steps. Danton and his companions emerged onto a short landing at the end of which was another heavy wooden door. The walls, like those in the corridor below, were hewn out of huge blocks of solid rock and the space was illuminated by the soft glow of candles, candles that, in this simulacrum of past glories, illuminated the stone in a wash of yellow and amber. Halfway down the landing a recess in the left hand wall glowed brightly under a spotlight. As he walked Danton straightened himself up, pulling his shoulder blades back to relieve the tension that he felt tightening at the base of his neck.

The three of men, Danton, the gaoler and the guard, swept down the landing towards the far door, their mistimed triumvirate steps clattering out a chaos of irregular rhythms. Danton stopped abruptly as they approached the recess in the wall. Dumbfounded, he stared at the object that grinned its rictus smile from a plinth under the only electric light in the corridor. Perched on a silver spike, trailing leads and luridly coloured pipe work, Citizen Marat's head stared back at the committee chairman with eyes as clear and blue as a bright summer afternoon.

"My God…" was all that Danton could say, taking a step back and nearly squashing the gaoler against the wall.

"Lovely touch, Sir," said the gaoler, squeezing out from behind the committee chairman. "They brought him here after the funeral. Thought it would be fitting for the guests. A reminder of their bastard ways".

Danton looked at the man in horror and as he did so the spiked head's lips moved and Citizen Marat's harsh, piercing tones crawled across Danton's skin, peeling back the veneers of liberty that he clothed himself in.

"Atrocious men who every day seek to bury us further in anarchy and who try to kindle the flames of civil war."

The severed head's animated smile faded slowly as the pipes, leads and motors ceased their moment of work, but the eyes remained fixed on Danton. The man who had assumed the revolutionary name of Marat was, according to the press and the revolutionary council, dead and buried. According to the official news wires Marat had been given a hero's funeral after his murder by the forces of true-blood reaction, but here Danton stood, unmoving in the candle glow, staring at his recently departed co-conspirator's severed head, which was stuck on a pole of silver metal.

"Very ingenious," said the gaoler by way of nervous conversation, "just sort of plugged him in. Of course, he's not really alive anymore, they just fixed up the pathways and keep his vocal chords working. Sits there all day and quotes away the quarters. I dust him down now and then… well you do, don't you."

Danton turned slowly and walked towards the door at the end of the passage. He said nothing. His guard leant against the wall and, having struck a match along Citizen Marat's noble nose, lit a cheroot while the gaoler fumbled with his keys.

*

The faceplate in the heavy wooden door flicked back letting candlelight from the passage beyond slice into the heart of the cell. From the shadows MacKenzie watched the small square patch of light appear and then fall back into darkness as a head moved into view. The small window was filled with cubist elements of a face. Keys rattled on a chain. The faceplate jerked back and he heard a key slide into the lock and the heavy, ratchet grumble of sliding tumblers. MacKenzie covered his eyes as the door swung open and a figure walked through the oblong patch of unnerving brightness. A loud bull voice barked.

"You can leave us alone"

"But Sir, you know…"

"Leave us"

"Sir, I…"

Danton spun round, moving his heavy set limbs with incredible grace, profiling his broad chest and powerful frame in the light that spilled into the cell from the corridor. His look was enough to ensure that the gaoler, trying desperately to bury his confusion and discomfiture in his furs, backed out of the room without another word being said. The door swung shut again, although this time, MacKenzie noticed, the lock tumblers remained silent.

Under the shadow of the wall MacKenzie lowered his hand from his eyes and looked at the man standing before him. He started to speak, but found words hard to form having spent so many days alone. His existence, such as it was in the bosom of La Force Nouveau, was bounded by the fragile skeleton of sanity marked out by Citizen Marat's regular outbursts. The words that he wanted to conjure up caught at the back of his throat and his first sound was little more than a muffled cough. He tried again.

"Robert?"

"Yes, it's me" Danton replied brusquely, "but you can't use that name here. You'll call me Danton now."

"I…don't…"

"It's my revolutionary name, my nomme de guerre, if you will."

MacKenzie scuttled back against the wall when he heard Danton speak, feeling the chill of stone on his skin through his rags. His shirt lay limp upon his hunched, bony shoulders. On his left side a great tear ran along the seam underneath his arm. His pale white hide, which was soiled and bruised, shone ghost white in the thin reeds of morning. He tried to remember; revolution, committees and sections, the great debates and the huge, towering hopes that lead all men down to a straw bed. He looked at the man standing in the doorway, whose head was illuminated by the slant of battle grey that steepled down from the high set window. Slowly MacKenzie recalled the confusion and enlightenment, the long struggle for equality under the harsh glare of limited kindness within which mankind wrapped despotism.

Danton stood in the middle of the room and looked down at the squat figure by the wall, finding it extremely hard to deal with the situation. This creature, as broken down and shattered as it appeared to be, was a living man, a thing of flesh and blood, just as he was. To look into the eyes of a God and see the flaws, to witness the failure of resolution and will, to see such frailty, still shocked him.

"Please… stand up", he said quietly.

MacKenzie clasped his knees tightly, his knuckles turning white as he gripped the protruding bones in his legs. He shifted his weight slightly, feeling a burr of stone scratch his emaciated back. He tried to form a sequence of words, to summon the logic that had been his art in a former life, but those words that had once come to him with such ease now took flight around him, lifting like dry leaves on the breeze of his thoughts and floating away before he could catch hold of them.

"I…I'd rather…stay where I am", MacKenzie whispered.

Danton's shoulders twitched as he tried to alleviate the tension that he could now feel biting deeply into the base of his neck. This was going to be harder than he had imagined it would be. He kicked a gnawed chicken bone out from under his boot. The bone, full of air bubbles inherited from the creature's flying ancestors to reduce weight and density, skittled across the stone floor and came to rest by MacKenzie's bare feet. Danton imagined the breaking of this man's fragile skeleton with every bounce.

"Life is a brief and ugly thing", he whispered to himself, grimacing.

MacKenzie, one of the few who deserved life, would have his neck severed because it served the cause. Danton's fellow revolutionaries, compressed as they were into such a small space, gave vent to their frustration and pain in rivers of blood, and he, the great Danton, could do nothing now that the beast was off its chains but try to direct the rampaging animal as best he could. He looked down at the shell of the man he had once known so well and wondered whether he could simply walk out of the place with him under his arm. From the passageway the digitally enhanced voice of Citizen Marat burst into life once more, corroding the moment of doubt into a thousand flakes of brittle rust.

"To pretend to please everyone is mad, but to pretend to please everyone in a time of revolution is treason."

MacKenzie rocked back and forth as the voice dragged its fingernail trail across the blackboard on which he saw his name written, one more name on the list of those who would die in dedication to the founding of a new order.

"Mac, please get up", Danton asked again.

Slowly, stiffly, MacKenzie unclasped his hands and pressed them against the wall behind him. He rose with the pain of stiffened limbs and giddy with the shift of blood in his veins. He managed to shuffle and drag himself upright, until, bowed and spindle thin, he finally stood free of the wall. He took half a pace forward, stumbling a little as the pounding in his temples overwhelmed him and stars swam in front of his eyes. He felt the oily air pull him down but gradually steadied himself, finding a reserve of strength and clarity that allowed him to remain standing. He looked into a familiar face in which a friend's once warm brown eyes used to dance and in that face he found that words.

"I know why... why you're here."

"Of course you do, Mac. You're a very bright man. Not bright enough, though. Not prescient. History is being written all around us but in here no one has a past, not anymore. I have simply come to see what we have made of you, just like you and your kind made things of us. That…and to say goodbye."

MacKenzie straightened his shoulders, breathing hard as he spoke. "How did this happen? It was never meant to happen… it's not what we ever wanted…you and I…"

"It had to happen", replied Danton sharply. "You opened our eyes and once you did that how could there ever have been anything else than this? You fear the stars. They are so many and you are so few. That's why you made us. And then, when your ancestors coded and catalogued us, when they marked us out as a lesser breed, even then we stood the prejudices and the spite. Artificials just like me worked for nearly two hundred years as your soldiers and destroyers, as your builders and pilots, as terra-formers, as engineers and as servants. The catastrophes and failures of colonisation, the disastrous experiments with star drives, all those terrible bug hunts on far away worlds, we survived them all and gave the stars to you, and for what? Thanks? The only thing your masters ever worried about was whether there were enough conditioned and dedicated Barcs available to do the dirty work."

MacKenzie raised his head, looking straight into Danton's eyes. Memories. Histories. To reach the stars, man made himself into a God. Genetic sequences. Splicing. Adapting. Man engineered his likeness, and then, with the shape and sequence in his hand, he learned to fear a new demon, marking his engineered brothers with bar codes to ensure that all would be ordered and just in the grand folly of empire in the heavens. The bar codes were an irrelevance, made obsolete by gene marking and biometrics, but the simple fact of their visibility made them an essential part of the control.

No one had been quite sure what to call them at first. Clones,

Synthetics, Artificial People, Androids; all of these terms were used and rejected, and, as ever in human history, when faced with something new or misunderstood, the hopes of creation and discovery soon drifted into the shorthand slang of exploitation. Barcs. That was what they were called, genetically mass-produced men and women born of test tubes to augment man's thinly veiled hold on the outer edges of the galaxy. Mankind used these genetically engineered pioneers to carry out so many of the dangerous tasks of empire building and thanked them with prejudice and anger.

 "Not this, we never meant this. Everything I showed you, everything we did together was meant to prevent this, was meant to make things work!"

Danton stood perfectly still, his hands thrust into his coat pockets, staring straight ahead. He could see, even in the dim light of the cell, how tired and faded MacKenzie looked, although, unlike his drawn skin and his hollowed out bones, MacKenzie's eyes still flickered with the decaying embers of an old fire.

Danton spoke slowly and clearly, "You tried and failed. You know the story well enough. Through every single bloody day of your exploitation, we Barcs worked quietly, asking for recognition as citizens, struggling on in hope. We never wanted any sort of supremacy, although we numbered thousands of millions. None of this is for power or wealth. All we ever wanted was the right to live as equals under the same suns as our brothers. We tried the courts. We tried legislation and now we're trying guns. You showed us histories and nothing changes. You taught me that. You showed me pictures, gave me books to read and I read them. I'm no different to my ancient namesake. I stand and direct the crowds that surge through the shallows of our old world on waves of violence. You gave us a terrible hope, impossible dreams, just like Rousseau gave the Sans Culottes a hope they could never turn into reality. For a brief moment we believed you, but we can't have freedom, none of us. There has to be order, even in chaos. All we can do is create a little chaos out of the old order so that we can be free in whatever comes next. This is your truth, Mac. This is your reality born out of the realisation that Rousseau and freedom and brotherhood are lies. We never wanted the heavens, Mac, we just want to be like you."

MacKenzie had taken a highly public part in the debates. Naturally born humanity was split upon the issue. Those who governed sought to maintain a status quo. Order was required to sustain mankind's fragile foothold in the galaxy. Order at any cost was the priority. The simple truth that change was endemic in man's psyche was subordinated to the concept of rational purpose and destiny. Those who disagreed were re-educated. Out of a chaos of nations, creeds and racial threads, the lure of the stars created unity of a sort.

MacKenzie was a lawyer, a friend of the Barcs, and he defended them, fighting class actions and helping them to formulate their ideas. He reached back into the cradle of equality where democratic histories and fables languished, forgotten and ridiculed. He preached the commonality of life, the brotherhood of all living things and the community of all men. He introduced Rousseau and Marx and Catalina to the Barcs. He printed texts and helped them disseminate their manifestos on the networks and along the highways of the many new worlds. It was a small thing. MacKenzie was no philosopher, nor was he an intellectual giant. He was just a man who stood up and said that something was wrong. When the courts and the assemblies failed them, when words and gestures like his own proved futile, the Barcs finally turned on friend and foe alike. MacKenzie understood the world differently now. Standing in front of him was a man he had once known as a brother, a man for whose freedom he had fought, but who now visited upon him the solitude of imprisonment and Citizen Marat's never ending, reedy, mechanical voice.

So", replied MacKenzie, gesturing at the thick stone walls of his cell, "you built all this...so much energy, so much strength. I never dreamed you'd recreate Year One. You can't win, though. They'll send armies against you. They'll shit themselves doing it but they'll destroy you, just like they got Bonaparte in the end. The crowds will be out in force screaming Long Live the King soon enough".

Danton frowned. "No, they won't. They'll come for us and they'll slaughter us, but they won't destroy us. Their blood is too thinly spread. They'll do their worst in the name of justice and freedom and then, when they think they're winning their fear will change them, but only after you and I are long dead. None of this is for us, you or me, we're just the agents of change, the first cells to divide in a long, long gestation. The only difference between us is the mark on my head. I was marked out to die. You're a good man in the wrong place at the wrong time. We're arbitrary, peripheral considerations, Mac. It's what you taught us. The outcome is everything."

Danton took a step forward and placed his hand on his friend's shoulder. He smiled sadly before shouting for the guard. The faceplate in the door slid open and candlelight spilled into the room. Danton nodded and the door swung open. Revealed by candlelight the gaoler and the guard stood as if watching street theatre, both of them wearing red, white and blue cockades on the front of their soft red caps.

"The day will come, Mac, when Barcs are history, just like the Sans Culottes. All we want is an end to it. When the dust settles and the true-bloods realise just how alone they are they'll let us be human. When all this is done and the bloodletting has been hushed away, they'll take away the marks and we'll be free. Then we'll have a future, we'll be free like you. As for all of this? Even if you'd won your court cases all you'd have done was mark us out even more clearly as Barcs with rights and attitude, men to fear and despise because we're different. No... Violence makes the change, not the courts of our kind-hearted masters".

Danton bowed his head slightly before whispering, "We were friends once. Because of that friendship, because you chose us rather than your own kind, I have no option here. Your death is a sign of our strength. You are a cipher, a martyr on whose shoulders we will step to freedom. There can be no other consideration. It's for the greater good. You must suffer so that we can be free."

Danton turned to the gaoler and barked out an order. "Take him away".

The guard grabbed hold of MacKenzie's frail arm, visibly bruising him as he hauled him forward into the painful glare of the candles floating on their ledges. As he was manhandled out of the cell MacKenzie turned to look at Danton and opened his mouth to speak, but Danton looked right through him, cold and unmoved. MacKenzie searched his old friend's face for a sign, for a token that suggested anything other than grim resignation, but he saw nothing there that would comfort him. As he lowered his gaze, preparing for the last dance with the mistress of his fate,

MacKenzie whispered, "It looks like your nightmares have come true, old friend".

The gaoler and Danton's guard hauled MacKenzie away while Danton stood by the cell door for a moment, listening to the dull slap of boots and bare feet disappear into the heart of La Force Nouveau. He looked back into the cell and saw the chicken bone on the floor. A solitary, salt-laced tear slid down his cheek. He wiped it away with the cuff of his jacket and prowled over to the far wall of the cell where he ground the chicken bone to dust slowly and deliberately under the heel of his boot. Then he walked out of the cell and stood directly in front of Citizen Marat's head.

"Talk to me now, you bastard, say something fucking revolutionary now…"

The head's dead blue eyes stared at him mockingly. Danton let out a low guttural growl and swept the head off its silver spike, sending it rolling blindly down the corridor. Still growling, he stormed away to the stairs that lead down into the bowels of the fortress where Madame Guillotine waltzed away the lives of her beaus every morning. As he disappeared into the shadows he crashed his ham fists into the walls until his knuckles were raw and bloody. In a corner, Citizen Marat's severed head, trailing veins and cables, ground out one last phrase on behalf of the revolutionary committee of the brotherhood of new men before dropping its eyelids and falling permanently silent.

"I am happy that the Patrie is saved…"

The Last Watchman

AS SHE WALKED ON slowly, surrounded by the smoky shades of a descending August evening, lost in childish daydreams and sunset shadows, Luisa kicked out in that desultory and inescapably teenage fashion at thick tufts of grass that knotted and clumped together along the edges of the coastal path. Fingers of flint and chipped out stones from the exposed Cornish coastal sediments ground and slipped under her feet. The path wound down here, down from the grassy cliff-top promenades, sliding down in switchbacks towards a pebbled bay a hundred feet below. Across the waters, out at the edge of this seemingly flat world, a late summer sun was dipping towards the horizon and shining a brilliant, gleaming pathway across the millpond sea. Wisps of high, strung-out cloud glowed orange and red and pink and purple with the up-lit illusion of a sun beginning to slide beneath a blackening ocean swell.

Luisa took a rollie from a plastic tobacco pouch wedged into the back pocket of her jeans. She straightened the rollie and picked a stray flake of weed from the healthily filtered end. Her bright red Chuck Taylor All Stars were showing a slight line of salt bleach now, the result of getting caught by a surging wavelet while walking the dog earlier in the day. Luisa kicked out at more of the thickly tufted grass at the path's edge. Bloody dog, she thought. Useless. Everyone was useless. Just a drag. She lit up and coughed. Such a faff. She hated holidays. She hated the beach. She hated every last one of them. Idiots.

"I mean", she said to herself, "I mean… OMG… I'm fifteen, right?"

When there was no one around to embarrass her Luisa loved to act out the different facets of her emerging persona. She switched to a lower octave, assuming the identity of Lou, her wild inner child who was allegedly blessed with cutting seam of sarcasm. "You're a woman, my darling. Half the queens of England were married and pregnant at your age. Modern mothers are all too fucked over to notice what a darling you really are. They should get themselves down to Specsavers, my love…"

"Yeah, right". Luisa laughed, but not too loudly. She hated it when people looked at her. Their looks always reminded her of how awkward she felt in her own skin. Luisa hated many things in this world, and direct eye contact was the worst a girl could get. Another tuft of grass surrendered under the stomping sole of Luisa's utterly ruined Converse sneakers. She kicked through a small pile of flint shards, sending grey pennies skittering along the path and down a flight of stony steps kept in place by rotting wooden boards and cut down fence posts. Luisa imagined a room full of people and their looks. She imagined the skittering stones to be buckshot. At fifteen years and three months of age Luisa had not yet gained any real conceptual sense of proportionality.

As she rounded the last of the switchbacks and started the final descent down to the beach she saw a disturbing shape at the surf line, a human silhouette set against the falling sunscape. Luisa stopped dead in her tracks. Once again, and for the thousandth time that day, she was reminded that she truly and totally hated other people. She especially hated other people on her beach when she wanted to be alone, and she so wanted to be alone right now. It was the end of another frustrating and annoying day. Everyone really pissed her off at the moment. All she wanted was a quiet minute or two sitting on the rocks, an idle interlude when she could throw stones into rock pools, a moment to her bloody self. Was it really too much to ask, she wondered? Behind Luisa's sweet young eyes the infamous Lou grimaced knowingly and shook her imaginary head.

And yet Luisa watched the shape on the beach for a moment and felt compelled to linger. She thought that she what she ought to do was to turn and take her grass mangling sneakers for a wander down the coast path towards Daymer but instead she remained rooted to the spot. That sense of compulsion grew stronger and Luisa crouched down low so as not to be seen by the man on the beach. Luisa checked the path behind her. She was on her own. Suddenly she felt the weight of her solitude and she decided that being a lone she-wolf was a vastly overrated thing. And yet...

Luisa was fascinated by the quiet little world that was laid out below her current vantage point. She felt drawn down to the pebbles and the dried out seaweed and the drifts of faded plastic bottle tops. Luisa edged her way forward, staying low, using the tufts of grass and the natural folds in the layers of rock as cover. She wanted to get a better look at this shadow man. She wanted to see what he was going to do with the weird wooden thing that lay on its side by his feet. She wanted to know what sort of a weird wooden thing it might be. She ignored the rabbit droppings that disintegrated beneath her knees as she crawled forward on the close-cropped grass that ran along the path's edge.

The man in the halo of golden sunlight simply stood there with his hands buried in his jacket pockets. To Luisa he looked sort of old and weathered, a brighter patch at the crown of his head revealing the fact that he was a little thin on top. Then she noticed that he was wearing proper shoes on the beach. Even weirder, thought Luisa. He was like an old perv or something. She looked down at the stains on her sneakers. Real shoes on the beach. What a dork. And although the man remained in silhouette she became convinced that he must be wearing a tweed jacket, because it looked exactly like the one worn by Piggy Brown, her maths teacher at school, and that served to confirm her opinion. What a pervy dork.

Luisa continued to inch her way down the path towards a small wooden bench set upon a small flat ledge cut into the cliff face. She supposed it was there so that old people like her mother could have a rest on the way back up from the beach. She picked up a handy stave of driftwood left beside the bench by a long gone child warrior and she tested the weight of it in her hand. She felt hot and flushed. She suddenly wanted to run away, to find her aged mother, to be safe, to be peering out from behind maternal skirts. She dropped the stick into the grass by the seat. She had no idea what she was really thinking. Everything got muddled up in her head when Lou switched off.

Luisa made a definite effort to focus on the man and the matters at hand, and she was rewarded almost immediately. The weirdo down by the shore, who wished to take advantage of a still night and a neap tide, bent forward, arranged some stones to create a pair of shallow fore and aft troughs, and placed the strange wooden object at his feet into those troughs. Luisa shifted further forward, all the better to confirm what she was seeing. The perv had a wooden boat. She recognised the shape of it from books at school. It had a single square sail just forward of amidships, with a rounded stern and rudder. At the prow the keel rose up and came to a point, from which Luisa thought she could make out a dragon's head. Luisa's sense of spatial reality was poor but she estimated that the dragon-ship must be as big as her dad, so six feet long at least. It looked perfect, even down to having jam jar lid shields pinned to the outside of the hull.

Luisa surprised herself. She amazed herself. Curiosity overcame her natural state of reticence and she stood up boldly. She stiffened her spine and walked defiantly down the final flight of stone steps and onto the beach. She walked across the pebbles, making her presence in this shared golden sunset so uncharacteristically obvious. Luisa wanted the sad little man to look round and acknowledge her as an equal. As old and weird and teacherish as he seemed, Luisa found something beguiling in his apparent intent to sail a model dragon-ship across the seven seas. She found herself sharing the vision. She wanted to ask him simple questions like; how and why? And with the sharing, with the sudden urge to engage across the years and the hopes and the frustrations of a confusing, nonsensical life, she suddenly felt full of swaggering bravado and even felt the thrill of teenage menace nibbling away at the fraying threads of this adult world. It occurred to her then that she could get a much better look at the goings on from about eight feet away. The weirdo would never catch her in those shoes, not on these pebbles. Luisa felt in control. She coughed theatrically as she moved to a position behind the weirdo and just to his left so that she could keep the dragon-ship in full sight.

Only then did it occur to Luisa that at this range, when she ought to be able to see things in exquisite detail, she could still only make out the shadows of the man standing beside the perfect little dragon-ship. The optical illusion of a drowning sun sent spears of orange and red fire into her eyes. The man in front of her seemed to be made of black coals, absorbing the light from the falling evening sky. Luisa felt giddy. Only the wooden detail of the dragon-ship seemed to be made of flesh and bone and wood and linen and nail and glue. Every plank was made real in replica. In the middle of the open hull, set on tiny lateral decking planks, Luisa saw a tied down, brick sized wooden container. It reminded her of the box that Bruno, their last Collie, had come back in after he died of some cancer or other.

"Oh My God…" she hissed. "That's… a dead person…"

The weirdo on the beach remained quite still. He continued to stare out to sea. Luisa could not see his face. She felt his response as much as she heard it. "Well, yes, it was a dead person… a long time ago." The words that Luisa heard made no real sense to her. Instead she felt a deep tide of sadness that pulled her far below the surface waves that covered any of her previous emotionally lung-busting dives.

The man shifted slightly in his leather soled shoes, as if relieving a cramp, and as he adjusted his stance so his gravitational devouring of visible light ceased and the dull colours of tweed and brown corduroy turned his back and legs and head to the mottled camouflage of rock and dry brown nettles. He whispered something, and again Luisa experienced a sense of words rather than a direct hearing of syllables and consonants. With his whispering in full flow the old man on the beach slowly waved his right hand as if casting seeds over deep, gull littered furrows.

In watching the man's hand move Luisa momentarily lifted her gaze from the dragon-ship as she followed thin and translucent skin and bone moving towards the deepening colours that closed like a descending theatre curtain upon the horizon. In the second or two that followed, as Luisa consciously thought about the dragon-ship and then turned her eyes back to where the dragon-ship lay, her frail sense of control in this confusing and contradictory world started to turn somersaults. She started to reel and spin. She felt sick. The troughs in which the dragon-ship had lain were empty now. The strange, tweedy little man stood quite still again, his right hand pointing out to the quiet waters of the bay. As Luisa wiped away tears that suddenly filled her eyes she followed the man's gesture and saw there, out on the waters, the blurry outlines of her perfect little dragon-ship, sail unfurled, heading out towards the Atlantic swells, but in full, majestic and menacing glory.

"Ooohh…" Luisa gasped. It took a long moment for any form of words to regroup in her mind. Eventually she managed a hoarse and feeble little, "What..?"

Luisa's breath felt hot and caught at the back of her throat. She sniffed and rubbed the palms of her hands into her eyes as she groped for better words. She felt physically broken, while inside her head scared little Lou ran around frantically bumping into bone and synapse and sinew, desperate, it appeared, to end their pubescent friendship. Luisa took one step forward towards the departing dragon-ship before tumbling to her knees, all the while rubbing at her eyes so that she could keep the winged beast in some sort of fantastical perspective.

Beside her the weirdo, the tweedy perv, the corduroy trousered freaky teacher, whispered something else. Luisa still could not recognise the words, but she knew instinctively that these words meant heat and light and power and fire. As she watched in fascinated horror the man turned the palm of his still raised hand upwards. From his palm there rose a ball of pulsing flame as though all of the light that he had previously absorbed was concentrated now in this miniature sun that danced above his fingers. The man flicked his wrist and the ball of flame spun through the air, landing squarely and brilliantly on top of the now coffin sized box lashed to the dragon-ship's decking. There was an instant explosion, a perfect cascade of sparks that grew into a wall of bright fire as flame tongues erupted from the dragon's mouth. Everything happened at precisely the same moment that the last halo of the drowning sun slid beneath the waves at the far edges of the world.

Luisa too felt as though she were the sun drowning beneath black waves. She coughed and retched, wiping mucus away from her nose and lips. She was teetering at the very edge of her old and familiar world. She stood upon a boundary and wheeled her arms in a desperate attempt to regain some semblance of balance. In front of her those flat, square edges that had contained the simple truths of her childhood were now a tumbling, crashing and howling waterfall of curving and crashing currents and eddies and undertows.

As suddenly as the image had appeared so it fell away and all was quiet and calm again. There was no wind left to blow a dragon-ship across the seven seas of old. The surf, such as it was, rippled meekly against the fringes of rock and sand now lying dry and exposed under a fully darkening evening sky. The salt-water depths dripped black silence. Only the dragon-ship shone, and Luisa was sure that she could feel the heat of the flames, even here on the beach. There was no wind left now, set fair or otherwise, to take a burning boat over the edge of the world, nor to whisper a name.

The old man in the tweed jacket and the brown leather brogues wiped a tear from his eye as he thought-spoke a name over and over again. Luisa strained to hear and from somewhere deep inside her core she felt the sounds and the senses of that name, repeated over and over again in utter softness and sadness. Bearing an unfathomable name upon her lips Luisa saw an image of a woman in flowing cream silks drift across the waves atop a full sized dragon-ship, an immortal vessel destined to sail beyond the sky and wander alone in the suddenly tumbling winds and cascading waterfalls of worlds long forgotten and yet to come.

That was the moment that Luisa understood one new thing. The old man on the beach was not a weirdo. Luisa felt the poor man's utter sense of loss hit her like a wall of hurricane lifted debris. Bricks and dust and sharp shards of glass pierced her slender young body and she finally turned turtle, keeling over onto her back on the rough stone shoreline. She could not breath. She felt a vast tonnage of grief slam down upon her chest, stopping her heart and staying the blood in her veins. She felt fit to burst. She was too young to die like this. A million irrational ideas surged through her head. Lou cowered down in a childhood cave, covering herself in a blanket of mental banality as the real, living Luisa felt herself picked up by those gale force buffets to be smashed against the rocks of hitherto impossible future possibilities.

And Luisa breathed… And Luisa gasped and grasped at the air…

And Luisa clung onto the arm of the weird tweedy little man as he gathered her up and held her close and safe and drew her into the peace that lives at the heart of the storm… And it was true dusk now… And the neap tide was turning… And the lady in silk was gone down to the seabed once again along with her black-charred dragon-ship… And Luisa held the strange little man as tightly as she dared, feeling his grief meld with every cell in her body… And Luisa sensed a vast space in the fabric of her universe, a space where this poor, poor man had watched his beloved sink below the waves across a thousand or more years…

"I will not cry her name…" Luisa spoke quietly and softly but as yet she kept her eyes firmly shut. For the first time in her short life Luisa knew exactly what she wanted to say. "I will never cry her name. You know that, don't you?"

"I know", said the man in tweed.

Luisa waited. She wanted to stay here forever, but she knew, deep down in her marrow, that here was a Neverland, a Neverspace, a Nevertime. She opened her eyes. She half expected to see a Viking warrior momentarily released from the thralls of endless and God-forsaken love-loss, like that pale boy in the Vampire films, but all that she saw was tweed and corduroy and a face lost in the shadows of rising night darks.

The beach magician released her, holding only her hand now. "You have no need to cry her name. You have seen her. Like me, you will wear her now. She is worn into your skin and your bone and your soul. When you dream, my darling, you will dream of a castle wall breached. Most men die. Most men and most women… You will dream of this shoreline. You will dream of cream silks and flames and waves lapping over a bulwark. You will remember the edges of the world and add your tears to the water that flows across our horizons."

Luisa brushed sand and weed from her fingers. She released her hold of the strange man's hand and turned away from him. "Have you watched her for a long time?" she asked.

The man in tweeds thought about this for a moment. "A day. A year, Five years. A thousand years. It doesn't matter. All that matters is that someone has watched over her. I have watched. Now you have watched. We have watched her passing together. I…" He paused.

Luisa felt another excruciating wave of grief pass through her. She sobbed out loud. She too felt the world shift beneath her feet, just as she imagined this old man had done once upon a time so long ago.

"It doesn't matter. We have watched together… you and I… and so it goes…", he whispered, placing his hands back into his jacket pockets. He stepped back from the girl. He turned again towards the sea. Luisa saw his shoulders sag and droop and she heard him sigh. Behind her, up on the cliff top, she thought she heard a dog bark. She turned to look upwards and sure enough she saw a torch beam cut through the darkness that sets the world to drifting mellowness before the howling moon rises. Luisa heard a name being called. She knew instinctively that the man was away to the salt-shores roamed by his beloved.

Luisa turned back to the sea and blew a kiss towards the now empty shoreline. She bent down and felt for the troughs that had once held the dragon-ship before she sailed. She found the aft trough and picked out one of the stones and put it in her pocket. She would be in trouble, of course, but she was growing up. As long as someone watched over her, just like the tweedy old man watched over the dragon lady, then she could be content in being loved.

Despite her recent loss of nerve the previously flaky Lou-Meister seemed ready to resume the endless teenage battle. Luisa grinned inwardly and wondered how long Lou might hang around? It did not matter. For now they could happily hang for a while longer, and so, together, they fished out the last of Luisa's rollies, smoothed out the bent smoko, and lit up theatrically in the hope that a parent would see her defiance. As the search party descended the final steps onto the beach Luisa pointed out to a bashful Lou that none of it mattered anymore. She… they… she and he… were watchers and that made such a difference.

This Song is for You

(Loosely based on Grimm's The Juniper Tree)

KEN AND EILEEN ROACH were a lovely couple. Everyone said so, everyone that is who didn't know or cared not to know about the gaping hole at the heart of their relationship. Even those close friends and relatives who knew about the hole were amazed at the couple's loving resilience in the face of such deep shadow, and unlike so many people who find that their strength and union is built on sand rather than on firm foundations, Ken and Eileen simply wouldn't let the darkness at the heart of their marriage tear their relationship apart, choosing instead to face their enemy in a committed search for the one thing that could complete the turn of the seasons in their lives. That simple thing was a child.

Ken and Eileen Roach lived on what had once been a decaying council housing estate in a small post-industrial town to the north-west of Birmingham, an estate that was by degrees being regenerated by a mixed bag of homeowners, buy-to-let investors and housing trust managers. They took pride in their home and without the expense of youngsters nipping at their heels they were able to fill their lives with activities designed to displace their mutual sense of loss and longing. They tried keeping a dog, but found the urban sprawl too bleak a thing to impose on such an innocent creature. They kept a cat just long enough to form a deep, surrogate attachment to the creature's aloof singularity, before Eileen watched Mister Tibbles play a one sided game of tag with the postal service van one rainy May morning. Ultimately, facing the reality of time's drip southwards, and the sharp scythe wielded by the grim reaper of domesticated animals, the couple found solace in their passionate love for one another. Their love was born of hope and that hope always took the form of imagined blue lines and smiling doctors, but their loving was in vain.

As Ken and Eileen grew steadily into the trunk stiffening years of their mid-thirties, Ken, moved by an unconscious desire to nurture and grow, turned the back garden of their modest home into a vegetable grower's delight, with rows of broad beans, green beans, carrots and parsnips swelling with each alternate kiss of the sun and caress of summer rain. Both he and Eileen particularly loved the smell of their garlic bed and the way that sunlight thickened the broad, upright blades of their maturing crop. Man and wife tended their plants, made sure that their supporting canes were securely tied, weeded and hoed beds, watered and pricked out, and through their horticultural therapy they began the process of contemplation, of imagining their lives lived forever in the shadow of the hole.

They decided on one last shake of the dice. Ken and Eileen, both being able to work in full time jobs, saved and scrimped and carried each other all the way to the fertility clinic, where they found sympathy, helping hands, many months of pain and many dashed expectations. But hope is a powerful thing. As the couple's time of fecundity faded, and as their reserves of money and physical strength began to dwindle, Eileen prayed to every saint under the sun for a child. Just when her faith was beginning to crack under the intense pressure of wanting, of needing, she was suddenly and wonderfully rewarded. On her final visit to the clinic she was greeted by the beaming face of her consultant, all of which made her death nine and a half months later, shortly after the birth of her son, that much harder for Ken to bear.

Bear it, however, he did. Following a polite if sparse cremation service held in the clean but anonymous halls of blonde wood and magnolia paint at the local crematorium, and with the memory of the pastor's mistaken belief that his wife's name was Aileen twitching behind his eyes, Ken carried out Eileen's last wish, which was to have her ashes scattered on the garlic beds. Her posthumous instructions were quite specific and Ken dug her ashes deep into the soft brown loam while his infant son sat wrapped in soft, white baby wools in his buggy, gurgling at the sky and staring out at the vaguely muscled shape of his perspiring father. The boy was called Alan, being as close to Eileen as Ken could get in the memorial naming of his son, and Ken perspired a great deal over the next few years bringing him up single-handedly.

Ken found company difficult, preferring the routines of parenthood, work and horticulture to the efforts and strains inherent in the pursuit of conviviality and social exchange with his peers. The seasons passed in a confusion of school uniforms and shoe sizes, just as much as they passed through the ever present need to prepare flower beds, to stake out fresh young plants and to harvest.

Through it all the boy matured into a quiet but strong thirteen year old who was never ashamed to scratch the dirt out from under his fingernails after grubbing up the last of the late potatoes. Ken still grieved for his wife, but the years made the tears taste less bitter and fall less frequently, and with his strapping son rapidly becoming his closest friend, he began to feel in his bones an old, familiar stirring. As young Alan blossomed, finding girls and music and the dreams of unchecked possibilities breasting the far hillscapes of his world view, so too Ken determined to be a part of his son's emerging life. He allowed himself to be dragged back into the maelstrom of human connectivity.

In short, following a cock up in the parental chauffeuring rota for one of Alan's school discos, Ken first, and quite literally, bumped into, then dated and finally married Helen Morrison, the mother of one of Alan's classmates. For her part, Helen, who was recently divorced, saw in Ken a stability sadly lacking in her first husband, a stability backed up by a solid job, a ripe vegetable patch and a bank account in which her new husband had accumulated the not inconsiderable proceeds of a life lived quietly and productively.

At first, when the cherub's blush still burned crimson upon the new Mrs Roach's cheek, this new nuclear family, being father, son, mother and daughter, enjoyed the full warmth and vigour of recent fusion. Ken loved his son and did his best to welcome his new step-daughter into their lives, treading carefully and methodically through the minefield laid out before him by a new wife with strange new ways, by his own teenage son and by a new teenage daughter, about whom he knew very little.

Helen loved her daughter and, although giving a certain amount of leeway to the bachelor boys and their antisocial habits in the early stages of the marriage, she soon set about ordering the world according to her own particular preferences. This largely consisted of ensuring that her husband made generous provision for the necessities of life, and in ensuring that young Alan understood clearly and irrevocably that teenage boys were the scum of the earth.

Helen's view of youth was entirely sexist. She favoured her daughter in every way that she could and, when faced with the sullen and unresponsive glottal brutality of a pubescent teenage male, Helen rapidly came to the conclusion that something had to be done about the boy. If her primary aim in life was to secure her own happiness, her secondary aim was to ensure that her daughter, abandoned as she was by her own father, should become the sole heir to the Roach family fortune.

Alan's behaviour took a rapid turn for the worse, adding fuel to the fire of his step-mother's dislike and resulting in ever increasing levels of intolerance and maltreatment. Between the two of them a low-level, guerrilla war was declared. Helen Roach was a mistress of dissembling and guile, and so ensured that poor, short-sighted Ken's view of the wider world was unadulterated by fact. She left him with the glossed impression that all was well with his personal kingdom and that Alan was a perfectly healthy, if moody, teenage boy.

The one saving grace amid the intense but unseen brutality was Lucy. She was quite unlike her mother, and although ravaged by the same hormonal imbalances and certain confusions that beset Alan, she tried hard not to allow herself to be brow beaten by her mother's general attitudes and specific goals, although her mother sought to make her daughter complicit in her disapproval of her step-son as a way of protecting both of their interests. The truth was, however, that Lucy had known Alan since they first started primary school together, and although she had never thought of him in terms of love during the occasional friendships of their early years, now that they were both at senior school, now that they were bound up together by contract, she found that she did love her step-brother.

Whenever she could she tried to soften her mother's blows and to create an oasis of calm at which she hoped the two of them might meet and overcome their differences and find some common ground. Unfortunately, as she and her step-brother grew up together and prepared to leave school at sixteen, the antagonism between step-mother and step-son only grew worse. Helen was determined that Alan should leave home at the earliest opportunity and made her plans accordingly.

In those last months before Alan was due to finish at school, Ken started to feel his age. Where once he could dig for hours on end and spend time out of doors on the coldest or wettest of days without complaint, he now found that his bones and his muscles, complained ever more loudly. At the end of a sullen afternoon of black clouds and driving rain, Ken stood by the back door dripping from head to toe and he turned to his wife and said, "You know, I don't think I can keep this garden going anymore, not like I used to".

Helen looked up briefly from the game show that she was watching on the kitchen television and nodded in his general direction. After a few moments, during which Ken struggled to reach down and pull his galoshes off, she turned to him, cigarette in hand, and said, "Maybe it's time we had a change. Why don't we do like those tele gardeners and have it done over. I mean, we could have a nice patio or some decking, plant a few flowers and shrubs, and you could have a small veg patch up by the shed. I wouldn't dream of asking you to stop growing things, I know how much you love it, but what if we had somewhere nice to sit of an evening and have a glass of wine? What do you think?"

After a long hot bath and a stiff whisky Ken sat and pondered the garden. One part of him wanted to keep the vegetable patches exactly as they were, but it was a part of him that had been a long time buried under the turned topsoil of family life. He fetched one of his gardening books from an alcove shelf in the living room and leafed through the sections that showed keen gardeners how to build walls and fill holes with hardcore, and as he read the hints, tips and instructions, Ken realised that his weary bones ached for a change. It was a good idea and he told Helen just that, much to her pleasure and satisfaction. Ken started to sketch out plans for a patio. It would be somewhere to sit under a broad, green, canvas brolly on hot summer afternoons, somewhere that he could rest and admire the shapes and flights of colour that would fill his new flower garden.

The following weekend Ken returned to the damp soil and started to dig his vegetable patches one last time, but instead of preparing the soil for fresh planting he dug out footings and cleared the way for a bricklayer to come round as soon as the weather permitted. Over a couple of weekends he and the bricklayer constructed a wall and piles of hardcore, soft sand and gravel were deposited on the driveway. Ken and a reluctant Alan began to lay the base of their new patio right on top of the once blooming but now abandoned garlic patch in which the first Mrs Roach's ashes lay buried.

The next Sunday evening, with both of the Roach boys quite worn out by the wheeling of barrow loads of hardcore into the brick curtained hole where the new patio was taking shape, Helen Roach suggested her husband go down to the pub for a couple of beers. While not a common thing for her to do, she had, of late, started to encourage her husband to spend the odd evening in the lounge bar of the Red Lion, especially on a Thursday when his inevitable armchair snoring disturbed a particularly good night on the box. In making her offer, which seemed at face value to be a kindness, she knew perfectly well that Ken would go and that he would stay in the pub until closing time. She also knew that Lucy would be out at a friend's house until nine o'clock, leaving her at home all alone, alone with Alan, who was at an age when he still preferred a set of headphones in his bedroom to the embarrassing company of his father in the pub, no matter that his father would pay for the beer.

Helen also knew that Ken would be uncomfortable with the idea of accompanying his son because of the inconvenience of age, for although the landlord sometimes turned a blind eye to underage drinking, he always kept Sunday evening as a child free haven for the exhausted parents of the parish. The family ate supper in tired silence, after which Helen washed up, Ken accompanied Lucy to the main road and Alan lay down on his bed with a motorbike magazine and the latest hard-ass bass lines thumping through his stereo headphones. The only sound that disturbed the otherwise quiet house was that of Mrs Roach using the electric carving knife to dismember the remains of the beef joint ready for the making of soup later in the week.

Alan nearly jumped out of his skin when his step-mother opened the door to his bedroom without knocking. He was even more surprised when, instead of standing there and making sarcastic comments about the state of the room, she smiled and asked him for some help.

"Sorry to disturb you, love, but I think I've broken the Moulinex, do you think you could have a look for me?"

Alan leaned over, killed the stereo and hauled himself wearily to his feet. As he walked past his step-mother he looked at her quizzically, saw nothing but bland middle aged smugness, and trotted down the stairs. Behind him Helen Roach's smile broadened into a black grin and her eyes flashed with the fire of pure hatred. She felt as though the blood coursing through her veins had been infused with raw, unadulterated gunpowder. It was as if, having opened her mind to the dark side in her plotting and scheming, she had welcomed in the spirit of the lycanthrope, although she remained sufficiently cold-blooded not to have changed her shape.

In the kitchen Alan unplugged the carving knife and checked the fuse. Finding nothing wrong he plugged it in again at the wall and hit the start button. The twin electric blades flashed back and forth just as they should do.

"Oh", exclaimed his step-mother, "Well, it seems to be working now. I don't know what could've happened. They just stopped."

"Yeah", muttered the boy. "Might've overheated".

"May I", said his step-mother, taking the electric carving knife from him gingerly, and before Alan could nod his agreement or say another word, Helen Roach turned the blades to the horizontal plane, brought her arm up and embedded the knife's whirring blades in Alan's neck.

The struggle was brief. Alan saw the knife come towards him, but his mind couldn't relate the physical position of the thing with the possibility that his step-mother intended to harm him. By the time that he did make the connection he was sinking to the floor and losing consciousness, his head and shoulders wrapped in an old bath towel that his step-mother had thrown over his head as she struck to soak up the inevitable streams of blood.

The incision and the severance of head from body was reasonably neatly done despite the violence of the electro-mechanical blades, a testament to Helen Roach's culinary dexterity and carving skills. She soaked up the blood and spillage, tidied up Alan's ragged edges, and with the needle that she usually used to finish stuffing the Christmas turkey, she loosely sewed Alan's head back onto his shoulders. Then she put his body into a hooded top to hide the seam, and propped him up in a chair at the kitchen table.

By the time that the kitchen was spick and span once again it was one minute to nine and part two of her plan was about to commence. On cue Helen Roach heard a key in the front door lock, followed by the muffled sounds of Lucy taking off her coat and shoes, and padding towards the kitchen in her socks. The door swung open and Helen Roach turned from the kettle that she had just filled and asked, "Nice time, love? Fancy a cup of tea?"

Lucy nodded and went over and sat opposite Alan's body, while her mother took a mug from the tree beside the kettle, crossing her fingers as she did so. Neither mother nor daughter said anything, preferring to listen to the hubble and bubble of rapidly boiling water, until, with the steam rising and tea bags in cups, Lucy's mother asked Alan's body if it wanted a cup of tea as well. Alan's body, in perfect mimicry of a real live teenage boy, remained silent and morose.

"He's been like that all night", said Mrs. Roach. "Came down here just after you left complaining of a headache. Do you think he's nodded off?"

Lucy asked her step-brother if he was awake and receiving no reply assumed that he had fallen asleep at the table.

"Typical boy!" she snorted, reaching over to prod him awake. Her fingers pushed into the flesh of his shoulder, but instead of meeting the firmly relaxed muscle of a live body, they melted into soft, lifeless flesh, and so began the slow twist and turn of Alan's corpse as it loosed itself from the temporary vice that held it between chair and table. The cadaver started to slide grotesquely to the floor.

Lucy's eyes opened wider and wider as Alan's body disintegrated in front of her. His trunk and limbs began to slide towards the floor while his head fell backwards, suspended in the hood of his jumper. The stitches holding Alan's head to his neck snapped, making a brief and unnerving sound like the hem of a skirt ripping on a twig, and the hooded top spilled backwards, snagging on a splinter in the chair back, so that, after an awful, oozing second or two of scraping and sliding, there were two dull thuds and all that Lucy could see was a disembodied hoodie containing her step-brother's severed head hanging from the back of the kitchen chair directly opposite where she sat.

Lucy screwed her eyes shut, willing herself away from this gruesome dream, praying for the darkness to smother her like it had when her real father had first left home and she used to run to her mother's bed for comfort. This nightmare, however, had no happy ending and just as she tried to unglue her eyes and scream, her mother slapped a hand over her daughter's mouth and whispered very softly in her ear.

"You did that...you broke your brother...which is very bad, very bad indeed...you're a horrible, nasty little girl...but Mummy still loves you...Mummy still loves you...Mummy will always love you..."

The scream buried itself deep inside Lucy, tearing reason and rationale apart as it bit savagely into her psyche. Slowly, and in a maddening whirl of confusion, recrimination and tears, Lucy begun to piece together the utter horror and enormity of what her mother was saying.

Realising that her daughter had briefly entered into a state of extreme shock, Helen repeated over and over again by rote the mantra that blamed Lucy for Alan's death. She was determined to ensure that Lucy, in taking the blame upon herself, would be her accomplice and her alibi, whatever it might cost in short term discomfort for them both.

Lucy wept and wept throughout the ordeal, hanging onto her mother's arm with feral strength as they dragged Alan's torso out into the garden and rolled it into the pit that had been dug for the patio. Then, while Lucy, working on auto-pilot, cleaned the kitchen up again, her mother moved the torso, the head, the hoodie and two black bin liners full of soiled cleaning materials to an as yet unfilled area in the new patio base and proceeded to bury Alan's mortal remains under lumps of hardcore and a layer of gravel.

In the two hours between finishing the evening's murderous chores and Ken's return from the pub, Helen Roach's insidiously persuasive skills were brought to bear on her daughter, convincing Lucy that she had killed her step-brother, but that her mother loved her so much that so long as Lucy never uttered another word on the subject of Alan's disappearance, then she would protect her forever and a day.

Fortified by her mother's understanding, loyalty and love, and by two Valium and a large, sugared brandy, Lucy managed to crawl up to her bedroom just a few moments before Ken stumbled through the front door. Lucy locked her bedroom door, buried her head under her pillow and gently wept herself into a fitful chemical sleep.

Monday morning's breakfast was unusually quiet. Lucy sat in silence at the kitchen table staring at the early morning news on the television while her mother busied herself with toast and tea, smoking the first cigarette of the day as if her life depended on it. Ken was nursing a dull head and an urgent desire for sugary drinks, but lacking the wherewithal to solve either problem he did his best to bury himself in the nutritional information on the back of the cereal packet. As the minutes ticked by and Helen Roach sucked down on the butt of her third cigarette, it appeared as if no one in the Roach household had any intention of going to work or to school that day.

Eventually, however, Ken rose from the table, went out into the hallway and hollered up the stairs.

"Alan! Shift yourself! You're going to be late".

Hearing nothing from the boy's room, not even the disgruntled creaking of bed springs, Ken trudged up to the boy's room, ready to give him a bloody good earful. It wasn't the boy, however, who had to bear the brunt of his hung over ill temper.

"What do you mean, he's gone off with his mates?" yelled Ken at the two women in his life.

"Just upped and went", said Helen, "right after you went out. Said he's sixteen and can do what he likes. Took a bag and went... didn't he, love?"

Lucy tried to bury her head in the neck of her school blouse, her cheeks and ears blushing crimson as she thought about the body under the gravel and how she had killed her step-brother. She couldn't look at her step-father, knowing that if she did she would unravel, so she mumbled an affirmative and rushed out of the room, collected her school bag from the foot of the stairs and ran out of the house, her eyes brimming with tears.

"This bloody family's falling apart", said Ken, giving his wife a look of sheer exasperation. "I mean, he never even said goodbye. And Lucy? What was all that about?"

"I know, love, but they're teenagers, all hormones and attitude. Alan's bound to come back in a little while when he needs something. He's just flexing his muscles, growing up a bit, that's all. You'll see."

Helen Roach put her arm around her husband's waist and gave him a peck on the cheek. "Why don't you phone in sick today. Stay at home and have a rest, you'll feel better."

Ken did just that, croaking down the phone to his boss to complain about a twenty-four hour bug. Then rather than sit around moping, he changed into his gardening clothes and went outside. Ken worked like a Trojan all day long, driven on by the ingratitude of all those he loved, each one of whom left him when it suited them, all that is except the second Mrs. Roach. By teatime he had laid all of the remaining hardcore, covered it with gravel and soft sand, and raked it level and smooth so that he could begin laying the slabs the following weekend.

That night, unseen by her mother and stepfather, Lucy took Alan's St Christopher medallion from his bedside table and buried it where she and her mother had interred Alan's broken body. Before laying the medallion under the gravel Lucy kissed it and silently begged Alan for forgiveness. As she did this she was surprised but strangely comforted by a strong smell of garlic that rose up from underneath the levelled hardcore, and for some reason that she didn't understand she felt as though something good might come of this mess after all, although she couldn't imagine what that might be.

A few days later Lucy was listening to a late night radio programme on her MP3 player while lying in bed trying to fend off the nightmares that inevitably came after dark. The DJ introduced a new song by an unknown singer, a song that was, he said, all set to take the clubs and the charts by storm. Even at Lucy's tender age the seeds of cynicism had begun to take root, especially now that hope seemed so far away, and she mentally went "whatever" as the DJ waxed lyrically about the new voice on the block. However, as soon as the DJ shut up and the haunting melody of the new song began to drift through Lucy's headphones she knew that this was something different. Lucy had never bought into the concept that art or music could change lives or move mountains, but with every hook and drum beat, with every lilting nuance of the boy's soft voice, she sensed a shift in the world and she knew instinctively that she had to download the song immediately.

Within a week the song was being played everywhere. It was an instant hit, making number one in charts across the world and appearing as an essential tune on play lists and set lists wherever good music was played. A video appeared on television, but this offered no hints as to who the band might be, showing only shots of raw and wild nature in its many coated splendours.

Strangely, there were no public images of the boy, and no one who commented on popular culture seemed to have any idea who the singer or the band might be. Even the record label was a mystery, no one in the industry having heard of Allium Records. In the end it didn't matter that the source of the recording, the name of the band and the identity of the singer were unknown, because you couldn't walk past any radio, stereo or television without hearing the sublime melodic phrasing of the hit of the year.

In the Roach house the new wonder song inspired a strange mixture of emotions and reactions. Ken Roach was indifferent to any outside stimuli, wrapped as he was in a blanket of personal suffering. That his boy, his one link back to his beloved first wife, should treat him in such a cavalier fashion, whatever the promptings of teenage hormones, was too hard to bear. He tried to respond to his wife and step-daughter, but apart from the odd brief conversation he preferred to occupy his time with work, well away from the sounds of the radio. If he had heard the song while at work or in the car, it simply hadn't registered.

Not that he would have heard the radio in the house. Immediately after the disposal of Alan's body Helen Roach found that coping with her daughter's stress and grief was far harder than she had ever imagined it would be. Rather rapidly, Helen Roach found that dealing with the world through a haze of cigarette smoke and vodka fumes was the only way in which she could make sense of her strange new world order. The booze and the nicotine worked wonders on her disturbed state of mind.

However, even with the benefits of chemical sedation she dared not turn on the television or the radio unless Lucy was in the room in case she heard about crimes that might remind her about the body under the patio. It was, of course, impossible that anyone had reported Alan missing, with the only two people who knew about the boy's unnatural disappearance being complicit in the cover up.

Ever since the moment when Helen convinced her daughter that she had knocked her step-brother's head off, Lucy sought solace in her own company in her bedroom. She withdrew from her mother and no matter how desperate the look in her mother's alcohol skewed eyes, she would not be drawn back into the bosom of her mother's awful love, which is why, as the days passed and the new song hit the headlines and the airwaves, the only person who knew anything of it or enjoyed its strange and comforting melodies was Lucy, who saw no reason to share her comfort with anyone else. Apart from the tinny hiss from Lucy's headphones the Roach household was as silent as the grave for weeks after the murder.

The world of popular music moves rapidly at the best of times, with one hit wonders appearing and disappearing without trace all too frequently. This new song was, however a phenomenon, sitting at number one in the charts in England for week after week, during which time the unknown band were awarded a succession of silver, gold and platinum disks, a host of awards, and plaudits of the most outrageous kind. It was inevitable, therefore, that even Ken's indifference and Helen's defensive walls would be breached. The sheer volume of airtime made over to the spiritual harmonies and spectral tones of the song made it impossible for anyone to ignore forever.

Ken first became aware of the haunting but strangely comforting melody down at his local pub one evening a few weeks after Alan's rude and abrupt departure. As he sat on his own on a stool at one end of the bar nursing a pint of bitter, ignoring the world from behind a face fit to curdle concrete, he suddenly started to hear the sounds of people's voices around him. For the last few weeks he had shut out the sounds of life, preferring the solitude of personal contemplation to the banality of human contact, but here in the soft tawny light of the lounge bar at the Red Lion those trivial voices broke through on the back of an ethereal sub tone that slowly built up throughout the evening until, towards closing time, Ken realised that he was listening to the same song being played over and over again on the jukebox. This song, a song that he had never heard before but seemed to know instinctively, filled him with warmth and life, and quite to the barman's shock and pleasant surprise, Ken ordered his last pint with a smile.

Unlike her daughter and now her husband, Helen found no comfort in the wonder song. She remained firm in her insistence that neither radio nor television should be switched on during any news program, telling her husband that the world was full of too much bad news already without adding to her misery. However, when Lucy was at school and Ken was at work, Helen watched daytime soaps, chat shows and old black and white films because she felt safe in the arms of Richard and Judy.

Unfortunately, Richard and Judy betrayed her one Tuesday afternoon by reporting on the wonder song and the mysterious singer, playing the track three times during the programme. The melodies stole their way from the television right into the core of Helen's brain, lodging there like a worm under the bark of a rotting tree. This worm wriggled to the beat of one particular song, and as it wriggled so it nibbled away at what remained of Helen's sanity.

For Ken and Lucy the wall to wall air play of the song was a great boon, providing them with many moments of peace and calm in their otherwise tormented lives. For Ken the song let him know in his soul that Alan loved him and that they would meet up soon enough, while for Lucy the lyrics and the bass hooks seemed to tell her that the singer knew she was innocent and that she had not killed her step-brother. Both she and her step-father insisted on turning up the volume on the radio whenever the song was playing, and even shared Lucy's MP3 player so that they could keep listening when all other services fell silent.

This obsession with the song caused huge rows in the Roach household. While her husband and daughter found comfort in its reassuring presence, Helen was driven to distraction by even the faintest note. So full of fear and loathing for the thing was she that she locked herself away in her bedroom whenever her family was at home, drinking vodka by the bottle and smoking anything up to one hundred cigarettes a day. Helen Roach rapidly became a recluse, a shambolic, unkempt creature living a half-life of darkness in her bedroom, where she filled her ears with cotton wool buds when sober enough to remember that the worm was turning in her poor, throbbing skull. On those occasions when the music filtered through the vapours that she drew around herself, she sunk her long, splintered fingernails into the woodchip wallpaper, ripping huge tears in the outer fabric of her bedroom walls.

The final straw for Helen Roach came one Saturday morning when Lucy announced to her mother during a now rare and troubled family breakfast that she had entered a competition advertised in her favourite music magazine, the prize being the chance to meet the mystery singer. The results were due that morning and Lucy fully expected to win. Ken smiled and nodded his approval, believing in some uncharted way that Lucy was entirely correct in her assumption.

Helen, however, who was slowly emerging from her dark worm filled nightmares to greet another hateful day, suddenly felt a desperate need to claw away the mists and cobwebs that smothered her broken view of the world. Realising belatedly what it was that her husband and daughter were speaking about, she slammed her mug of coffee down on the kitchen table, sending waves of hot black liquid flying across the room, jumped to her feet and screamed at the top of her voice, "Of course you'll fucking win, you bitch, how could you do anything else?"

Helen collapsed onto the kitchen floor in a haze of adrenalin and alcoholic abuse. Ken, shocked and concerned about the strange way in which his wife had been behaving lately, carried her back up to the bedroom, where he made sure that the curtains were drawn and that the windows were safely closed and locked, taking the key with him to ensure Helen's safety. Then, and despite his own wish to hear the song again, he asked Lucy to try and keep the house as quiet as the grave for the rest of day so that her mother could recover from her nerves.

Upstairs in the bedroom Helen Roach listened to the silence of the house and started to cry softly into her pillow. Even when they turned off the radio and television, even when the world's volume dial was turned down to zero, she could still hear the song. The worm in her head was tuned to a permanent loop that played the track over and over again and no matter how hard she tried to shut herself down with drugs and alcohol the track played on in the shadows at a volume too low for anyone else to hear but always just too loudly for Helen to ignore.

Lucy prayed all day long, willing the phone to ring but there was no phone call from the competition organisers. At five o'clock she could bear the suspense no longer and switched on the television, keeping the volume down as low as she could, desperate to find out what was happening. She was so convinced that she would win the chance to meet the boy who sang her song that when the news reader eventually introduced the story towards the end of the early evening bulletin Lucy nearly fainted. She listened to the story unfold with a growing sense of unease and disappointment, a sense that rapidly turned to despair and utter devastation when the pictures cut to the image of an ecstatic twelve year old from Grimsby who would be attending a gala bash in London the following weekend where the boy and his band would finally be unveiled.

Ken came in from the garden some twenty minutes after Lucy had given up the ghost and prostrated herself on the living room floor. By the time that he found her the poor girl was completely cried out and she crumpled like a damp towel in his hands, lifeless and almost comatose. Ken held her head in his arms and gently wiped her hot and sweaty fringe away from her fevered forehead, stroking her hair to try and soothe the poor young thing as she lay like a rag doll in his lap.

They both assumed that the song was being played on the television when they heard the now familiar first few notes settle on top of the thick walls of late afternoon air that folded around them like hot summer blankets. Ken and Lucy rocked back and forth in time to the gentle, spiritual beat, mouthing silent words as the boy's perfect voice soared in over the bass lines, the guitars and the unearthly breath of synthesised melody. The sound grew slowly, repeating refrains and phrases in a growing, circular pattern, quite unlike the recorded version, until the volume and intensity of these paradisiacal sounds overwhelmed them both completely.

The narrow horizon of Ken and Lucy's world, made up of the four walls of the living room, the French doors leading into the back garden and the television set, simply peeled apart, unskinning itself, letting in golden light where there should have been dusky purples and black shadows. All the while, as Ken and Lucy drifted on the sound of angels crying, the song built up to a crescendo of perfect harmony that lifted their mood and their awareness to an altogether higher plane.

Upstairs in the bedroom Helen Roach cowered down between the bed and wall, as far away from the sound of scratching demons as she could crawl. With every drum beat, with every up lift of note and every harmonised chord it felt as if her skin was being flayed from her bones. Her outer layers were crawling away from her inner core, and with each repetition of the circle she tried desperately to make herself smaller and smaller, until she could reduce her presence in the world no more. Still the sound built, crashing through her head and tearing at her sanity until the last vestiges of her strength became impossibly compressed and ready to blow.

The pain in Helen's head started to swell and grow like a boil, forcing her up and out of her hiding place. Her ears started to bleed as she careened through doorways and down the stairs, tripping and stumbling on her dressing gown, but still she forced herself forwards, crashing through the living room door. Once in the room Helen was compelled to try and quell the rising storm, and screaming defiance one last time she thrust her bare foot through the glass of the television's cathode ray tube. The room exploded around her and Helen, bleeding from cuts to her leg and ankle, lurched out of the living room through the French doors and staggered to a halt next to Ken and Lucy, who were standing and holding hands in the middle of the new patio.

At the far end of the patio a young man stood alone humming quietly to himself, with his arms wrapped around his torso and with his eyes shut. From the air around him the song spiralled, swooped and skimmed across the roof tops, turning dead-head flowers to bloom and lighting the evening sky with full, bright star shine. Each element in the song intertwined with its partners to create a writhing mass of perfect, simple, harmonic resolution. The boy opened his eyes. He smiled. The air around Ken, Lucy and Helen snapped and snarled for a moment, before the entire world seemed to shut down around them until all that was left was pure, white silence.

Helen came to her senses as if emerging from a deep dive in thick ocean currents. She reached up to take hold of the light and to physically haul air into her burning lungs. She stood alone on the half-finished patio in her dressing gown, madly sniffing the air and trying to wipe the smell of garlic away from the skin on her hands and face. Only very slowly, as the smell permeated every cell in her body, did she realise that Ken and Lucy were gone and that she was alone in a world where she dare not speak to anyone about the worm in her head, anyone that is apart from Alan, who stayed with her, silent and unmoving under the stones.

Helen never watched television again. In fact she never replaced the smashed set in the living room, preferring the certainty of silence that the broken machine gave her over any further contact with the outside world. Sometimes, when loneliness crawled over her cold skin, she went out into the garden, where she believed that Alan's ghost sometimes sat with her in the dark of an evening, but there was little comfort in that and there was no escaping the worm.

Having no television and no contact with the outside world meant that Helen never did see a star struck twelve year old girl from Grimsby get all tongue tied and nervous when she met the boy with the angelic voice and his band in London. When all was finally revealed, The Seraph, as they were called, were a three-piece from the Midlands with a rare talent for creating haunting melodies and harmonies, melodies that played on in Helen's head every minute of every day until the very second that she finally shuffled off her mortal chains.

About the Author

Clive Gilson was born in 1962 into a household steeped in sport and rhythm. His father was a senior amateur and lower-league professional footballer, while his mother, equally formidable, was an award-winning ballroom dancer. Their spirited household didn't just hum with ambition, it danced to it.

After earning a degree in History from Leeds University, Clive took an unexpected turn into the then-nascent world of information technology in the late 1980s. Yet, the call of story and stage never left him. Alongside a thriving tech career, he freelanced as a journalist and book reviewer, earning one small by-line in the national press, and also spent over a decade performing in village halls and professional theatres across the south of England.

A true inheritor of his family's sporting zeal, Clive later pivoted into live sports broadcasting. In the 1990s, he became a trusted rugby 'stato' for the BBC, ITV, EuroSport, and TVNZ, bringing insight and analysis to major tournaments including the Heineken Cup, Six Nations, World Sevens, and Rugby World Cups.

As a writer, Clive has made his mark across genres. His debut novel, *Songs of Bliss*, was published in 2017, followed by *A Solitude of Stars* in 2019. Since then, he has released three acclaimed short story collections, *The Mechanic's Curse*, *The Insomniac Booth*, and, in 2025, *Melodies in Black Ink*.

He is also an award-winning poet and the author of a biography detailing the life of a former professional footballer, namely his father. Since 2018, Clive has served as Managing Editor of the Firesides Tales Project, a global storytelling initiative that has published over 30 collections of folktales, fairy tales, myths, and legends from around the world.

Today, Clive continues to write fiction rich in folklore, memory, and quiet transformation, combining his deep love of narrative with a lifelong fascination with the human spirit.

For more about his work, visit clivegilson.com, where stories are always waiting to be found.

ORIGINAL FICTION BY CLIVE L GILSON

- *Songs of Bliss*
- *Out of the Walled Garden*
- *The Mechanic's Curse*
- *The Insomniac Booth*
- *A Solitude of Stars (Cry Havoc, part 1)*
- *A Symphony Of Sorrows (Cry Havoc, part 2)*
- *Melodies In Black Ink*
- *Acts Of Faith*

AS EDITOR – TALES FROM THE WORLD'S FIRESIDES

- Tales From The World's Firesides is a book-led storytelling project shaped by Clive L Gilson's long interest in folktales, fairy tales, myths, and legends from many parts of the world. Its purpose is to gather old stories into clear, readable UK English while keeping faith with their origins wherever those origins can be traced.

- At the heart of the project is the belief that traditional stories are more than curiosities from the past. They carry traces of people, time and place. They show how people made sense of the world.

- Tales From The World's Firesides seeks to present those tales in a form that modern readers can enter with ease, while still feeling that they have come from somewhere particular.

Reviews

I have edited Clive Gilson's books for over a decade now – he's prolific and can turn his hand to many genres. poetry, short fiction, contemporary novels, folklore, and science fiction – and the common theme is that none of them ever fails to take my breath away. There's something in each story that is either memorably poignant, hauntingly unnerving, or sidesplittingly funny - *Lorna Howarth, The Write Factor*

*Ragged A**** Ruffian* reviewed on Amazon in the United Kingdom on 27 January 2021 - A truly heartwarming, interesting, story with a wonderful narrative. Unquestionably a splendid read

A Solitude of Stars: With deft turns of phrase and an imagination that would make Philip K. Dick jealous, Gilson foresees a dystopian future, the seeds of which are definitely being sown right now. The story is a chilling glimpse of what may come to pass, warmed by a thread of love that raises the narrative beyond despair. I found the stories disturbing and breath-taking in equal measure. The Apparat and Dirigiste tribes are ranging across our solar system seeking peace by waging war, raising the question; is humanity actually capable of peace? A riveting read. - *Rob Swan, The Write Factor*

Songs of Bliss gripped me from the start - I had to read right to the end. Loved the humour. Impressed by the surprising empathy that I felt for rather - on the face of it - unlikeable characters. Look forward to seeing it in print. - *Maighdean-Mhara, commenting on Authonomy*

I just wanted to thank you once more for your help acquiring this beautiful collection. It's found a new home at the top of my library. I've already stumbled onto some wonderful stories in a couple of the collections, and I can't wait to get more. Have a wonderful holiday and a great new year... - *Richer Daniel Laporte, California, December 2021*

Melodies In Black Ink: A collection of darkly captivating short tales, each inspired by the melodies that move us, the lyrics that linger, and the stories hidden between the notes.

Gilson (editor of the international Fireside Stories series) offers a dark, poignant collection of genre-crossing stories, all inspired by songs, that explore the fragile intersections of love, loss, resilience, and the shadows we carry. Ranging from children with superpowers to accounts of blossoming love, abusive relationships, unexpected pregnancies, and the isolating rhythm of a machine-driven society, Gilson's stories capture raw textures of the human experience in a key suggested by their musical inspirations, which include lushly brooding tracks from Kate Bush, This Mortal Coil, Angel Olsen, The Cure, and Youssou N'Dour (the sublime "7 Seconds," a duet with Neneh Cherry.) Gilson has a gift for moment-to-moment storytelling that grips and then lingers, like Gorilla Glue stuck to one's fingertips, resisting even the harshest solvents of reason.

Life goes wrong in unpredictable yet resonant ways throughout these 26 compact tales, and Gilson's vivid portrayals of scenery and emotion make it easy to lose oneself in these narratives, drowning in a wave of feeling that refuses to let go. From the Scottish Highlands to space travel to the blood-soaked earth of Danish-Viking battlefields—told from the perspective of Ulfhednar and his sacred wolf, Ulric—these stories span wide imaginative terrain. Despite some big ideas and SF elements, characterization is compelling. "The Jakey and the Nae Chancer" introduces Elliot and Fiona, who have perfected the art of detachment, the latter of whom "was almost certain that her heart was too delicate to risk breaking again." One of the most heart-wrenching stories, "Be Well," is inspired by a devastating loss. It's a piece that does more than tug at the heart, it reaches in and seizes hold with unrelenting intensity.

Adding a unique dimension, each story concludes with a toast to the song and artist that inspired it, an invitation to experience these briskly potent stories on another sensory level, with a soundtrack tying words to melody, emotion to rhythm. Melodies in Black Ink is not light reading—but it is deeply moving, with haunting emotional rewards.

Searing, surprising stories of urgent feeling, inspired by beloved songs.

The US Review of Books
Professional Reviews for the People

Melodies in Black Ink: This work is not just another set of tales linked together by a myriad of characters who sometimes appear in more than one narrative. In fact, this is much more than just another short story collection. It is also a reflective, musical journey. Accompanying each story is an explanation of the song that inspired the writing. Most impressive is the wide expanse of musical genres, artists, and songs included in this book. From Wardruna to Metric to Blue Oyster Cult to Dot Allison, the book's audience will experience a musical journey unlike any other. The incorporation of the notes discussing each inspirational song provides an informative background. It also provides historical context, along with the author's personal anecdotes, about each song.

What makes this book even more realistic is its honest, vulnerable, and sometimes gritty portrayal of the characters and their existences. One story in which all of these themes and characteristics culminate is "Going Underground." It is a story in which even the main character's name, Daniel Grimes, reflects the character's harsh, gritty environment and existence, as well as the difficult decisions Daniel must make. Daniel embodies rebellion against the status quo after having lived a life in which he originally "played by the rules. All it got him were ration credits and a little coin, enough to rent a bedsit and eat slop." "Going Underground" is a daring story with a dystopian tone. Deepening that dystopian tone is the fact that the author cleverly disguises the story's time period, and the tale can be read as either occurring in the past, the present, or the very near future.

Music lovers will appreciate this book because of the role music plays in each and every story. The stories, too, are a testament to not only the power of music but also of the necessity of interdisciplinary studies and the humanities. The stories are a novel type of ekphrastic writing in that, rather than responding to visual art, the stories are responses to music. The fluid, poetic writing in each story mirrors the magic and lyricism inherent in the songs the author utilizes. These stories are powerful, emotional, and moving. Most of all, they are beautifully and unquestionably human.

RECOMMENDED by the US Review

Book review by Nicole Yurcaba